SEND ME A SONG

Send Me A Song

Deborah J Rhoades

ISBN: 979-8-9869836-3-9; 979-8-9869836-4-6; 979-8-9869836-5-3

This book is dedicated to the high school teachers and college professors who inspired my love of history and writing. They are true champions.

Preface

Several years ago, I became a fan of the Irish singing group *Celtic Woman*. I have Irish and Scottish ancestors and have enjoyed this genre of music for most of my life. When I discovered this group, I wanted every song that they had recorded, many of which I had never heard. My husband purchased two of their DVDs and their companion CDs for my birthday. I was immediately in love with the song, *Send Me A Song*, sung by Lisa Kelly and written by David Downes. I told myself, "Hey, that would make a terrific novel." The song reflects the theme of distance and separation, particularly between parents and their children and vice versa. It is a theme that all of us can relate to.

Years later, while listening to Peter Hollens, I discovered another terrific song with a connection to Ireland. This song is an ancient one, having been written sometime between 1615 and 1635. There are no records that inform us as to who the writer of the song was, but we do know that the song, originally titled *Good Night and Joy Be To You All*, became popular in the 17th Century. Today in the United States, the song, now known as *The Parting Glass*, is sung more at funerals than at other times; but in the 17th Century, it was sung at all types of occasions.

After publishing my first novel. *Finding Faith* in December 2022, I was considering the topic of my next novel. I knew that I wanted to stay in the historical fiction genre. Having worked as a genealogist for many years, it was hearing so many fascinating stories of courage, tragedy, and faith that I discovered a desire to tell these kinds of stories. Previously I had only been an academic writer. I was not certain I could be successful, but I wanted to try. Reading reviews of my first book convinced me that I needed to keep telling stories of our ancestors and how their lives directly influence ours. Writing historical fiction allows me to do what had always been my favorite part of academic writing—research coupled with my love of history. I could lock myself in a library doing research and never want to leave.

In this novel, I have also incorporated a story from my own ancestry, though loosely. In researching my ancestry, I discovered stories of ancestors that I could never have anticipated. One of those stories is that of my fourth great-grandfather, Robert W. Kennon. Kennon was the son of Richard Cocke and a slave woman named Becky Short. It was not a story of abuse between slave holder and slave, I believe Richard loved Becky. He had known her most of his life. The Cocke family was unique in Virginia during the colonial period through the Civil War; they were devout abolitionists. John Hartwell Cocke openly educated his slaves, in clear violation of the law.

John Hartwell Cocke was a close friend of President Thomas Jefferson. He assisted Jefferson in the founding of the University of Virginia. Appalled at his behavior with Sally Hemings, Cocke wrote an article condemning Virginia planters who engaged in these relationships. No doubt, he would have been unhappy that his own son had done the same. The difference between Jefferson and Richard Cocke was that Richard claimed his child, freed the child and his mother, and provided financial support. Robert Kennon, the child named for a family friend, spent his entire life passing for white. It is unknown if he realized his situation. He was only five years old when he left his mother's home to be raised by Richard's sister Elizabeth and her husband William Taliaferro.

As I was doing my historical research and developing the story I wanted to tell, I remembered these two songs, the story of Richard and Becky; and, I thought to myself, "What if I put them altogether?" I had what I believed would be the perfect story. It is a story about the love of family, of tradition, and of perseverance. It takes place during the earliest days of this country and goes forward through ten generations to the near present. I hope that you will come to love these families and to appreciate their struggles. While they were not perfect (none of our families are), they stood beside each other through life's hardships and triumphs. I believe that these attributes are what bind us together as humans and lift us out of despair when life brings us challenges.

Send Me A Song by David Downes performed by Lisa Kelly of Celtic Woman

Take the wave now and know that you're free
Turn your back on the land, face the sea
Face the wind now, so wild and so strong
When you think of me, wave to me and send me song

Don't look back when you reach the new shore
Don't forget what you're leaving me for
Don't forget when you're missing me so
Love must never hold, never hold tight, but let go

Oh, the nights will be long when I'm not in your arms
But I'll be in this song that you sing to me
Across the sea, somehow, someday
You will be far away, so far from me
And maybe one day I will follow you in all you do
'Til then, send me a song

When the sun sets the water on fire
When the wind swells the sails of her hire
Let the call of the bird on the wind
Calm your sadness and loneliness
And then start to sing to me
I will sing to you
If you promise to send me a song

I walk by the shore and I hear
Hear your song come so faint and so clear
And I catch it, a breath on the wind
And I smile and I sing you a song
I will send you a song
I will sing you a song
I will sing to you
If you promise to send me a song

"If you don't know history, then you don't know anything. You are a leaf that doesn't know it is part of a tree." —Michael Crichton

Chapter 1

"Come on kids! We've got to get going," shouted Ross from the bottom of the staircase. "Gram is waiting on us."

"Don't forget your coats!" added Anne. "It may snow in Tennessee this weekend."

In two minutes, Hannah, Celia, and Sean came running down the stairs. "Geeze, you don't have to yell. We were coming. I can't believe I have to miss the ski trip with my friends! Everyone will be there, and I will be on this stupid trip," moaned Hannah, the oldest of the three Walsh children at age 15. The other two children, Celia, age 12, and Sean, age 10, were not much happier. They each had events they had rather be participating in than traveling to Tennessee to help their grandfather clean out his home and pack up for his move to their home, especially since this was a break from school.

It wasn't that they were not looking forward to their grandfather living with them. They adored their grandfather, but they didn't want to miss out on their activities to help him clean and pack. Their grandmother, Amanda, died ten months earlier, and their grandfather Alexander's health began to decline since her death. Their daughter, Anne, agreed to take in her father rather than place him in a retirement home. Her siblings, Mary Beth, John, and Charles lived further away from their father, and none had volunteered to take their father in. After a discussion with her family, Anne, Ross, and their children invited Alex to live with them.

As the family piled into their SUV, each child pulled out their electronic devices, popped in his or her earbuds, and settled in for the lengthy drive to Tennessee. Anne and Ross, who met in high school, moved from Tennessee to Washington, D.C. after graduate school. Ross was a historian at the Smithsonian and Anne was a history professor at George Mason University. Both were well-known in their field of study. Their children attended Georgetown Day School, a private school in the district. Each excelled in academics and athletics.

After a few hours passed, they decided to stop for something to eat. They pulled into Staunton, Virginia, and found a diner. "Your ancestors lived in this area long ago," informed Ross.

"They did. I didn't know that" responded Celia.

"I have never heard you talk about this before, Dad. Why did they leave," questioned Hannah.

"I don't know, Hannah. I suppose for more opportunity. Tennessee was a new territory and the government encouraged people to settle there."

"Wow, that must have been a long time ago. It must have been scary," concluded Hannah. "I don't think I could do that."

"I'm sure it was scary, but they believed they could be successful, so it was worth the risk," added Anne. "Our family has been in Tennessee since that time."

"Well, until you guys moved, right? I mean all of Gram and Nanna's kids left Tennessee," Sean corrected his mother.

"That is true. Sort of sad to think about that, but Gram has a sister and brother who still live in Tennessee and so do their children. You may not remember our aunts and uncles. You have not seen them in a long time. We need to make time to see them sometime."

"Maybe we should schedule a family reunion sometime soon," said Ross.

"Yes, we should. Maybe I can coordinate that with our cousins. It might be nice to bring Dad back to Tennessee to visit while he is still able to do it."

"I absolutely think we should do that but don't wait too long. You just don't know how long he will be able to get around like he can now."

"You're right, Ross. Well, we'd better get back on the road."

After returning to their vehicle, the children watched as they drove along the highway toward Tennessee. "It is so beautiful here. I love the mountains, the trees, and all the farms," noted Celia.

"This part of Virginia is called the Shenandoah Valley. Did you know that George Washington started his career as a surveyor in this part of Virginia?" asked Ross.

"No, I don't think I learned about that," responded Sean. "What does a surveyor do?"

"They help to partition the land. In those days this area was a wilderness, so a surveyor would come out and establish boundaries for people buying or being given land by the government."

Anne continued, "Many families were given land for coming to the colonies and after the Revolutionary War as a benefit for their participation in the war. The same happened after the Civil War for those who fought for the Union. It was a way of paying the soldiers back for their participation, but it was also of benefit to the country because it helped us to become more self-sufficient and prosperous."

"Sean, a surveyor also helps to plan the building of a city, like Charlottesville. Many of the earliest cities in America were patterned after those in Europe. Washington came back to this area when he led the Patriot Army during the Revolutionary War." Ross continued hoping to garner more questions from his children. A few moments of silent contemplation followed.

"Where did we…I mean our ancestors come from? How did they get here," questioned Hannah. "I don't think I've heard either of you talk about it."

Anne was quiet for a few minutes trying to think about her knowledge of her own family's history, as did Ross. "You know, I am ashamed to say that I don't know. We both have studied this nation's history and the history of other nations, but we haven't put much effort into knowing our own," answered Anne sadly.

"I bet Gram knows. You should talk to him about it. I'm sure he'd love to tell you about it. I know he loves history as much as we do. He taught high school history, you know," instructed their father.

"Hmm, I forgot that" replied Celia. Looking towards her siblings, Celia added, "I think we should ask Gram. It might help keep his mind off missing Nanna." Hannah and Sean shook their heads in agreement.

The rest of the drive was spent in quiet, except for the low sound of the radio. The children returned to their devices and Anne read a book as Ross drove. They would arrive in Knoxville in the evening. They made a quick stop at a Wendy's Restaurant to buy food for everyone before going on to Alex's home.

When they pulled into the driveway, Alex came from the house to welcome the family. "Oh, Anne, Ross, kids, I am so happy to see you all. Come on inside, we can get your luggage later."

"Hi, Daddy," Anne responded as she leaned over to kiss her father. Anne remarked about how well her father looked, which he promptly disregarded and changed the topic of conversation.

"Hi, Gram," responded Ross as he put his hand out to shake his father-in-law's hand. "We are happy to see you."

"Gram!" All three of the children screamed in unison as they ran for the door. Each of the children hugged their grandfather before going inside.

Once inside they all went into the kitchen to get the food ready to eat. The children pulled out paper plates and napkins. Anne gathered glasses for drinks while Ross unloaded the food from the bags.

"It is so wonderful to have you all here," announced Alexander. "I miss you when you aren't here. Your brothers and sister rarely call much less visit. They always seem to be too busy."

Anne reached over and pulled her father towards her, "I'm sorry, Daddy. They could do better, but I don't want to get into that right now. We are here for you, and we are thrilled to have you come to live with us. The children and I have arranged your room in the basement. They've labeled it, 'Gram's Suite'; I think you will like it. You have everything you need." The family sat down together to eat their meal. Gram commented on how fast-food burgers used to taste better. Sean stole his sisters' french fries, while Ross perused the local newspaper. Anne quietly looked around the table and realized how blessed she was to have such a beautiful, loving family. After dinner, the children returned to the SUV to bring in the suitcases and other items. They took the suitcases to the rooms where they would be sleeping over the next few days. After finishing the chore, the children arrived in the living room where their parents and grandfather were sitting watching television. Their grandfather watched *Jeopardy* ev-ery night without question. He adored being challenged by the questions and kept a running tally of what his winnings would be if he was actually on the program. The children, while they didn't fully appreciate the challenge of the game show, found humor in his relentless pursuit of the answers if he did not know them, especially now that he could Google the questions on his iPad!

At the end of the show, Alex turned the television off and asked his family if they'd like to play a board game. The children went with their grandfather to choose a game to play. After seeing their choices—*Monopoly, Scrabble, or Chinese Checkers*, the children cheered for *Monopoly*.

"We just got a new *Monopoly* game…it's a Washington, DC, version and it has related properties and game pieces. It is so cool, Gram," commented Sean. "We love to play it, but Hannah gets vicious when she plays," he added giggling.

"I do not, Sean! I just play to win," retorted Hannah. Because no one had won the game by bedtime, they agreed to leave it until the following evening.

Chapter 2

The next morning seemed to come quickly. Arising at 7:00 a.m., they each sauntered into the kitchen looking for food. Alex, who was an early riser, had already been awake for an hour and a half and had begun to cook breakfast. The smell of coffee and bacon permeated the house.

"Dad, I'm sorry, I should have gotten up earlier to help you with breakfast. We slept through the alarm clock," reported Anne.

"It's fine, Annie. I have been doing this for decades. Today is no different. Your mom and I always ate a hot breakfast, and so did you kids. Do you remember what your favorite breakfast was before school?"

"Oh, I sure do. You made egg McMuffins before egg McMuffins were even a 'thing'," replied Anne. "I loved them so much that I wanted them every day."

Sean looked puzzled at his mother, "You ate the same thing every day? That's weird."

Laughing at Sean, "I guess it may seem so to you. Each of you has always wanted something different. None of you was patient enough for me to cook breakfast. You have always wanted just a Pop Tart or cereal."

"I guess that's true," Sean confirmed.

"What about you, Daddy," Celia asked. "What did you eat when you were growing up?"

"Well, you know, I grew up on a farm. Your uncle Evan and I had to wake up very early, having to help with chores, while my mother and my sisters made breakfast. We usually had eggs, bacon, and biscuits. Other days we might have pancakes."

Changing the subject, Ross asked, "Do you have a plan for how you want to handle this process today, Gramps?"

"Ross, I think today I want to work on cleaning out Amanda's things. I want to take her clothes, the nicer ones, to the church for their clothes closet. The other clothes, furniture, and such things will be taken to Goodwill. This will probably take most of today and possibly tomorrow to accomplish. Ironically, your mother and I cleaned out most of the closets six months before we lost her."

"That's fine, Daddy. I can help you with this and Ross and the children work on cleaning up the yard. Is that okay with you?"

"Oh, I think that would be wonderful. I haven't felt like getting out there to work." While Alex was mostly in good health, pain in his knees made mobility more difficult. Pushing a lawnmower wasn't something he could do anymore. As a frugal person, he also did not want to pay someone to do the work for him. The yard had become unsightly as a result.

After finishing their meal and cleaning up the kitchen, each returned to their room to get dressed. Before going outside to help their father, Sean, Hannah, and Celia were instructed to clean the bathrooms.

Anne went to her father's room to begin the process of cleaning out her mother's closet and dresser. When she entered the room, Alex was quietly sitting at the end of the bed. There were several empty boxes that he had brought in to fill with Amanda's things. Anne walked over to her father and sat down beside him. Reaching her arm around his shoulder, she pulled him close to her. "Daddy, I cannot imagine how difficult this must be for you. You and Momma had been married for so long. I know how much I miss her; it must be so much more difficult for you."

"Your Momma and I met when we were in first grade. I think I always loved her. I never wanted to date anyone else. We married young. I was in college, you know? I just couldn't bear the thought of her meeting and marrying someone else."

"Oh Daddy, that is so sweet. I felt the same way about Ross."

"You got a good one with Ross, Annie. Well, I guess we had better get started if we want to finish today." Sadly, Alex walked into their closet to pull his wife's clothes out. Anne took them, folded them, and placed them into boxes. Looking at one of the dresses, Anne held it close to her chest. "Oh, Daddy, I remember this dress. She wore it to Sean's christening. I remember how pretty she looked in it." Wiping away a tear running down her cheek, Anne continued to pack boxes.

After they finished with Amanda's clothes, Anne went to her mother's dresser. "Some of these things will just have to be thrown away, Daddy. They cannot be resold."

"I understand. It's fine." Alex reluctantly responded. He continued cleaning out the closet. "I think I will donate some of my things, too. I cannot take all of this with me to your house. Some of this is just too worn out and old."

"Okay, Daddy. I will go to the garage and get a few more boxes for you to put those things in," Anne agreed. When she returned, Alex was again seated on the end of the bed, this time, with a box of photographs. "What did you find, Dad?"

"I bet the kids would like to see these. There are photos of you, Mary Beth, Johnny, and Charles when you were kids. Funny to look at them now. We had some bad hair and some crazy clothes back then, didn't we?"

"Oh, my goodness, they would get a kick out seeing these. What's this," inquired Anne.

"That's our wedding album. I guess it must seem small compared to those today. We didn't have a professional photographer. My Uncle Thomas took these," Alex sighed. "We were so young then. We had a wonderful life together. It was difficult at times, but it was worth it."

"Wow, look at you both. You look like babies. Momma was so pretty with her dark hair. I remember thinking how beautiful my Momma was when I was a girl. I thought I looked like a wash rag compared to her. Mary Beth looks like Mom, doesn't she?"

"You were a beautiful wash rag, my girl! Mary Beth does look like your mother, but she has my personality. You're much more even-tempered like your mother. Nothing seemed to rattle her. I am much more emotional and quick-tempered."

"So, who would you say the boys are like?" asked Anne.

"Johnny is more like my brother, Jimmy. He has a great mind for math and science, but he isn't always common-sense smart. Charles is more like my Uncle Neil, I think. He was sort of an oddball. He was a wonderful person: he could always make me laugh. He was a hard worker, which made up for what he lacked in other areas. He went to work at a dairy farm after dropping out of school. He did all the jobs no one else wanted to do, but once he was old enough to drive, he became a delivery man. Charles was much the same; he never cared about school. It wasn't his strong suit, but he is a hard worker. Your brother has done well for himself despite not having an advanced education like you, Johnny, and Mary Beth. But all you kids were good. You all never gave us any trouble," patting Anne on the knee, he continued, "We were lucky for that." Alex went to the linen closet to pack up all the sheets and towels. "I think we'll take these to the church, too. Maybe someone can use them. Some are almost new."

After Anne finished packing up her mother's things, she went into the closet to remove anything left by her dad. She saw a garment bag hanging alone. Her father had gone downstairs to get a glass of water. Anne walked over to the bag and unzipped it. Inside she found her mother's wedding dress. It was a beautiful ivory satin, swing skirt dress with lace bodice and sleeves. It had a bow in the front just at the waist. In the bottom of the garment bag were matching satin pumps and a pill-bottle style hat in the same ivory satin and lace with a short ivory veil in the front. Anne was surprised that her mother had kept the dress and that it was in such good condition. Anne yelled, "Girls, come here!"

"Okay, just a minute, Mom. We need to finish the tub." A few minutes passed when the girls came walking into the closet taking off their gloves as they came in. "Is there a problem, Mom?"

"No, I want to show you both something and ask you a question. Look, here is your grandmother's wedding ensemble." Anne took the items over to her parents' bed and laid them out as they would have been worn. What do you think?"

Hannah sat on the bed and felt the fabric. "It's lovely, Momma. It's very vintage."

"I guess so, Hannah, she wore it over sixty years ago. I was wondering what you two might suggest we do with it."

Hannah and Celia responded in unexpected unison, "We have to keep it." Looking at each other they laughed. Hannah continued, "This is popular now. Celia or I might want to wear it one day." Hannah and Celia both kept touching it and commenting on the beauty of the dress and shoes. "Why didn't you or Aunt Mary Beth wear it?"

"I don't know that we thought of it as an option at the time. It was not the style then."

"Let's keep it, Momma," added Celia.

"Then that is what we will do," Anne concluded. "You girls go on out and help your dad and Sean and we will have lunch in an hour." The girls did as their mother requested.

The process of cleaning out, throwing away, and packing continued after lunch until 4:00 p.m. Anne then went to make dinner for the crew. After dinner, the previous evening's routine was repeated—*Jeopardy* then *Monopoly*. The *Monopoly* game ended with Celia as the ultimate victor. Before retiring for the evening, the family shared ice cream sundaes.

Chapter 3

Over the next two days, each bedroom was cleaned out and packed up. Some items were saved for Anne, Mary Beth, Charles, and John. Others were donated or given to family and friends as mementos. Some of Alex's friends felt awkward taking the gifts but relented after feeling that they'd be hurting their friend if they refused.

On the third day, Ross' brother and his family came over to help move out some of the heavier furniture. Evan and his wife Emily had four teenage boys who could lift anything. Everyone felt some sorrow in the finality of watching bedroom furniture, kitchen, and dining room furniture, and finally, living room furniture leave the home. The children helped occupy their grandfather by helping him to clean out the attic.

The home had an enormous attic by modern standards. It was large enough that it could have been converted into a living space if it had been needed. Alex's children often played in the attic on rainy days while they were growing up, and Amanda hung laundry in the attic on hot, rainy days. Over the years since they had grown up and left the home, it became a place to "stick" things that Alexander and Amanda wanted to keep or that they thought their children would like to have. Unfortunately for Alex now, most of these items could not be kept.

The group began to sift through the many boxes in the attic. Some contained old toys and books that belonged to their mother and her siblings. There was a box of yearbooks. The children laughed as they glanced through the various books at the odd clothes and crazy hairstyles. Other boxes held old clothes, purses, and mementos. Sean was drawn to a steamer truck in the back corner of the attic. He knelt in front of the trunk and tried to open it but was unable. "Gram, could you help me open this?"

"Oh, wow, that belonged to my great-grandfather Richard. Let me see if we can get that open." Alex attempted to open the trunk, but it was locked. "Hmm, I think I might know where the key is. I will be right back." Alex went to his bedroom and opened the box where he had placed his wife's jewelry box. Inside the box was a key, which he believed went to the trunk. Returning to the attic, he announced to the group, "Let's see if this key will work. I think it is the right one."

"I hope so, Gram," said Sean looking at his grandfather with distress in his eyes. Alex bent over to put the key in the lock and with a wiggle and a turn, the key unlocked the trunk. Alex lifted the lid uncovering its contents for the group who had gathered around to watch.

"Let me go get you a chair to sit in, Gram. I know you can't sit on the floor!" Hannah exclaimed. She walked over to another side of the attic where several folding chairs were located. She brought the chair over to the corner where the trunk was and set it down for her grandfather.

"Well, let's see what we find," Alex uttered as he sat down feeling tired from the morning's activities. He began to pick up items from the trunk and to relate to his grandchildren the item's importance. "This is a photograph of my parents, your great-grandparents Campbell and Sarah. This photograph was taken after they married in 1936. They were both eighteen years old. Campbell studied to be a doctor. Because of the time and the Depression, they did not always make much money. People did not have the money to pay doctors. Often, they paid with vegetables from their farms, a pig, or even traded it for something he might need. When it looked like the United States would be entering World War II, he was called up for service as a doctor in Europe. He had to leave behind my mother and four very young children. Luckily, we had my grandmother to help."

Alex pulled a jacket from the trunk. "This is the Army jacket my father wore in the Army. Here is his hat." Sean grabbed the coat and hat and put them on.

"Look at me, Gram! How do I look?" exclaimed Sean.

"Ya' look like a million bucks, doesn't he girls?"

The girls began to giggle. "Silly is how you look, Sean!"

Alex rummaged through the trunk looking for something else interesting when he came across something he did not recall. "Hmmm, I am not sure what this is." In a box inside the trunk, he found a book. It was a leather-bound book with a leather tie closing it. Alex untied the strings and opened the book. He could tell it was much older than anything he remembered his father had. The handwriting on the inside also did not remind him of his father, and once he began to read, he realized that it did not belong to his father or grandfather, but to his great-grandfather. "Oh, my goodness, I don't remember ever reading this. I guess it could be possible that over the years, we combined items into this trunk after we moved my mother in with us."

"What is it, Gram?" Inquired Celia.

"It appears to be a journal kept by my great-grandfather, your great-great-grandfather, Richard Sean Murray. There's an inscription here at the front from him."

"What does it say?" Hannah asked. The children moved closer to their grandfather so that they could hear him read.

> *"This is the story of our family. It is written for future generations that they might know and appreciate the family who came before. Some of this story may seem to be a work of fiction, but I assure you that it is absolutely true. I, Richard Sean Murray, write this from my memory of the stories told to me by my grandparents, Alexander MacKenzie Murray, Jr. and Anna Brown Murray. I have also researched and confirmed this story which many might seek to hide. Each one of us is a book with a story to be told. We must pass on our stories so that our descendants know who we were, what we believed in, what we fought for, and even the mistakes we made. My blessings to all those who may read the contents of these journals. Know that your family who came before was respected and loved. Further, I make a simple request of said readers that you pass these books on to each new generation so that*

they may know us as well. Continuing with tra-dition, these journals is passed to the oldest son of the oldest son. If, however, a generation holds no son then, in that event, these should be passed to the oldest daughter. If at some time a manner of making copies of the journals exists, then I prefer copies to be shared with all members of the family, but the originals shall remain with the oldest son or daughter. Signed, Richard Sean Murray, Washington County, Tennessee, 1900."

"That's my name…Sean! I never knew my name came from your family, Gram. Please read the journal! Please?" Sean begged his grandfather.

"I will but you all have to keep cleaning while I do. Deal?"

"Yes, sir!" Each child responded.

As Alex began to read, each of the children began to imagine the story in their minds as they cleaned and threw away items which had not weathered the attic heat.

Chapter 4

Our story, the story of this family, begins in Ulster, Ireland. Despite being in Ireland for a few years when your ancestors left for the colonies, we were of Scottish stock, as was much of Ulster. Historians have called these immigrants Ulster Scots. These Scots originated in the western part of Scotland. They immigrated to Ireland because of a poor economy, an unstable political environment, and religious persecution. Many of these families were of the Presbyterian faith. Too many consecutive years of drought led to failures in the agricultural economy of Scotland. This was true of our family.

The first wave of Scots from Ulster to the Colony of Virginia began in the early 1700s. The Shenandoah Valley, where our family settled, offered opportunities to these early pioneers in the sparsely populated area. Other Ulster Scots stayed in Pennsylvania for a period of time before moving south into Virginia. You will be surprised to learn that our last name is not actually 'Murray', but that will be explained later. Our family traveled to Virginia around 1740 and remained in Virginia until about 1777-78. At that time, two members of the family relocated to Washington County, Tennessee, again hoping for better economic outcomes as well as dealing with a difficult family situation, which only life in the wilderness could hide.

Our first ancestor in America was Duncan MacKenzie, our direct ancestor, along with his older brother, Donald, and sister Eleanor. They came from Ulster, Ireland, with another Scottish family to work on a farm. The patriarch of the family, Alexander MacKenzie, and his wife Isobel, originally planned for the entire family to come to America, but Alexander and the youngest child James died before the others were scheduled to leave. This left Isobel with three children she could not support. Isobel worked for Robert and Mary Fraser in their Donegal home. Robert's father William Fraser descended from an aristocratic family who supported King James I in his supplanting of Ulster. This made the Fraser family unpopular in Scotland. The King rewarded the Frasers with land. Eventually, even they wished to leave Ireland after finding the agricultural income of their tenant farmers to be less than desirable.

Isobel went to Mr. Fraser and implored him to take her children to Virginia as indentured servants. She too had become ill and believed herself incapable of making the journey. The Fraser family was quite fond of Alexander and Isobel. She was a trustworthy and dedicated servant in their home. They agreed to take the children. She signed indentures for each child for a period of ten years, after which they would be given land of their own and money to buy equipment needed to begin their own farming operation. As for her daughter Eleanor, she would work in their home as a housemaid until her brothers were emancipated. Then, Mr. Fraser would assist in finding a proper marriage for the girl. Each of Isobel's children would be provided with the means and skills to start successful families.

Before the family left for the colonies, Isobel told her children to work hard and not to give the Frasers any reason to dismiss them. She promised them that, should she become able, she would come to Virginia as soon as she was able. When they arrived in America, she asked that they, before they left the docks, turn and face the horizon in the direction they had come from and to remember her with a song she sang to them each night before bed. She asked, "Send me a song, my loves, that I might hear it and know that you are well." I do not know if the children did as she asked, but I would like to think that they did. It was a beautiful request from a loving mother who, in the end, would not join them in their new country.

The MacKenzie children and the Frasers arrived in Virginia in 1740. They settled in Staunton, Virginia. Before setting out for Staunton, however, they spent a month on the coast of Virginia gathering the necessary provisions. The travel from the coast to Staunton was treacherous given the terrain and the possibility of encountering Indians along the way. In addition to the land given to the Frasers by the King, Mr. Fraser purchased an additional three hundred acres of land from Staunton's founder, William Beverley. This proved to be a wise decision for both the Beverleys and the Frasers. Staunton grew to be the economic center of banking, shipping, brokerage, and other businesses in what would later become Augusta County. From 1738 until about 1770, Staunton served as the capital of the Northwest Territory for several years. Mr. Fraser's tobacco farm, later to be called "Dumbarton Hall", was just one of many successful farms in the area. Years later Robert Fraser purchased an additional thousand acres.

Chapter 5

The following is all the information I have been able to acquire regarding the eldest son, Donald MacKenzie. At the time the MacKenzie children traveled to Virginia, Donald was fourteen years old; Eleanor was twelve; and Duncan was ten. Don was a mature young man for his years. He was a thin child with black hair, ivory skin, and light eyes. He was described as tall for a child of his age. Despite his thin frame, he was remarkably strong.

His father taught him to hunt, prepare meat, and plant a vegetable garden. Alexander tried to pay his son money when he had some left over to teach his son how to handle money. He made certain that his son understood the importance of paying his rent promptly and the burden that debt could cause a family. He encouraged his son to avoid debt at all costs. Don would later pass these lessons on to his younger brother, and later he made certain any future spouse for his sister possessed the same values.

Once they arrived in America, Don became a father figure and an advisor to Duncan and Eleanor. Mr. Fraser, in turn, took Don under his wing. If an issue were presented involving his siblings, Mr. Fraser would discuss it with Donny first. Donny attempted to handle the situation with his sibling first before involving Mr. Fraser. After the household was established and they could begin to farm the land, Mr. Fraser taught Donny everything he knew about farming. The Fraser farm primarily grew tobacco. Over time, they would expand to growing vegetables and apples. Donny made it a habit to be up before the sun rose without having to be awakened by Mr. Fraser. He went right to work milking the cows, bringing in firewood to the kitchen and other rooms, and then being out in the field ready to work after eating breakfast. If he had any extra time, Donny could be found chopping wood or playing music. Don was a remarkable fiddler. Because of his diligence, Mr. Fraser gave him more responsibility and both Donald and the farm matured well.

It was about 1742 when Mr. Fraser and Don traveled back to the coast. I do not know if the boy knew the purpose of the trip. Undoubtedly, Donny would have known of the existence of African slaves in the colony having encountered them on other farms in the area. It wasn't until this time, though, that Mr. Fraser decided to become a slaveholder. The work on a tobacco farm was labor intensive. While Mr. Fraser did not approve of the practice, he felt compelled to participate to be a profitable farm. When the pair arrived at the coast, they arranged for a room and then went to the waterfront where the slave market was. Once at the market, Donny became visibly disturbed by what he witnessed. The men, women, and children, all barely clothed, were bound together at the hands and feet. They walked onto a platform in front of the crowd. He could see intense fear and sadness in their eyes. He felt deep sorrow for their circumstance. That day, Mr. Fraser bought four men, two women, and a small boy and girl, both of whom looked to be about Duncan's age. Mr. Fraser told Don that most of the men would help in the fields, and the children would help Eleanor in the house, while the women would cook and assist in the fields as needed.

During their time on the farm, Mr. Fraser proved to be a kind and generous man. Unlike other planters, as they were called then, in the area who often mistreated their slaves, Mr. Fraser did not. He discovered that when treated with fairness, they worked harder and were less argumentative. He also believed that at some time in the near future, slaves would be emancipated like indentured servants. He believed that they should be educated and taught skills that would help them to be successful when such emancipation happened. This practice was frowned upon by his fellow planters. Nonetheless, Mr. Fraser did as Mr. Fraser set his mind to do regardless of the sentiments of his fellow planters.

All the children, including Donny, Duncan, Eleanor and the older negro children, were educated in the evenings by Mrs. Fraser. She taught them to read, to write, and to do simple math. All of them were eager students. They spent an hour before bedtime going over their studies with each other and correcting any errors they may have made. It should be no surprise that this farm became quite successful and admired by many.

As Donny matured, he became a handsome young man. He eventually became the foreman of the plantation and assisted in managing the operation. Don enjoyed the work and felt a deep sense of accomplishment. He went on to have his own farm and to marry the daughter of the local bank president. They had eight children.

Chapter 6

The only MacKenzie daughter, Eleanor, was twelve years old when the group came to Virginia. She was a blonde-haired, light-green-eyed, little beauty. As a child, she was timid and shy until she became comfortable around others. Mrs. Fraser appreciated the quiet nature of the child. Eleanor seemed to miss her mother and father more than her brothers. In the beginning, she could often be heard crying at night. This changed, however, after the slave children arrived at the home. The children became close friends. Mrs. Fraser allowed the children to have playtime after their chores had been completed. She knew that exercise was important for the well-being of the children. Being a rather vain woman, she did not want fat children no matter their race.

Each of the children had chores. The little slave girl, who had been named Rebecca, assisted the cooks in the kitchen. The little slave boy, Lucas, brought in the firewood, but Rebecca was responsible for starting the fires in each room, keeping them lit, and cleaning the fireplaces three times a week. Both Rebecca and Eleanor cleaned the house, except for fragile items which were left to the older women. As the girls grew, they became responsible for all the cleaning.

As with the boys, the girls were educated. They were taught to read and write; but unlike the boys, the girls were taught to garden, sew and cook. Mrs. Fraser wanted to make certain that each girl would become an appropriate wife when the time came. While reading and writing were taught by Mrs. Fraser, other housekeeping skills were taught to the girls by the slave women, Agnes and Esther. Eleanor came to love both women as substitute mothers. Mrs. Fraser, unlike her husband, could often be cold and curt. She did not treat "the help" with the same kindness that her husband did. It was not unusual for Mrs. Fraser to be overheard scolding her husband for being too "soft" to those in his employment. Mr. Fraser often chose the path of least resistance, but there were times when he would correct his wife and demand that she apologize for her behavior. It was clear to all that Mrs. Fraser felt herself above them. This behavior placed a clear line of demarcation between Mrs. Fraser and those who worked in her home, which could make for a tense environment.

Mrs. Fraser gave birth her first child a year after the family's arrival in Virginia. Her first child, a son named Robert Junior, was born sickly. Mrs. Fraser had a difficult time bearing the child and was bedridden for several weeks thereafter. Agnes became a makeshift Nanny to the tiny boy because she had birthed a child six months prior. Agnes was allowed to bring her baby into Robbie's nursery and to assist in the care of the boys until the boys were a little over two years old. At this time, the family brought in an older negro woman to take care of the small children. Another family nearby was planning to send the old woman away because they did not want the responsibility of caring for her since she could no longer work in the fields. Maybelle was thankful to be taken into the Fraser home. They were acquainted with one another from attending social events at their neighbor's home. Robbie, who had always been a scrawny boy, gained five pounds after Maybelle began caring for him.

As Eleanor grew older and Maybelle died, she took over the nanny duties for the Fraser's children. Mrs. Fraser gave birth eight times in ten years. Only six of these children survived to adulthood. Eleanor loved all the children, and she treated them as if they were her own family. The Fraser children loved Eleanor as much as they loved their own parents, despite Mrs. Fraser's opinion of social propriety. There were times when the children confided in Eleanor rather than their mother about situations they encountered. One of those subjects was the presence of African slaves on the farm. They were not immune to the difference in opinions between their parents or those of their friends who lived in Staunton. The topic was often discussed and overheard by the children at church on Sundays. Eleanor related this story to her children years later when they too inquired about the subject.

"Miss Eleanor, why do Momma and Daddy argue so much about the negroes?" inquired Sara Beth, the eldest daughter.

"Well, children, this is a most difficult situation. I believe your father understands, as our Lord has taught us, that all people should be treated with respect and kindness. Your mother was raised differently than your father. While both of their families were aristocrats in Scotland, your mother's family, the MacDonalds, were more involved in society and government. They lived in a castle and had many servants. In those households, the servants were never allowed to interact with the family. That was, and I suppose still is, the custom. That is how she expects it to be here. It is what she knows. I understand it because my mother worked in your parents' home before we came here. It's just how it is."

"So, you don't hate her for acting like she does? She can be quite mean," inquired Emily, the middle daughter.

"No, certainly I do not. I could not hate her," responded Eleanor. "She and your father promised my mother that they would take care of me and, once I am old enough, they will assist in finding me a suitable husband. That meant so much to my mother because she did not have to worry about what might happen to my brothers and me after we left Ireland."

"Would they do that for Agnes and Esther," asked Edwin with a puzzled look on his face.

"Well now, Agnes and Esther were married to Abraham and Isaac not long after they came here. Your father believed that they would be happier if they were married. Reuben and Caleb are unmarried currently, but they will find them wives at some point."

"Oh sure, I guess I hadn't thought about it because of Lucas. Who are Lucas' parents," asked William, the youngest and twin of Richard.

"We do not know, William, and that makes me sad. Esther and Isaac care for him and Rebecca. I think they love them as their own," continued Eleanor.

Richard who was obviously sitting and thinking about what he had heard interjected, "Why are the negroes treated differently than you and your brothers?"

"I know it seems strange. Truthfully, it is strange. You see me living in the house, though my room is in the attic and not on the second floor with you all. But you also know that my brothers do not. They have a separate house where they live, but they come here to eat and sometimes I go out to their cottage to spend time with them apart from your family. The negroes, for the most part, do everything separately from us. I understand why you would wonder. Unfortunately, I do not have a reasonable answer to your question. In my mind and belief, we are all the same. In many ways, Abraham, Isaac, Caleb, Reuben, Agnes, Esther, Rebecca, Lucas, my brothers, and I have been treated the same. We all have been taught to read, to write, and to do arithmetic. Agnes and Esther are teaching Rebecca and me how to sew and cook. In these ways, we've been treated the same. I simply believe that the only differences between me and the negroes is our skin color and where we came from. Many of your parent's friends do not believe as I do, and they certainly do not do any of these things for their negroes. I hope that soon all of them will be freed. Have any of you seen what happens when Agnes cuts a finger in the kitchen?"

"No, I haven't seen her cut her finger," responded Robbie, "what happens?"

"Well, her finger bleeds. Do you know what color her blood is," inquired Eleanor of her audience?

They looked at each other puzzled at the question. Richard piped up, "Nope".

"It is red! What color is your blood, William?"

"It's red!" A look of awe overtook the children.

"You see, God made us mostly the same."

As soon as the conversation with the children began, it was over. They were content with the answers Eleanor had given them. Each went their own way to read, play in the yard, or ride horses. As time went on and the negroes had more children, as did the Frasers, they became friends and Mrs. Fraser's attitude softened. Most seemed happy and content despite the nature of their relationships.

Chapter 7

The youngest of the MacKenzie children was Duncan, the red-headed, freckle-faced, little spitfire. When the MacKenzies arrived in America, Duncan was ten years old, and unlike his scrawny older brother, Duncan was a hearty boy. He loved to eat. He was always eating something. Mrs. Fraser worried at first that the child might have some illness that caused his stomach to bulge. Before leaving Ulster, Mr. Fraser had his physician examine Duncan to determine if he would survive the long voyage. The last thing he wanted was for the child to die aboard ship. The doctor assured Mr. Fraser that Duncan was a healthy, thriving boy with a great metabolism.

As I have related to you, Duncan worked in the Fraser home as a houseboy until he was of sufficient age to begin working in the stables and fields. Duncan worked hard for the family, often finishing his chores early. When he did, he could be found reading every book he could find in the Fraser library. He excelled in his studies. He enjoyed reading about science and history. He appeared to have a mind for education which Mr. Fraser both acknowledged and encouraged. Mr. Fraser believed that an investment in the boy's continued education would be well worth the cost, so he put aside additional monies for that purpose after Duncan was emancipated.

At about this time, William and Mary University was the second oldest school of higher education in the colonies, hav-ing been founded in 1693. Mr. Fraser's desire for Duncan to attend the university. By the time of his emancipation in 1750, Duncan was thrilled to discover Mr. Fraser's plans. Duncan enrolled that same year and graduated two years later. He studied agriculture, animal husbandry, and botany. It was in Williamsburg that Duncan met his future wife, Elizabeth Cameron, the daughter of a professor at William and Mary. Mr. James Cameron, who taught Latin, often invited students to his home for meals and discussions. It was at one of these events that Duncan met Elizabeth. She was a petite, dark auburn-haired girl with a milky white complexion. Like Mr. Fraser, Mr. Cameron also believed in educating both men and women. Elizabeth and her siblings were taught the same subjects as Mr. Cameron's male students. Duncan found this to be attractive. He enjoyed strolling along the Camerons' yard with Elizabeth discussing the many subjects of the day. Duncan described Elizabeth as being as intelligent as she was beautiful. He fell deeply in love with her.

As the time of his graduation neared, Duncan asked to speak with Mr. Cameron privately after class one day. Mr. Cameron suspected why his favorite student requested a pri-vate meeting and he was not wrong. A most eloquent speaker, Duncan was now stammering like a child. As he began to make his best argument for Mr. Cameron to agree to a mar-riage between Elizabeth and himself, Mr. Cameron interjected a resounding, "Yes, of course," and stuck his hand out to shake the hand of his future son-in-law.

From that moment until the wedding day, the couple was showered with parties and gifts. Duncan was introduced to the Who's Who of Virginia society. His brother and sister were also welcomed as a part of the merging family. It was a bonus for Eleanor as she needed to marry well so that she would be provided for. She could not afford to wait too long for the planning of a marriage because she was two years older than Duncan. While there were gentlemen of good stature in the Staunton area, the choices were not like those on the coast of Virginia. Many of those families were much wealthier and well-connected.

Chapter 8

As I stated earlier, Isobel Murray MacKenzie and her husband Alexander were employed in Ulster by Mr. Robert Fraser's father, William Fraser. Robert was his only son, having three daughters. William Fraser was given land in Virginia because of his support for the British king in Ulster. This made Mr. Fraser unpopular with his Scottish clansmen and made life difficult for his family and their tenant farmers. Being an aged man, Mr. Fraser decided to give the land in Virginia to his son who had just married. He would retain partial ownership in the land, and thus receive a percentage of the profits made until his death.

Isobel, having been born in Scotland, was the niece of the governess to the children of Earl William Home. When Isobel became of age, her aunt assisted her in obtaining employment as a housemaid with the Earl. Their service to this family came to an end when Isobel met Alexander MacKenzie, a farrier for the Earl. As was the custom, people working in service were required to remain unmarried. If a servant decided to marry, they were required to leave their employment, except for the more progressive Fraser family. They determined after a period of experimentation that happily married couples stayed longer in their employ and were more productive. They further believed that, because the Bible encouraged marriage, they should encourage marriage as well. These beliefs, too, made the Frasers hated by their fellow aristocrats in Scotland, like the Homes.

When Isobel and Alexander met with the Earl, he thanked them for their dedicated service to his family. He mentioned to them that he had heard that the Fraser family was planning a move to Ulster and that they had other servants who were married and who were provided cottages on the grounds of the Fraser family home. He heard, however, that a few of the servants would not be joining the Frasers in their move to Ireland. Knowing that they would have to employ new servants, he believed they might prefer to employ people with good recommendations from kinsmen. The couple was encouraged by this news. The Earl asked for time to contact Mr. Fraser and inquire on their behalf. He asked that they wait to make any decisions until he could report his findings.

About three weeks passed before the Earl sought out Isobel and Alexander. As soon as they made eye contact with the Earl, a smile washed across his face and his cheeks flushed. They knew it was good news. At the brief meeting, the Earl related that Mr. Fraser was happy to employ the young couple, especially after receiving such a fine recommendation from him. He further related that the move was expected to occur within the next two months. This gave the couple cause for concern, believing that they would lose their employment and be without another. The Earl assured them that he would not leave them without work and that he and Mr. Fraser would work out the details of a transition from one home to the next. He understood their reservations and allowed them to remain in his home, as a married couple until the transition; however, they had to reside in separate quarters until after they left his service. The couple was thrilled and agreed to his conditions.

As should be abundantly clear, the marriage of Alexander and Isobel was a blessed one. The Frasers provided a cottage on their property for the couple's use. Within a few short years, they would have an increasing family and a feeling of contentment and happiness. Until, of course, they prepared to move with the Frasers to America. At this time many new illnesses were circulating that could kill in days, if not hours. Unfortunately for Alexander, he contracted influenza and died. Isobel was forced to quickly prepare her children for the trip to America.

Eleanor learned to clean and cook quickly. She enjoyed singing as she worked. She had a lovely singing voice, and she often sang traditional Scottish songs, especially those taught to her and her brothers by their mother. She was petite but mighty, as Mr. Fraser often described her. She was not tender-hearted like many young girls. The criticism and rudeness often heaped upon her by Mrs. Fraser did not seem to affect her. She listened and made mental notes of the comments, and then moved on with her chores.

Because of her small stature and bone structure, she was a quick runner. Her brothers and sometimes the negro children were thrilled to play hide-and-seek or chase fireflies in the evening. The adults enjoyed the spectacle of wild children running about as they sat in their rocking chairs sipping their evening cocktails. To say it was at times idyllic would not have been untrue.

When Duncan and Elizabeth neared their wedding day, Eleanor assisted in many of the preparations. The wedding took place on the grounds of a plantation just outside of Williamsburg which was owned by a friend of the Camerons. The residence was a large, two-story, white home that sat on almost a thousand acres. The property was on the western side of the James River which could be seen from the back porch of the home. Beautiful river birch and dogwood trees dotted the grounds from which paper lanterns had been hung. The smell of honeysuckle and jasmine wafted through the warm air. Musicians played chamber music and a few more popular tunes of the day. The MacKenzies felt out of place in such surroundings, but in their hearts, they knew that this was the life that their parents had wished for them.

Eleanor was daydreaming when Elizabeth's brother Walter brought over some of his friends to meet her. It was one of these friends who would become Eleanor's suitor. Malcolm Campbell was a classmate of Walter's at Harvard. His family lived in North Carolina. Eleanor found Malcolm to be handsome, charming, and well-spoken. She delighted in quizzing him on his knowledge of literature and history. He was equally impressed by her intelligence and quick-witted humor. He found Eleanor to be enticing and mysterious, qualities which were intriguing to him.

Malcolm approached Donny and Mr. Fraser to speak with them about being permitted to court Eleanor. This request thrilled them both. Arrangements were made for Malcolm to visit the Frasers' home a few weeks later. The evening continued as the couples waltzed and mingled into the wee hours of the morning.

After Donny, Eleanor, and the Frasers returned home, Mr. Fraser called a meeting between the parties and his wife. They needed to discuss the terms under which Eleanor would live until marriage could be negotiated. Mr. Fraser felt it would be awkward for Eleanor to be working as a maid and nanny when Malcolm came to visit. He might not understand the situation and Mr. Fraser did not want to make Eleanor feel uncomfortable. Mr. Fraser proposed that Eleanor be allowed to live on the second floor of the home until her marriage. Mr. Fraser would continue to pay her wage into the account he was keeping for her. Robert believed that the negotiations would be quick and that the money paid would not be great.

"This is what I promised your mother when she asked me to bring you to America with your brothers. The money I have saved for you will become your dowry. This way Malcolm's family will not be concerned about your status. I will tell him that you are my niece. Don, you will also be allowed to stay in our home until all of this is concluded." Looking at his wife, he continued, "I need you Mary to assist in gathering appropriate attire for Eleanor and to continue working with her on proper etiquette."

Mary reached her hand over and took Eleanor's hand, smiled, and assured Eleanor that she would help her to ready herself for courting. "You are already a beautiful, smart girl, Eleanor. We won't have to work too hard. We've been preparing you for this since you came to us. I know sometimes it may have seemed that I was hard on you; harder on you than my own daughters at times, but it was necessary because you do not have a family to support you and to make these decisions on your behalf. We will keep our promise to your mother. You do not need to worry."

"But is it a wise decision not to tell him the truth? What if he finds out from someone in Staunton who doesn't know that it isn't common knowledge? I would not wish for him to find out in that way. I want you to tell him the truth and allow him to decide if he wishes to continue the courtship," implored Eleanor.

Between the time of their first meeting and his visit, Malcolm and Eleanor wrote letters. The letters were long and filled with all sorts of topics. They both anxiously awaited the arrival of each letter. Emotions began to swell in their hearts. They discussed the importance of family, commitment, faith, and…love…everything they felt was important to a good marriage.

When the time came for Malcolm's visit, everyone feverishly prepared the home and menus. Everyone looked forward to getting to know the young man better. He arrived at the Frasers' farm on a Wednesday afternoon. At the time of his arrival, the men were in the barn hanging tobacco. The ladies were in the sitting room. Mary Fraser was sewing as her daughter Sarah played the piano. The other young ladies were either reading or sewing. As they heard an approaching carriage, they left their places to gather on the front porch of the home. As he disembarked the carriage, he greeted each member of the family with a hug or handshake.

As Malcolm was finishing greeting each of the ladies, Don, Robert, and his sons appeared looking quite disheveled. "Good afternoon, Mr. Campbell, it is a pleasure to see you again and to have your company for a few days. I hope your travels were not too unpleasant. I apologize for our presentation; we were in the barn bringing in the tobacco to hang. I know you are familiar with that process." Robert patted Malcolm on the back as the group entered the home. Upon entering the sitting room, Robert asked for some time for the men to clean up and prepare for the evening. Malcolm cheerfully consented. As he exited the room, Robert instructed Lucus to deliver Malcolm's suitcase to the room where he would be sleeping.

After eating dinner that first evening, Malcolm and Eleanor went for a walk. Eleanor took him by the hand, "I want to take you somewhere special."

"Do you think that Mr. Fraser and your brothers would approve of this? I wouldn't want to do anything to upset them," questioned Malcolm.

"It will be fine. We aren't going far. When we first came here, my brothers and I started coming here to sit and talk away from the rest of the family." The couple walked up a path toward the top of a hill. The air was cool, and the trees were covered in the colors of autumn—reds, golds, oranges. "This place reminded us of our home in Ireland. In the summer everything is colored in rich shades of greens, like the hills at home. It became a place to come and talk about our family. We miss our parents and our little brother." Eleanor lowered her head for a moment to hold back tears.

"Oh, Eleanor, I understand why you love it here. This place is amazing. The colors are so vivid. I love the crisp smell of the air here." Malcolm turned to look at his intended in the eyes. "It is as beautiful as you are." He leaned over and kissed her lightly on the cheek. "Would you like to sit for a moment?"

"Yes, but we cannot stay too long. It will be dark soon."

"I thought we might discuss for a moment my plans after I graduate from university," Malcolm added.

"I suppose you are correct. Have you made plans for your future? Will you return to North Carolina?" Eleanor inquired.

"A law firm in Charlottesville has offered me a position as a clerk initially. As I become more accomplished and confident, I will be given cases of my own to handle. I will make more than enough to support us both and…," Malcolm paused for a moment, "and a family later." He smiled at her with a boyish grin.

Letting out a breath she had been holding, Ellie replied, "That sounds so wonderful, Malcolm. We wouldn't be so far away from here." Eleanor smiled and laid her head on his shoulder. The pair sat quietly gazing out over the valley below. "You know I don't think I have ever asked you what your full name is."

Eleanor giggled, "No, I don't suppose you have. It is Eleanor Grace MacKenzie."

"Um, I think I would like to call you Grace. Only I shall call you Grace. It's my special right. How do you feel about that?"

"I think I like it. But what shall I call you?"

"My full name is Malcolm Isi Campbell. Isi means 'deer'. Each of us has an English name and an Indian name."

"That is beautiful, Malcolm. I will let you know what name I choose on our wedding day," Eleanor spoke playfully. They laughed and then headed back down the hill towards the house. The darkness was quickly moving upon them.

The next morning the family gathered for breakfast. Upon finishing his meal, Mr. Fraser asked Malcolm and Don to meet him in his study. "I think I may speak for all of us, Malcolm, when I say that we are overjoyed to have you with us. I hope that you found your room comfortable. We would have liked to have had Duncan here, but he was unable to travel this week. He had other commitments. He has related his feelings to me and his brother, Donny regarding Eleanor. Thus, we wanted to speak with you today about Eleanor and to make you aware of some things before you make any further considerations about marriage."

Malcolm appearing puzzled asked, "Is there a problem with Eleanor? I don't think I could bear it if...."

Don interjected, "No, no, she's probably healthier than any of us here. We simply wanted to inform you of the truth about my family so that it doesn't come as a surprise to you and your family later. That is if you do not already know our specific circumstances. We do not wish for you to feel you have been misled in any way."

"I am not sure that I understand, Don...."

Mr. Fraser handed each man a cigar and then sat down in his armchair. Then Mr. Fraser told the story of how Donald, Duncan, and Eleanor came to live with his family, and the promises made to their mother regarding their futures. He explained that each had been emancipated and that he was holding monies for Eleanor as a dowry, as was the custom for girls of his social standing. He explained that all he had done up to this point was to fulfill the promises he and Mary made to Isobel MacKenzie. At the end of the story, Mr. Fraser paused for a response from Malcolm.

"Well, I certainly had not expected this to be the story, but I did suspect that this was not a conventional arrangement. I thought maybe Don, Duncan, and Eleanor were part of your extended family." He laughed for a moment and then added, "It is not unusual for extended members of one's family to reside within the same home. I have no concerns here, sir. I love Eleanor and I am honored that you believe me worthy of becoming her husband."

Donny looked seriously at Malcolm, "I understand that you are fine with this situation, but what reaction might your parents have knowing that Eleanor was once an indentured servant to Mr. and Mrs. Fraser?"

"It will not be a problem. To be honest, this type of circumstance is not unusual in my family. My father's family came from the highlands of Scotland to the colonies after a brief time in England. They arrived in an area near Wilmington and lived there for a few years. Then they decided to move inland to be closer to my father's brothers near the settlement of Campbellton. My father and his brothers began growing tobacco together. He met one of the daughters of the local Coharie tribal chief and fell in love. That girl is my mother. While not everyone was accepting of my mother, the relationship has proven beneficial to my father in his pursuits. He has often been called in to mediate situations between the residents and the tribe. I have no issue with being a bit different, sir."

The men began to laugh, and it felt as though a dark cloud had been lifted and the sun began to shine. Insecurities and fears had been assuaged. The men then planned for the return visit for Malcolm and his family to celebrate the wedding.

The couple decided to marry the following autumn after the tobacco had been harvested and taken to market. In late October, the Campbell family arrived in Staunton early to assist with the preparations. The Frasers threw a party the afternoon following the arrival of the Campbells—Malcolm's parents: Colin and Abigail, brothers Elias and Levi, and sisters Caroline and Beatrice. The closest friends of the Frasers were invited to the welcoming shindig. The home was decorated with autumn leaves, pumpkins, gourds, and dried fruits.

Mr. Fraser made certain that there would be plenty of food for all the festivities. He slaughtered pigs and cows, and Agnes and Esther baked for several days. He sent Abraham and Isaac to the river to fish for trout and Bartholomew doubled their output of cider for the festivities. The bedrooms were filled with autumn flowers and crisp, clean linens. Robert Fraser even hired a bagpipe player to play at the evening's festivities. No one would have ever suspected that Eleanor had once been a part of the home's staff. Eleanor was thrilled to meet the Campbells, especially Malcolm's sisters. She had become quite close to the Frasers' daughters, Sarah Beth and Emily, but they were much young-er than she, and she hoped Malcolm's sisters would like her as they would soon be her sisters-in-law. Eleanor found the Campbells to be just how Malcolm had described them—kind and welcoming. Eleanor did not know what he had shared with his family. Just after dinner, she sat beside Abigail to talk. "It is nice to finally meet you, Mrs. Campbell." "Oh, my dear girl, we do not stand on formalities and you, sweet girl, will soon be a part of our family. Please, call me Abigail. You are as lovely as Malcolm described you. He shared your history with us. We were all quite moved to hear how the Frasers took you and your brothers in and made you part of their family despite being indentured. It is an unusual circumstance, but we are accustomed to unusual circumstances in our family. I hope Malcolm shared that with you." Abigail's voice was warm, and she had a soft, sweet-sounding dialect. Eleanor was awestruck by her beauty. She had seen many Indians in the area, but she did not recall any of the women being as beautiful as Abigail.

"He did. You and your daughters are more beautiful than I had imagined given his description of you all. He is proud of you and to be your son. I look forward to getting to know everyone."

"There were some small-minded people who shunned my husband after he married me. There were times when we have been mistreated, but he has always protected us. As time has progressed, that mistreatment has diminished, and I also think we care less about it when it happens. It is not as unusual where we live now to have Indians married to white men. I hope that you will find some time to visit us in our home after all these festivities are completed. We would love for you to come."

"Yes, I would love to visit. As you know, my parents have been gone for a long time. As much as we love the Fraser family for taking such great care of us, this will be different. You all will be our children's actual grandparents." As they were speaking Malcolm's sisters came over and sat near Eleanor and their mother.

"You are so lovely with your light hair and light green eyes. You're as beautiful as an angel. Malcolm told us that you like to challenge him to quizzes. He said that you are very smart," provided Caroline.

"I'm glad to be getting such a smart and pretty sister," added Bea.

"I look forward to getting to know Elias and Levi, also. What should I know about them?" She asked in a whisper because they stood not far from them.

"Well, you know Malcolm is the oldest, Elias is next, then me, then Levi, and finally baby Bea. Personally, I think Malcolm got all the brains and Elias got the brawn. Levi is handsome and all the girls love him. He's funny. He loves to tell jokes," Reported Caroline.

"And you, Bea, how would you describe them?"

Bea thought for a moment, "Malcolm is dependable. Eli always needs to be right, even when he isn't. That can be annoying. Levi is always making jokes and keeps us laughing, which can be nice when Eli is being too serious."

"When the boys were little, they were always wrestling and getting into mischief. Malcolm could always talk his way out of trouble. Eli would storm off to sulk, and Levi would try to lighten the mood with a joke. They are quite a threesome!" Concluded Caroline.

The wedding was held the next day in the Presbyterian Church in Staunton. It was decorated with all the fall foliage the families could gather. It was filled with candles which created an intensely romantic atmosphere. When the time for the vow exchange came, Malcolm turned to the minister and asked for a moment. Malcolm looked Eleanor directly in the eyes and began to speak.

"Eleanor Grace, I promise that I will always love you, care for you, and protect you no matter what may come. I have never met anyone as beautiful, intelligent, and sometimes silly as you. Life may deal us challenges, but I know that I will never stop loving you, trusting you, or believing in you."

Malcolm paused for a moment as Eleanor quickly lifted her veil to wipe away her tears. He then bowed his head at the minister to continue.

When it was Eleanor's turn to recite her vows, she began by saying the name she had chosen to call her husband—Isi. Malcolm smiled at her and shook his head in agreement.

As with most life events, this one was over quickly. The wedding party was celebrated with a large reception at the Frasers' home. It was a magnificent day. Everyone spoke of Malcolm's words to Eleanor. No one remembered anything more emotional and special, and some women speculated about how their husbands might learn something from this well-raised young man.

Malcolm became a successful attorney in Virginia, representing some of the most influential families. He and Eleanor had a deep and lasting love for each other. Eleanor, who desperately wanted to be a mother, had difficulties in carrying her babies to term. She would give birth eight times, but only three would survive. Nevertheless, from what I have gathered, Malcolm and Eleanor became a significant part of society in Charlottesville, and their children grew into well-respected adults.

Chapter 9

As the reader hereto may understand, at this time there were rumblings of problems in the upper colonies between the natives, French, and British. Tensions were rising as Donald, Duncan, and Eleanor began their adult lives. For those families in the Shenandoah Valley, the decision on which side to take was not as obvious as it was to those living in Boston or Philadelphia. Many of the Scots Irish, as we became known, sided with the British King because it was profitable to do so. Others chose the French side because they felt it to be the moral choice.

This was a decision that the Frasers, MacKenzies, and Campbells would have to make. In 1756 after the defeat of General Braddock, the British needed substantial troops to continue. A law was passed conscripting men throughout the colonies. Given their predilection for being independent thinkers, these families wanted no part in a fight that did not directly affect them, but with the passage of the law, there was no choice. This meant that these men would be called to arms in support of the cause, leaving behind their wives, children, and farm operations.

As Donald, Duncan, and Malcolm had determined to be faithful and kind masters, taking on the examples set by their families, they were not concerned with leaving their families and farms in the hands of their slaves. The Frasers, MacKenzies, and Campbells set an example of kindness, education, trust, and responsibility which produced dedicated and trustworthy servants. When the men returned from their service, they were greeted with hugs and well wishes from everyone in their households.

Duncan and Elizabeth, who now lived near Blacksburg and had a tobacco farm, were blessed with four children— Donald, Mary, James, and Eleanor, whom they called Ellie. Duncan was injured in the war, having been shot in his left arm near the elbow. He lost the use of the arm which greatly diminished the amount of work he was able to do on the farm. (I suppose I have not made the reader aware that, unlike many of the tobacco planters of this time, these men worked alongside their slaves. They believed that hard work made for successful hearts, while laziness bred a more sinful nature and that by working alongside their slaves, they would set an example for everyone.) He and Elizabeth increased the number of slaves who worked in the fields but tried to keep the household staff as lean as possible. Like Mr. Fraser, they educated their slaves and encouraged them to have families. None of these families were happy with the practice of slave ownership; but like the older generation, they felt it was impossible to do much about it.

The war, which became known as the French and Indian War, ended in 1763. Although each fought for less than a year, Donny returned with minor injuries, Robert Fraser was killed, and Duncan died a couple of years after returning home from the war. His doctor believed that the round lodged inside his arm caused his blood to become poisoned. Those years were filled with much pain and agony, but Duncan forced himself to work through his pain. Realizing he would not have the chance to know his children and grandchildren, he realized that he must prepare Donald for the time when he would be responsible for the farm.

When Duncan's day arrived, his family was, of course, devastated. The children were still quite young—Donald was sixteen years old; Mary was fourteen; James was ten; and Eleanor was three. Donald felt the loss more than his siblings because he understood the responsibility he had inherited. He knew that his family was dependent on the decisions he would have to make. The farm was to be maintained for the benefit of their mother until she died. At that time, each would be given some furniture, farm equipment, and a portion of the farm for the benefit of themselves and their future families. Elizabeth lived for five more years. Mary, unfortunately, also died young.

During the years he had with his children, Duncan raised them in the same manner as he and his brother and sister were. They were raised alongside the children of their slaves, and they were taught the value of hard work and perseverance. His children played, studied, and worked alongside the slaves on his farm. Certainly, there were distinctions between the slaves and the MacKenzie children, but it was not a harsh one. It had to be this way because Duncan and Elizabeth recognized that Donald would need to have a close relationship with everyone because his success would be dependent upon the support and input of everyone. Their mother was certainly capable of decision-making along with her son, but Duncan knew his son needed to be independent.

One of the slave girls on the MacKenzie farm was named Mollie. Mollie was the same age as Mary, having been born a few months after her. Her father, Bartholomew, was a foreman on the farm and Tabitha, her mother, was an exceptional cook. Bart and Tab came with Duncan when he and Elizabeth moved away from the Fraser farm. When Mollie was about ten, she began to work as a maid. She was a beautifully outgoing and well-mannered young lady. Bart and Tab were strict parents who demanded their children behave appropriately and work diligently. There were four children in their family—Mollie, Ruth, Jacob, and Macajah.

After Duncan's death, James became withdrawn. At times he was depressed, and his studies suffered. Mollie, who was a dedicated student, assisted James in finishing his work so that his mother would not discover that he was not finishing his schoolwork. She went so far as to wake James up when he tried to stay in bed. Mollie and James seemed to be as close as siblings.

A few years later when James was about fifteen years old, his attitude and disposition changed; he was happy again. All the children, despite their advancing ages, still enjoyed playing games on the lawn in the evenings. On one such evening, the children were playing hide-and-seek. James was the seeker, and he was running about trying to find each one, but it seemed as though he was making a more concerted effort to find Mollie than the others, though the other children did not seem to notice or care. Mollie ran to hide in one of the empty stalls of the barn. When James reached the barn, he was calling out her name. He went to one of the empty stalls, quickly yanked open the gate, and yelled, "Gotcha!" Mollie could not contain her laughter. James went into the stall and closed the gate behind him. He threw himself down into the straw beside Mollie breathing heavily from all the running around he had done.

"Mollie, you always come in here. You knew I would find you here, silly girl!" Just then Mollie tried to get up to run away, but James caught her by the back of her dress and pulled her back down. "Come on, don't run away so fast. Can't we talk for a few minutes?" He impeached her.
"You know I need to get back to the house to help Momma with the supper dishes," Mollie retorted.

"Just wait, please," begged James.

"Fine, what is it you wish to talk about Master James?"

"Do not call me that! I don't like it." James became quiet and he looked away for a moment. Then suddenly, he leaned over and kissed her. "I love you, Mollie."

"Don't be ridiculous, Master James. It ain't appropriate. You know that," Mollie exclaimed.

"I don't care, Mollie. We've known each other our whole lives. I have loved you since we were little running around here playing games together. You know my family doesn't care about *propriety*!" James retorted harshly. Then, being sorry for his tone, he pulled Mollie over towards him and he kissed her again.

Mollie whispered as softly as she could praying no one was around who might hear her, "Oh, James…I…I…I love you too, James MacKenzie; but you know it would never be allowed, no matter what you or I might want. They will make you marry someone of their choosing, and then they will find someone of my own kind for me. We have no control over these things, James." Mollie was visibly upset.

"I don't want to marry *anyone*, Mollie, not if I cannot marry you. There is no one as beautiful and kind as you." As they looked at each other, the emotion of the words and the moment overtook them. James and Mollie gave in to their intense desires. Suddenly, Mollie, realizing what she had just done, jumped up, fixed her clothes, and ran from the barn to the house. She took a few moments to compose herself and then went back inside the house.

James stayed in the barn. He pulled himself together, but it took him a bit longer to compose himself, being emotionally distraught because he knew in his heart that Mollie was correct. At that moment he committed himself to never marry. He simply could not imagine loving anyone other than Mollie.

A few weeks passed and the pair tried to avoid each other. There was no playing in the yard. James worked late in the field and Mollie assisted her mother in the kitchen after she finished cleaning. One afternoon just after dinner, Mollie began to feel ill. Everything she smelled made her sick to her stomach. Often it resulted in vomiting. It was not long before she realized what the problem was, and she had to find James. Running from the house to the barn, she inquired from the farrier as to where she might find James.

"I just seen him in the back forty, Mollie," responded Toby to her question, "hey, you feelin' poorly, Miss Mollie? You ain't lookin' so good."

"I'm fine. Lunch must not have set well on my stomach; that's all," Mollie quickly replied.

"I's could hitch youse up a horse if'n you wants to go find Masser James, Miss Mollie."

Mollie thought for a moment and agreed. Toby saddled up an aging mare and set her on her way. Mollie forced the horse to run as fast as it could. Now, I suspect, maybe, Mollie might have done this thinking the horse might throw her and remove the problem and she'd never have to tell anyone. That, of course, did not happen. When James saw Mollie on the horse, he became fearful that something might be wrong, so he went running towards her.

"Mollie, everything okay up at the house?" James asked with panic in his voice.

"We must talk, James. Alone. Now." James was more frightened hearing her words. He jumped on the back of the horse, and they rode back towards the house.

"James...."

"Yes, Mollie. What is it?"

Mollie was quiet, but James felt her anxiety. "I'm with child. I am going to have your baby, James."

Despite an overwhelming feeling of excitement, James took a moment to ponder an appropriate response. He knew she was afraid, and he understood those fears. "Mollie, you know how I feel about this. I certainly want to take care of you and our child, no matter what others may think of it. Don't be scared."

"What are we going to do? We are too young for this. Donald just told me yesterday that he plans for me to marry Toby."

"What did Donald say? He has not spoken to me about it. Well, I am just going to have to tell him that it won't happen."

"No, James. You must allow me to marry Toby and marry him quickly. He needs to think this baby is his. It's the only way."

"Oh no, I will not! You know you do not love Toby. How can you say such a thing to me, Mollie? I know you love me!"

"Because, James, I am your brother's slave. I must do whatever he tells me to do. I do not get to refuse his will."

"I understand your feelings, Mollie, but there must be a way. I will find a way through this. I need to think about this for a bit. Please do not commit to Toby until we talk again. Please."

"I will give you three days. If you have not come up with another way out of this situation, I will talk to Donald." As the conversation was ending, the pair came near the barn. James slid off the backside of the horse and allowed Mollie to return to the barn out of sight of Toby. That evening, James excused himself from the table after finishing his meal, telling his family that he was not feeling well. He retired to his bedroom to think about this dire situation.

The next morning, James awoke earlier than usual. He needed to speak with Mollie before anyone else was awake. He snuck around the side of her cottage and whispered to her to come out. "Mollie, meet me in the field. Quick. Hurry." Mollie wiped her eyes and then put her shoes on.

"Hey, where ya' goin', Mollie?" Her sister Ruth asked as Mollie was slipping out of their little cottage.

"Just goin' ta tha outhouse. Be back in a minute. Go back to sleep." Mollie met James in the field behind the barn. "What's going on James? It is so early and cold."

"I needed to tell you what I decided last night."

"Okay."

"I am going to ask Donald to buy you so that I can free you and the baby. I will make arrangements for you and the baby to go with Ellie to Tennessee after she marries Thomas. You can work and live with them, and I will provide for the two of you. When I can, I will come, and we can be together as a family."

"James, I don't know what to say. What if Donald asks you why you want to buy me? What if he refuses? What if Miss Ellie and Masser Thomas don't wants me ta come wit dem?"

"I will have to think of a way to handle that, but I do not believe he will refuse. I don't know if you have ever heard of my Aunt Eleanor and her husband, Malcolm. Malcolm is part Indian. We are accustomed to unusual situations in my family. I know we cannot stay here, but at least I can find a way to get us somewhere we can be together and where we will all be safe."

"I must go, or Ruth will come lookin' for me. I will see you later. I love you, James." Mollie smiled and took a quick hold of his hand.

"I love you, too, Mollie. Please do not worry."

Chapter 10

Maybe I should back up. I am not sure that I related to you about Duncan and Elizabeth and their family as I should have. Duncan and Elizabeth had four children—Donald, the eldest who was named after his brother; Mary, the eldest daughter; James; and then Eleanor, the youngest, who was named after Duncan's sister. Mary only lived to sixteen. She became ill and took to her bed for several weeks. The doctor told the family that her heart was weak. She died soon thereafter. James and Don were not particularly close because, after their father died, Donald inherited everything, and he was often harsh in his treatment of his brother. James became resentful, though he tried not to let Donald see it.

James and Eleanor, however, were very close. Ellie thought James was the greatest. There was a rather large age gap between Donald and Eleanor, and she felt she could not relate to him. He seemed much more like a father than a brother, especially since she was young when her father died. James protected Ellie from Donald's constant criticism. Their mother made little attempt to change Donald believing it was for the best of everyone.

James understood that he was going to have to give some explanation to his brother regarding his wish to buy Mollie, but he saw Eleanor's upcoming marriage to Thomas MacGregor as the perfect circumstance to work out a bad situation. When he went to the study, he found Donald working on the books for the farm. He sat down in a chair just in front of the desk, slouching down.

"What can I help you with James? If you have problem, it may have to wait because I am doing the books right now." Donald said speaking in a slow, uneven tone not taking his eyes off his paperwork.

"Well, I have a matter that I need to discuss with you."

Piquing his interest because his brother rarely came to him about anything, Donald stopped and looked at his brother. "Is there a problem I am unaware of, James?"

"Not a problem, just somethin' I think you ought to consider is all."

"Okay, let's hear it. I don't have much time, James."

"Mollie is still young, and I know Ellie loves her. What if I were to buy Mollie from you and allow her to go with Ellie and Thomas to Tennessee?"

Donny leaned back in his chair and looked at his brother in bewilderment. "Have you run this by Eleanor or Mollie, by chance? I just spoke to Mollie the other day about maybe having her marry Toby. She is at the right age. But now, what you are saying does have some benefits as well. Are you saying that you want to give Mollie to Eleanor and Thomas as a gift?"

"Well, I guess you could see it that way. Mother, Mary, and Ellie have always had someone to help them around the house. Ellie did not pay as much attention in learning to cook as Mollie; she is an outstanding cook. Mollie would be a great help once Ellie and Thomas have children. I would reimburse you for the expense of replacing her should you decide to do so."

"How much were you thinking of?" Donald seemed to be pondering the idea as viable and practical.

"Well, I think it would cost you $100 to $200 to replace her with another young negro woman of the same age. I have saved money, and I can pay you."

"All right, then, I agree, as long as Ellie and Mollie agree. I will draw up a Bill of Sale in the next few days and we can execute it thereafter. I do think it is a wise decision for Eleanor; wish I had thought of that. She is not a great cook. I think the only thing she knows how to cook is cornpone, and it is truly awful! Thomas might starve or die from burnt roast!" The brothers had a great laugh.

Chapter 11

While James was waiting for Donny to obtain the sale paperwork, James proceeded to write his Last Will and Testament. He provided for Mollie and the child upon his untimely death. He also provided for the child's future education, and he officially acknowledged their status as slaves and provided for their emancipation. To financially provide for his family, James would give all rights of inheritance to his assets to his child and Mollie. At the time of his father's passing, Duncan had given each of his children an inheritance distinct from what Donald inherited. He wanted to make certain that each of them understood that he valued and loved them.

In his Will, James stipulated that, if Mollie were to die before the child reached the age of majority, her share of his estate would pass to the child. These provisions were quite radical for the time they were written. It was the late 1700s and, while white slave owners often had children with their female slaves (most often not by the choice of the slave woman), it was rare for the slave owner to acknowledge the mother and child. It was even more rare for a slave owner to free and financially provide for them.

The final provision related to the designation of a guardian who would raise the child should both he and Mollie die before the child reached adulthood. This responsibility was given to his sister Eleanor and her future husband Thomas. He felt certain that Eleanor would have no reservations about this provision given that Mollie would be living and working in her household and because he would provide income for the child's maintenance.

After the Bill of Sale and Will were executed, James went to speak with Ellie. "Sister, I need to speak with you about something important and our conversation must remain private until I have everything in place. Do you understand?"

"My goodness, James. I don't think I have seen you this serious since father passed. Are you all right?" Ellie appeared gravely concerned by her brother's tone and words.

"Well, I am not dying if that's what you mean! The situation involves Mollie and I need your utmost discretion, please," he urged.

"Oh, I do hope there is nothing wrong with her. I would not like that either."

"Well, she is not ill; she's pregnant." James paused a moment waiting to see her reaction.

"James, what are you saying? Did Toby get Mollie pregnant…against her will?" Eleanor appeared confused and afraid.

"No, this isn't about Toby. It…well, it's mine."

"Well now, that is something, James Alexander MacKenzie! You know better than to put Mollie in this kind of situation. I know you two have always been close, but this isn't fair. Mollie will have such troubles if she gives birth to a white baby. How could you? I'm very upset with you, James." A look of disapproval and anger washed over her face.

"I love her, Ellie; I always have. I intend to make this situation right, but I need your assistance to do that."

"Now, James, how on earth can I help YOU to make this situation right? I will not be around after Thomas and I are married next month."

"Today, I bought Mollie from Donny. I want to give her to you to go with you and Thomas to Tennessee. I will come later after I close out my business in Virginia. Then, she and I and our child will live together somewhere more distant from other folks."

"Well…hmmm…that is something to consider. It isn't something I would have thought of, but it just might work. You know that I love her, and I will need help. Do you have any idea when she might give birth?"

"I don't think for another 8 and half months; it has just happened. By that time, you might be with child yourself!"

"James do not try to make light of this situation. What you have done is not to be condoned by me or anyone else in this family. I will need to discuss this with Thomas, but I do not believe it would be a problem. I will talk to him tomorrow, and then I will let you know. Have you discussed this with her?"

"No, I have not because I needed to make certain you and Donald would both agree. Donald does not know of the pregnancy."

"Well, you must tell him."

"I will, but I need to know about Thomas first. I want you to know that I will pay all of Mollie and the baby's expenses should anything happen to me. You and Thomas need not worry about that."

"Fine. I will speak to Thomas tomorrow and we will all talk about this after dinner tomorrow night. Is that agreeable?" Eleanor firmly stated to her brother. While she may have been younger and a woman, she knew how to get her point across. "You know, it's a good thing our parents are not here. They would be disappointed in you, James."

Chapter 12

Alex came to the end of the journal. "I don't understand. How could he just leave us hanging like this?" Sean asked sounding upset.

Hannah, placing her hand on her grandfather's shoulder, said, "Maybe he died? It doesn't make sense otherwise. He's gone to such lengths to tell this story."

"Wait, Gram. I think I see something down in the bottom of the trunk," responded Sean. Sean leaned over, reaching down deep into the trunk. "I think I found it! I think I found it! Look Gram, it looks like another journal." As he was squealing in joy, Anne appeared.

"What in the world are you all doing up here? You've been here all day," she commented as she looked around the attic and noticed that progress had not been made in the cleanup effort.

"Oh, Annie, don't get upset. We found a real treasure up here. I had no idea these things existed. The children and I lost track of time and our work when we began to read this," he retorted as he handed the first journal to his daughter.

"My this looks old. I don't remember ever seeing this either, Dad. I don't have time to read right now. I must get dinner ready, and I need the children to help."

"It's a journal about our family's history. It was written by my great-great-grandfather, Richard Murray. It is a real treasure, isn't it children?" Alex said as he patted Hannah's hand which was still on his shoulder.

Hannah continued, "Mom, it is really something. I cannot believe you never knew any of this story. Gram, could we continue reading after dinner? I don't want to stop hearing the story now! You want to keep reading, don't you Sean… Celia? Right?"

Sean shouted, "I sure do!" Celia nodded her head in agreement.

"Okay, that is what we will do, but we need to get dinner, so come on kids!" As they were departing the attic, Ross appeared at the bottom of the stairs.

"Daddy, you have to hear about what we found in Gram's attic!!" Sean exclaimed as he, Celia, and Hannah rushed away towards the kitchen.

"Let's hurry so we can get finished with dinner! We have to find out what happens." Hollered Celia towards Hannah.

"Mom, what's for dinner?" Hannah yelled.

"Oh, my goodness, Annie, Alex, I cannot recall the last time I saw these children this excited, except maybe at Christmas. This must be something to behold," Ross noted.

"It truly is. I'm just flabbergasted that I have never heard any of this before." Alex shook his head in utter disbelief. "Your mother, Annie, would have just adored this story. It's scandalous, but intriguing at the same time. A soap opera, it is!"

"Well, by all means, let's get this show on the road so we can return to this scandalous moment in our family history!" Annie said laughing at her father's words.

During dinner the children related to their parents what they had learned in the first journal. They speculated about what they might discover in the next journal. Sean posited that Thomas MacGregor refused to take Mollie and her unborn child to Tennessee, which would leave James reeling with fear for what to do instead. Hannah argued that Sean must be wrong because Eleanor loved Mollie and would fight for her. In opposition, Celia felt that Donald would be angry that James had not told him the entire truth, and that he might tear up the Bill of Sale and force James to deal with the situation in Virginia.

The dinner meal flew as fast as a pelican trying to out-fly a hurricane. The children insisted on cleaning up after the meal was complete. The adults contemplated writing their own journals to hide and let the kids find them so they could get them to clean their rooms. They had a full belly laugh at the expense of their eager young ones.

Being pushed out of the kitchen, the adults retired to the living room for the evening's *Jeopardy* game. In a short time, Hannah, Celia, and Sean came into the room carrying a tray towards their grandfather. "Well, now, what is this?"

"We made everyone a bowl of ice cream to eat while Gram reads the second journal," Hannah said holding the tray tightly in her hands and trying to look like an adult.

"Now, I don't know if we can finish it tonight. We need our sleep because we only have tomorrow to finish everything up. We will all need to get a good night's sleep," Annie interjected.

"Annie, you are not my mother!" Retorted Alex. "Children, I love that you made everyone dessert. Let me have that journal and we will read until we cannot keep our eyes open." Annie rolled her eyes at her father as she plopped down on the floor next to her husband.

"Here we go. Let's see. Give me a second to wipe my glasses so that I can see," Alex continued. After breathing on his glasses and wiping them with his napkin, he opened the second journal and began to read.

Ellie met Thomas at the door the next morning before breakfast. Thomas MacGregor lived with his family on a neighboring farm. His family came to Virginia two years prior to the MacKenzies and Frasers. The three families had become acquainted after meeting at church. They had much in common and enjoyed being in each other's company. Thomas was the eldest child and he worked on the plantation. He attended William and Mary where he studied agriculture, animal husbandry, and forestry. Everyone was excited when Thomas proposed marriage to Eleanor. He adored her and she adored him.

"Is there a problem, Ellie? You look like you have had too much coffee," Thomas joked.

"No, silly, I have had no coffee yet today. I just need to talk to you in the study for a moment. It is important." Eleanor took Thomas by the hand and walked with him to the study as she took a deep breath preparing herself for the conversation she was about to have. "Sit down, please." Eleanor knew how important this discussion was, and she knew the answer she wanted from Thomas, so she knew how the subject had to be presented to get that answer. "You know how much I love Mollie. She has been with us her whole life. You know my parents did not approve of slavery, but they felt as though it was better that we have slaves so that we could make sure they were taken care of and educated. I know that your parents don't exactly share the same opinion, but I also know that they have not mistreated your slaves either. I believe we both believe that every human deserves to be treated with respect…"

"Ellie, where are you going with all of this?" Inquired Thomas whose stomach was growling rather loudly. "We need to move this along. I am starving."

"Thomas, I told you this is important. I cannot help that you did not eat at home. I want to take Mollie to Tennessee to live and work with us. I just couldn't bear it if something happened, and she ended up with another family and they did not treat her well. She is like a sister to me. Can we? Please?" Eleanor looked into his eyes with an intense gaze.

"Is that all? Of course, she can. That's really a decision for you and Donny to make. You know I will help you with whatever you need. At the same time, though," Thomas said to Eleanor with doubt in his voice and squinting his eyes, "there is more to this than you are letting on, but I trust you, Eleanor."

"Thank you, thank you, thank you!" Eleanor exclaimed with both excitement and relief. "Let's go eat! I cannot wait to tell Mollie."

The rest of the day proceeded as usual with no one suspecting the events going on secret. James gathered the legal documents together and rode into town on his horse to take them to his lawyer. Mr. Edgar, who had been the family's attorney for many years, reviewed the documents and gave James his approval. He informed James that he would need multiple copies of the documents so that he could provide them to anyone who might need them in Tennessee or Virginia. He quoted a price to James for his assistants to copy the documents. The price quoted was accepted and James paid the fees. Mr. Edgar told James to return in four days to pick up his copies. He did warn James to be careful with whom he shared the contents of his Will because it might cause unintentional consequences from others. Times were intense regarding the status of slavery in the country. The position taken by the Frasers and MacKenzies was unusual for Southern farming families. It could bring boycotts and hostilities.

In the early evening, James invited his brother to join him for a drink on the veranda. The brothers enjoyed a glass of whiskey in the afternoons before dinner, especially in the fall when temperatures cooled and the beauty of the grounds of their home were at its height. The brothers sat drinking and rocking in the rocking chairs while discussing the issues of the day. James segued the conversation from new farming implements to one regarding his purchase of Mollie. "Don, I spoke with Eleanor about Mollie. She was thrilled to hear my plan. Thank you for agreeing. I would not have been able to make this happen for Eleanor had you not consented."

"James, I know we have not always agreed on some issues, but you and Eleanor are my family. I was put into a difficult position when Father died, and I was forced to become the man of the house. I had to make decisions that I had no experience with. I know I did not always make the right decision, but nothing I have ever done was intended to hurt you or Eleanor. I do hope you understand that," Donald said sincerely.

"I haven't always made it easy for you either, Donny. I apologize if you feel I have ever been unfair towards you. I, too, was not intentional in any hurt I may have caused you. You have done a tremendous job carrying on after Father. Now, I have something else to tell you and I pray you will listen and give me the time to explain." James used an emphatic but sincere tone.

"I do not know of what you speak, but I will make every effort to be open minded and allow you time to explain whatever is so important," assured Donald.

"Thank you. I intend to follow Eleanor and Thomas to Tennessee. I will not be traveling with them because I have some business that I must tie up here first. I hope to be in Tennessee before Christmas. I know that you wish for all of us to continue to live here in Virginia, but Tennessee is a new, open territory and I want to strike out on my own. Do you understand? It's like our dad, Uncle Donald, and Aunt Eleanor when they came here. They wanted a better life. I hope I can find and make my own way in Tennessee. I want to have a farm that is like this one—productive and successful."

Donald took a few minutes to consume the words his brother had uttered. He wished to make certain he did not jump to any conclusions for the reason James did not want to stay in Virginia. "James, believe it or not, I can and do understand that you desire to have your own life. If Father and Momma had not died so young, I am certain I would have felt the same way. As much as I would love to throw a temper tantrum right now just to get your goat, I will not." Looking at his brother with love overflowing from every pore in his body, he continued, "I love you and, of course, I want you to be happy. I would not want you or Eleanor to stay here only out of a sense of obligation. I have my family to consider. Maureen and I have three little MacKenzies running around causing all sorts of chaos. Our lives are here, and we are happy.

I want the same for you dear brother." Donny patted James on the shoulder as he walked back into the house to find out if dinner was ready. James breathed a sigh of relief and then took another deep breath as he now had to tell Mollie about his entire plan. He prayed that her response would resemble that of his brother—calm and reserved.

As James sat thinking of the best way to tell Mollie about his plans, she appeared behind him. "James, did I hear you talking to Donald about going to Tennessee?"

"Oh, Mollie, well…," James started to answer but Mollie interrupted him.

"How could you just leave me? I thought you loved me," she said with a tear coming to her eyes.

"Mollie, no, it isn't like that, dearest," James turned to look Mollie directly in the eyes. "Please sit so that we can talk." Mollie sat down in the rocking chair next to James. "Today I took steps to help us—you, me, and our child to be together. I know that this may sound crazy but hear me out. I have purchased you from Donny; I hate how awful that sounds. But I am giving you Eleanor so that you can accompany her and Thomas to Tennessee. I have some things to take care of here, but when I finish, I will be coming to Tennessee as well. When I arrive, you and I will live together with our child. I do not like the fact that I had to buy you, but you know how things work."

"So, I now belong to you, and I am going on to Tennessee with Ellie and Thomas. Do they know about this plan of yours?"

"Yes, they do. Ellie thinks that this is the best plan for us also. We need to be careful not to give ourselves away or we will become targets. I don't want that for you or our child. We will all live together until we can move further west where, maybe, slavery won't be an issue."

"I don't know, James. It sounds wonderful, but scary. And what about my family here? What will they think of this?"

"We will have to talk to them, but I know that they will want what is best for you and their grandchild. Your parents are getting older; moving them to Tennessee isn't really an option, and my brother needs them here. Don relies on your father and Maureen needs your mother. You know that he will always take care of them as well as your sister and brothers and their families. Maybe later as the farm grows, we can send for them."

"That might be nice, if it works out. James, we need to talk to them all as soon as possible," Mollie became silent and thoughtful as she pondered the response of her family. Her father was a no-nonsense man, and her mother had high standards for her children. They had benefitted from the progressive ideas of the MacKenzie family, but Mollie knew that they would not be happy about the current situation she had gotten herself into, but what choice did they really have?

A week passed before James and Mollie were able to sit down with Bartholomew and Tabitha. James asked Bart to meet him on the back porch after he finished putting the horses in the barn and cleaned up. Tabitha was finishing up supper when James walked into the kitchen. "Miss Tab, as he liked to call her, I need to talk with you for a few minutes before we sit down to supper," instructed James.

"Yessuh, Masser James. Somethin' wrong, sir?" Inquired Tabitha never having had a private conversation with James before.

"It will be fine. Bart will be here in a minute, and we'll have a little talk on the back porch," as he was finishing his sentence Mollie came up the back steps to the porch.

"Pap will be here in a minute," Mollie said looking at her mother's puzzled expression.

"Mols, what's a goin' on?" Tab looked disturbed at the notion of a private conversation, probably fearing one of them may be getting ready to be sold off, which was a common situation on southern plantations.

"Hold on, Ma, Masser James will tell you in a few minutes," Mollie said to her mother as James motioned to her to sit in the rocking chair on his right. Just then Bart appeared rushing towards the porch, taking his hat off and wiping sweat from his face.

"Masser James, please forgive my appearance. Dem horses was a fussin' and tis a peculiarly hot day today," Bart said softly. He had never been a man of harsh, loud tones, but he did not suffer fools in the behavior of those with whom he lived and worked.

"Now that everyone is here, let's all sit and talk for a few minutes." James glanced towards Bart and Tab, and he took Mollie's hand. Bart began to get upset by the gesture, but James quickly caught his expression. "Bart, it's fine. Mollie and I have some issues we need to discuss with you." There was no question about the expression that overtook James' face as he looked at Mollie and squeezed her hand. "Now, I know that neither of you will like what I am about to say, but I ask that you let me finish before you speak." After a brief pause, he continued, "Mollie and I love each other. She's carrying my child. I know that this is not something that either of you approve of given the status of slavery in Virginia, over which I have no control. I have arranged with Donald for Mollie to move with Ellie and Thomas to Tennessee after their wedding. I will join them later after I finish some matters here. I will always take care of Mollie and our child, even in the event I might pass while the child is still young. They will always be taken care of. I pray that you will not be harsh towards her. She did not get into this situation alone. I am responsible, and I will do what is right." James stopped and waited for Bart's response.

"Mollie, I is greatly disappointed in you, girl. Youse knows better than ta gets yo'self in dis mess. It ain't right, Masser James, but I knowd you two was sweet on each other, but you knowd that me and Miss Tab, we knows our place, Masser James. Your Pap and Mam always done take good care of us on dis farm, not like mose of dem otha massers roun' yonder. We ain't never been beat like dem others we knowd. Look, girl, yo done gone and made yo Ma cry. Masser James, I don sees that we gots a choice here, suh. I knowd you and Masser Don to be men of yo word, and I'll be a trustin' you ta do right by our girl," Bart lowered his head and shook it in disbelief.

"Ma, I am sorry to make you sad. We didn't mean to get into this. It was a mistake we made, but James IS a man of his word. Tennessee is a frontier where there ain't many folks yet. James says we can all live together with no one a knowin'."

Tabitha shook her finger angrily at James and Mollie. A tear had formed in both Tab and Bart's eyes. They were clearly saddened and frightened by the situation. "Masser James, I love you like youse my own boy. Yo oughts not ta let dis happen. Iffin yo' daddy was still aroun', he'd tan your backside! Like Bart says tho, we beeze at yo mercy. We ain't gots no choice but ta trust ya. No one else needs ta knowd ya'lls bidness. Until it beeze time for ya'lls ta go, Mollie, you'll beeze in da house carin' for Missus Ellie. You and Masser James needs ta keep yo distance. Iffin any folks roun' here gets wind, dey'll kill our girl and dey'll kill youse too!"

"I understand, Ma. I will. I promise, and so does James. Right?" She said looking intently into James' eyes.

"We will certainly do as you ask. I will do whatever you ask of me," James squeezed Mollie's hand again. "I guess we'd better get in the house and get dinner on the table before Miss Tabitha's dinner is ruined." James stood up from his seat and released Mollie's hand. The parties stood in an awkward silence for a few minutes as if to once again accept the situation and move forward.

Over the next few weeks Tab and Bart kept close tabs on their daughter and James, making certain they were not trying to sneak off to see each other. Tab kept Mollie busy with chores preparing for Ellie's wedding and packing up her clothes, dishes, linens, and other necessities for the move to Tennessee. Thomas often came in the late afternoon to help with the packing and making other preparations for the lengthy trip, going on over maps with Donald, James, and Jeremiah, James' horseman who would be traveling with them and helping him to establish his farm. They needed to have contingency plans if roads became impassable due to weather. They would also need to have pre-arranged stops in towns where they could sleep and refresh their horses. They spent evenings preparing their weapons and ammunition for protection along the way.

By the end of the month and time for the wedding, they had three buckboards prepared. Thomas decided to take two other young negro men with them to help drive an extra wagon. He felt certain that the extra help would provide added security as well as hands on the farm. Two black women would be going with the party as well—Addie, Jeremiah's wife, and Mame, her sister.

Thomas and Ellie would ride in the middle wagon, in between wagons driven by Jeremiah and Killian. After all the preparations were complete, the wedding and celebrations held, the group was ready to set out for Tennessee. Despite the difficult situation, everyone was in great spirits, looking forward to seeing this new frontier. Little did they know that there would be massive changes to come that would throw the group off their well-laid plans.

Chapter 13

Eleanor and Thomas became husband and wife in February 1775. The group would arrive in Washington County, Tennessee, near the end of March of that same year. Before leaving Virginia, no one had given much thought to the rumors of war. Living along the edge of the Appalachian Mountains, these families did not believe the rumors or that any would affect them. This was, perhaps, naive on their part. These young men were of fighting age and landowners. The representatives in the Continental Congress were beginning to put together militias throughout the colonies. There was no intentional plan to avoid participation; however, they were not interested in taking part in a situation that they felt did not affect them. They had also seen the negative effects war has on families, having lost their father when they were so young. Thomas' father had been wounded, but his wounds healed, and he was able to work again. He did, on occasion, have nightmares which the family believed were caused by the war. At times his nightmares were frightening to everyone.

James, though, had stayed behind in Staunton to close his business affairs and to help Don get through the spring planting. Unfortunately, both found themselves manipulated into service in the burgeoning Patriot Army before they were ready. Donny and James would join a local friend of their father's, Daniel Morgan, to form a militia in the Valley. No one believed that the war would last as long as it did. Their militia group, led by Morgan, became an elite force of hard-fighting and exceptionally accurate fighters. Daniel Morgan gained a reputation as a fighter who couldn't (or wouldn't) die after surviving being lashed 500 times for annoying his superior officer and later a musket ball wound to his face which left his jaw deformed and scarred.

His warriors would be called to fight alongside General Benedict Arnold and General Richard Montgomery, all of whom were of Scottish heritage, at the Battle of Quebec. General Arnold, severely wounded, left the command of the troops to Morgan. The troops, which numbered about 400, were later captured and held captive. The Tennessee branch of the family did not discover the circumstances of the war for many months because mail carriers were often delayed due to battles and to death. By the time the news finally arrived in Tennessee, Mollie had given birth to a baby boy she named Alexander MacKenzie Murray. James asked Mollie to name him using his mother's surname rather than his. Although he recognized the selfishness of his request, he believed using a surname other than MacKenzie would provide secu-rity for both the child and Mollie. Mollie decided, upon the suggestion of his Uncle Thomas, to call her son "Mack". The white community would not connect the relationship between his family and Mollie and the child. Ellie had also welcomed a bundle of joy herself near the end of the year—a little girl named Mary Elizabeth MacGregor. Thomas assured the women that James and Donald would be fine, and that James would be there soon. He kept his fears to himself.

A year and half passed with only a handful of letters from Virginia regarding James and Donald. Don died in captivity; James' condition was not known. The family prayed together nightly for his safe travels to his family and an end to the war. They worked hard and made their farm a prosperous one. The intense work and the raising of children helped keep the women's worries at bay, and the insular posture taken by Thomas would keep others from speculating about the farm and its inhabitants.

Then, one afternoon in the summer of 1777 as Ellie and Mollie sat on the porch snapping peas for the evening's meal, they saw a shadow moving down the dirt road. At first, they could not determine what it was they saw until the shadow moved closer. Then the realization of what…no who…they saw became apparent. Ellie jumped up from her chair throwing her bowl onto the ground. "Thomas! Thomas! Come quick! It's James! It's James!" Mollie ran so fast down the stairs that her feet seemed to fly. In an instant she was in James' arms.

"James! James! You're finally here! We thought you were… Oh! Thank God, you are home!" Mollie hugged James so tightly he couldn't breathe, but he didn't care. He was so relieved to finally see his family. He was dirty, hot, and exhausted from his travels.

Ellie and Thomas came from around the side of the house. Thomas ran up to James and hugged him. "These gals sure have been worried about you, old man. It's about time you found your way home. We've been working hard on this farm.

I think you'll be pleased. You should've let us know when you'd be arriving; I would have gone to town to pick you up."

"Thomas, I wanted to get here so badly, that I did not think of it. I apologize. I have no doubt that you and the boys have been working hard. I would've been here a long time ago had Donald and I not gotten caught up in the war. I feel like I have been walking forever...." James collapsed to the ground. Thomas sent Ellie to get water and cloths to wash off James' face.

"James, let's get you up and into the chair and we'll get you some water." By this time, everyone was at the house. The babies were playing on the porch. After cooling off and a brief rest, James held Mack for the first time. He was thrilled to see his young son and Mollie.

"I am so happy to be here. I might never stop smiling," glancing at Mollie, James continued, "I'm sorry to have left you all to do this without me. It was not what I had intended. I am very sorry."

Mollie took James' hand, "We understand that you had no choice. We did not find out what happened for so long. We thought something bad had happened to you. Imagine our shock when we finally received word from Maureen. I am sorry that you had to go through all of that and I am so, so, sorry about Donald." The group then went inside to show James the home they had built. It was modest but it met their needs. Thomas built a separate, smaller home in the rear for Mollie and Mack. It was close enough to the main house to provide security, but far enough to give them privacy. Thomas also built small houses for Jeremiah and the other men who had come from Virginia and their subsequent families.

That evening as they sat together for the evening meal, they shared stories from the past year and half with James. James watched the babies play together on the floor with toys Thomas and the others had made for them. James commented on the ebony curls springing from his niece's head. "Mary Elizabeth looks like mother, doesn't she, Ellie?" "She does. She's got a temper to go with that hair too!" Ellie chuckled.

"Mollie, I don't believe there is a finer looking young man, than our MacKenzie. I believe those are blue eyes I see! How marvelous! I do apologize. I am a bit tired from all the walking I have been doing. I'd like to turn in." He took her hand and picked up Mack and led them towards their little home. "Thank you. Thank you for taking care of everything."

Chapter 14

Over the next few weeks, James and Thomas went over all the details of the farming operation. James was quite impressed with the work Thomas and the others had accomplished. He was amazed at the barn which seemed enormous to him at first. They had cows, goats, sheep, and chickens. Ione Skye Plantation began with 100 acres, but now had grown to 350. Thomas tried to keep the expenses as low as possible by growing corn and oats to feed the livestock. The rest of the fields were planted in cotton and tobacco. Unfortunately, the expansion of the farm also meant that they needed more labor. This meant more slave labor. It was a constant source of stress for the MacGregors. Thomas fired a manager he once hired after catching him trying to beat one of the men for looking at him "wrong".

James had news of his own to share with Thomas. For his service to the Patriot Army, he had received a grant of an additional 250 acres. Thomas and the men were delighted by the news and were anxious to sit down and work out plans for how to work those additional fields. James told Thomas that he wanted to build a forge. He further suggested that they choose one of the negro men to train as a blacksmith so that they would not have to hire a stranger. This would cut down on the trips away from the farm to go to the blacksmith shop in Jonesborough. Thomas agreed that anything they could do for themselves was beneficial both economically and socially. Then, James asked to speak to Thomas alone. The others excused themselves to return to their duties.

James wanted to speak with Thomas about his position on abolition. It wasn't that he felt he would get pushback from Thomas regarding slavery, but that he wanted to make certain that there was a consensus regarding the goals for those living on their property. "Thomas," James began as he poured himself and Thomas a glass of tea, "You know my feelings for Mollie, my son, and slavery in general. My Father believed that slavery would have ended by now, especially since he believed it to be a sin; but, as we see, it is still very much a part of this country. I think we must be clear on our support for abolition, on how we will address emancipation when it happens, and how to move forward so that everyone here benefits. This means that we must teach our negro families skills like reading, writing, and arithmetic so that they are adequately prepared when that time comes. My family found it beneficial to have men and women who could read and do simple arithmetic. Now, I know these narrow-minded fools think it is a waste to teach them anything, but we only set them up for failure if we do not. Moreover, we have seen how this works in practice on the Fraser's farm. Once emancipation happens, and it will happen in our lifetime, we can develop a plan to provide each with land to farm and with an income for their work on ours. I see it much in the same way my grandparents were treated when they came indentured to the Frasers. What are your thoughts?"

"James, I certainly agree with you. In the past year in Washington County, a more positive attitude towards emancipation has grown here. I believe this county will support abolition efforts. Of course, we benefit from being out a distance from the city. We do not get many folks out this way; and again, the more tasks we can accomplish on our own, the more we can be a positive influence on the issue. You always have my support, James. I must, however, inquire about your health, James. I have not mentioned this to your sister, but I am concerned about the injuries you sustained in the war and during your imprisonment. Are you well? Don't worry, I will not betray your trust."

"Thomas, I appreciate your concerns. There was a time when I was not certain I would survive, and some days when I did not want to. The British prison was…well, I think you can imagine the horror. Donald, as you know, did not make it out alive. I was released not long after he died, and I took him back to Virginia to be buried on his farm near his family. I spent a couple of weeks with his family trying to restore my energy and to assist Maureen in employing help for the farm. Her boys are still young, so she needed a manager. But I was also anxious to get to Tennessee, to all of you, but especially to Mollie and my son. I hope that my energy will be restored to its full potential soon. I just need time, good food, and good company!" James patted Thomas' shoulder. "I do not wish to keep you from Ellie and Mary Elizabeth any longer today. Thank you again, Thomas. You are as much a brother to me as Don. It has been comforting knowing my family was in your good hands. Good night, sir."

"You are most welcome, James. Good evening to you and Mollie." Thomas left to return to his wife and daughter in the parlor as James left to find Mollie.

Unfortunately, James' health would not recover as he had hoped. He contracted malaria during his time as a prisoner of war. While he went for periods without symptoms, he would inevitably relapse. When these relapses occurred, he would be bedridden for weeks at a time. His level of frustration with his inability to work alongside Thomas or to play with his son began to affect his spirit. He felt immense guilt. Mollie doted on him making certain he ate well and rested. After some time, the periods between relapses narrowed and James remained depressed. His family felt powerless in spite of their best efforts.

Almost two years after his return from war James came to a time when he was not able to out of bed. Mollie's patience was wearing thin only because she had no idea what to do for him. She found herself exhausted from long days of taking care of the children and working with Ellie cooking, cleaning, and teaching, and then having to deal with James. One day out of the blue, James jumped from his bed early in the morning. He made coffee and went to the chicken coop to get eggs. Mollie was not yet awake. As James cooked breakfast for his wife and son, they appeared behind him wondering what on earth was going on. "James, are you alright? You haven't been up this early in months."

"It is a beautiful morning with my beautiful family. I know that I have not been myself for a while and that it has been a terrible burden for you. I apologize. I thought it might be nice if I made breakfast for my two very favorite people." James smiled at his son and picked him up to throw him up over his head. Mack squealed in delight. Putting Mack back down, James pulled out a chair from the table and motioned to Mollie to be seated. "I have made eggs, bacon, and I even tried my hand at biscuits, though I'm not sure they are edible. They seem a bit hard." He grimaced at Mollie.

"My goodness, I think I might be able to use these as a door stop!" They had a hearty laugh. A feeling of warmth and love enveloped the cottage that morning. Mollie thought their troubles might finally be over. She sent James on to work while she cleaned up the mess he had made. What a mess it was! After finishing, she took Mack to the main house to tell Ellie what had happened. She was thrilled with the prospect of having the man she loved back.

Ellie and Mary Beth were finishing their breakfast when Mollie and Mack appeared in the dining room. Mollie poured a cup of coffee and sat down at the table. She relayed everything that happened that morning. Ellie was excited about the news. She and James had always been close, and she missed him. She and Mollie were thrilled to get started with the day's chores, believing that everything from then on would be better.

An hour or so passed when Thomas appeared at the house. Ellie and Mollie were teaching the children in the parlor when they saw him come in the door. "Ellie, Mollie, have either of you seen James this morning?"

Mollie, looking puzzled, said, "What do you mean? He left me over an hour ago to meet you in the field. You haven't seen him?" Just as the words left her lips, there was a thunderous noise that echoed throughout the valley. They jumped from their chairs and ran toward the backdoor.

Stopping them at the door, Thomas instructed, "Ellie, you and Mollie stay here. If I need you, I will send Jeremiah or Killian to get you. Stay here." Ellie could see the seriousness in his eyes.

"We will. I promise," responded Ellie emphatically. She put her arm around Mollie to comfort her. Mollie rushed back into the parlor to make certain the children were there and safe. Ellie was right behind her. "Mollie, I'm sure it's fine. Maybe there was an issue with a horse or something…maybe a snake."

Quietly, Mollie whispered, "Yes, I am sure you are right." A feeling of dread washed over her.

Thomas rushed to find Jeremiah and Killian. He found them coming out of their respective cottages pulling their suspenders up over their shoulders. "What was that, Misser Thomas," asked Jeremiah?

"I don't know, but I do not think it is good. No one should be in the fields yet. Get our guns, Jeremiah. Killian and I will saddle up the horses. No one seems to know where James is." Within moments the three men on horseback headed towards the hilly, wooded area of the property. The wooded area was too steep to farm, so they had left it wooded for hunting. It was a beautiful area that came to a high peak that looked down over the valley where the farm was located. The men separated and went in different directions to cover more ground. Thomas instructed them to fire a shot if they needed help; the other two would come in the direction of the shot. Twenty minutes or so passed when Thomas heard a shot ring out from the west of his location. He and Killian met Jeremiah within fifteen minutes. As they approached his position, they could see Jeremiah standing down a few feet from his horse.

He turned towards them, "I's so sorry, Misser Thomas." No more words were needed.

Thomas and Killian dismounted their horses and walked to where Jeremiah was standing. At his feet lay the dead body of James MacKenzie. His horse stood nearby tied to a tree. "Dear Lord, how am I going to explain this to Mollie and his sister?" The men took their hats off and bowed their heads. Each quietly prayed before picking up James' body and draping it over the back of his horse. The men rode back to the farm in silence. All these men who had known each other for much of their lives were crushed by the loss of their friend.

When they arrived at the barn, Killian took James' body from the horse and carried it inside the barn where he laid the body on a table. Thomas went on to the house to inform the women of their discovery.

It was a soul crushing blow for Mollie after the lovely morning she and Mack had with James. She did not understand right away, but as she thought about it, she realized that he had not been the man she loved for a long time. He was a broken man. She came to understand that he wanted their last memory of him to be a joyous one in an attempt to temper the situation to come. They had almost two years together and it was those memories that she and Mack would have to cherish.

They buried James on a small hill overlooking a grove of apple trees. They gathered everyone together and had a small graveside service. Ellie spoke about their grandmother, Isobel, when her father, aunt, and uncle came to the New World. "My grandmother took her children aside at the docks in Ulster and told them, that when they arrived in the New World, to look back towards Ireland and to sing to her the song she taught them, and she would know that they were well. This was a song that she sang to them each night before bed. When they arrived near Jamestown, the children holding hands, did as their mother requested. The song became a tradition for both celebrations and funerals for the little MacKenzie family in this new land. Eleanor then began to sing…

Of all the money e'er I had,
I spent it in good company.
And all the harm I've ever done,
Alas! it was to none but me.
And all I've done for want of wit
To mem'ry now I can't recall
So fill to me the parting glass
Good night and joy be with you all

Oh, all the comrades e'er I had,
They're sorry for my going away,
And all the sweethearts e'er I had,
They'd wish me one more day to stay,
But since it falls unto my lot,
That I should rise and you should not,
I gently rise and softly call,
That I should go and you should not,
Good night and joy be with you all.

If I had money enough to spend,
And leisure time to sit awhile,
There is a fair maid in this town,
That sorely has my heart beguiled.
Her rosy cheeks and ruby lips,

I own she has my heart in thrall,
Then fill to me the parting glass,
Good night and joy be with you all.[1]

As she sang tears ran down her cheeks, but she did not let that stop her song. Her beautiful voice rang through the valley. There was nothing more beautiful than her love for her brother and their family. It was a fitting tribute to her brother and to the grandmother whose sacrifice had made this life a reality.

When the service was over, Mollie and Mack returned home for quiet time together. Ellie and Thomas took Mary Elizabeth back to the main house and ate supper together in silence. Ellie tried to hide her devastation at having lost both of her brothers just a few years apart.

"Ellie, honey, I know you are sad. I promise that the pain will not last forever. James was a wounded soul. He couldn't get past everything he had experienced during the war; his sickness was only one part of it. I suppose he felt he had nothing left to give. We know that isn't true, but it is how he felt. I saw the same thing with my father. No matter how much he wanted to be healed, to forget the horrors of war, he couldn't. My father learned how to work through it. There were times when he would go off to the woods to be alone for a while. He'd be gone and we just waited. When he returned, he would be better until the next time."

Ellie turned to look at Thomas. "I know what you say is true, Thomas. It doesn't make it hurt any less. We had just gotten him back and he seemed happy. I guess he was pretending."

"I think so. He did not want to burden us with his brokenness. We will always have each other. James provided well for Mollie and Mack. We will make certain that they have everything they need." Ellie sighed and hugged Thomas.

The following morning, Ellie found Mollie in the kitchen cooking breakfast at sunrise. "Mollie, what on earth are you doing here; I was planning to help Addie this morning. I wanted you and Mack to rest."

"I could not sleep. I was awake most of the night thinking of James." Turning towards Eleanor, Mollie continued, "Missus Eleanor, that song you sang…it was so beautiful. Your grandmother sang that song?"

"Yes, she did. We never met her. She, our grandfather, and an uncle died in Ireland. Our parents sang the song to us as we went to sleep at night. It reminded them of their childhood in Ireland. The family, though, was originally from Scotland. I believe they lived in Ireland for a few years before coming with Mr. Fraser and his family as indentured servants."

"Your family was indentured to the Frasers? James never told me that. I guess that is why he believed as he did, in freedom for my people."

"It absolutely is, Mollie. It is why he wanted to make sure you and Mack would be free and now you are. No one can question it. It is written in his Last Will and Testament. He provided funds for you both to make certain you both would be taken care of regardless of how the farm does, but you will receive an income from the farm for James' portion. Thomas will become Mack's guardian so that he can guide him throughout his education and later years into adulthood. Of course, Thomas would not do anything without consulting you. We will discuss this more after we've had time to grieve. Now, I do not expect you or Mack in the house today. Stay home and spend time together. I am sure that Mack would enjoy talking about his father. I would bet he'd love to hear some stories of his father's mischief as a young boy," Eleanor rose from her chair and patted Mollie on her shoulder.

"Thank you, Missus Ellie. I will do that, but may I ask a favor of you?"

"Certainly, Mollie. My name, by the way, is just Eleanor or Ellie. You are my sister Mollie."

"Will you tell me and MacKenzie more stories about your family? We need to hear them." Ellie smiled wide and assured Mollie that she would share her family stories and heritage with her and with Mack.

Running into the kitchen she found Addie in the kitchen starting the noon meal. "Oh, Addie! I wasn't expecting you; you scared me. I guess I was in the attic too long. Here, let me help you."

It did not take long for life to return to normal at Ione Skye. Thomas was required to travel to Jonesborough to execute James' Will, which would then free up the monies he had set aside for Mollie and Mack. Jeremiah became Thomas' foreman on the farm, essentially taking his position, and Thomas took James'. Thomas had always respected the financial position James provided in the initiation of the venture. Each of the men and women were provided specific positions to fill in the running of the farm and home. This provided a sense of purpose and later it would provide them with an income.

Chapter 15

Mack grew into an exceptional student. Much like his grandfather Duncan, he thrived on learning. He enjoyed learning science, including learning about the animals and crops grown on the farm, though his Uncle Thomas preferred that he focus on classical learning, teaching him Latin, mathematics, and literature. Thomas' desire for Mack was to become a doctor. Because of their closeness in age, Mary Elizabeth insisted that she be taught the same subjects as Mack. She was thrilled to show off her intellect when she conquered a subject, especially if she did so faster than Mack. The cousins were quite competitive.

Nevertheless, the reality of the situation was not lost on Mary Elizabeth. She knew she would never be fortunate enough to attend university like Mack or to have a job like he would have. He was not required to learn to sew, cook, or how to be a good father. Sometimes she became jealous of her cousin's gender. "You get to leave here and go to university. I will be stuck here forever, Mack! It is not fair for girls to still be treated this way. England and Russia have had women leaders for heaven's sake. I have heard about female historians, scientists, and authors. Times are changing Mack. Why will father not see that?"

"Mary Elizabeth, you need to be patient. You are correct that times are changing. We are still young. I do not know if that is what I wish to do. It is what YOUR father wants. I may want to stay here and continue my father's work building this farm into a one of the greatest plantations in America like the ones I have read about in Virginia, South Carolina, and Georgia. They grow rice, indigo, corn, cotton, and tobacco. New technologies are being developed each year and a new millennium is coming. There is so much more we could do here. Why would I want to waste years away in some stuffy classroom?"

"You better not let Poppa hear you say that! He promised your Father that you would go to university. Uncle James demanded it," insisted Mary Elizabeth. Turning her back to look out a window onto the front lawn of her house, Mary Beth pondered aloud, "I wonder what the millennium will bring to us, Mack? I think it will be splendid."

Standing behind her gazing out the window as well, Mack whispered, "I hope so."

Unfortunately for Mary Elizabeth, her time of study was becoming shorter. Her mother more often required her assistance in cooking and cleaning the home. Her discontent often resulted in grunting and groaning after being given instructions. Ellie, Mollie, Addie, and Mame, Killian's wife, often chuckled to themselves after her tirades.

Much of life on Ione Skye Farm went unchanged for many years. Each week came and went without much fanfare or drama. That would change in November 1785 as the family prepared for Thanksgiving. Cool air circulated through the hills and the leaves were painted in the colors of the season.

Ellie, Addie, and Mame met early one morning to discuss the arrangements for the holiday celebration. When Mollie did not appear, the women knew something was wrong. Addie and Mame rushed out the door, as Ellie ran to the bottom of the stairs to call for Mary Elizabeth and Mack, who had moved into the big house at his mother's request so that he would have more room and privacy. As the women reached the door and flung it open, they found Mollie lying in her bed. They called her name, but she did not respond. Addie, sitting on the side of her bed, touched her forehead. "She's burnin' up Miss Ellie."

"But she's breathing, Addie," inquired Eleanor?

"Yessum, but it ain't real strong, ma'am." Addie and Mame became visibly upset by the situation. By this time Mack and Mary Elizabeth had made it to the cottage. Mack rushed over to his mother's side.

"Mother, Mother, can you hear me? It's Mack. I am here, Mother." His look of fear and desperation led these women to begin organizing her treatment.

"Addie, run go get Jeremiah and tell him to ride to Doc Hammond's and bring him back. Hurry." Looking at Mame and Mary Elizabeth, she said, "You two go to the kitchen and bring water and clean linens. We need to cool her down. MacKenzie, let's get these covers off her. She's got too many blankets on."

Everyone jumped into action. Addie returned about ten minutes later. "Ma'am, Jeremiah done gone ta gets Doc Hammond. He tole me dat he done heard 'bouts a fever goin' roun' da valley. Two younguns over to Millwood died a few days ago. She gonna beeze okay, ma'am?"

"I do not know. I do not see pox, so that is good, but there is no way to know what will happen. At least not if we cannot wake her up." Just then, Mame and Mary Elizabeth returned to the cottage with a bucket of water and cloths. "We need to keep cool cloths on her head. Change them as soon as they warm. Keep the blankets off until the fever breaks. She may get chills, but we must keep the blankets off. Let's also see if we might be able to get her to drink water. I hope the doctor will be here soon." Ellie and Mack walked outside together.

"Is my mother going to die, Aunt Eleanor?" The 10-year-old looked fearfully into her face.

"Mack, I cannot lie to you. I do not know. All we can do until the doctor arrives is to get her cooled down and see if she will awaken. I am sure she would not want you not to worry. Let's pray, Mack." Eleanor squeezed his hand and the two bowed their heads and said a prayer for his mother. Then Eleanor walked toward the house. She went to the front porch so that she could hasten the doctor to the rear as soon as she saw him. It felt like an eternity, but it was about forty-five minutes.

As the doctor and Jeremiah approached the house, Eleanor pointed toward the back of the house and to the cottage. She followed. Doc Hammond asked everyone to remain outside until he had the opportunity to examine Mollie. The group paced outside wearing a rut in the dirt. Everyone stopped in their places when the door began to open, and Doc Hammond appeared. Stepping out of the doorway, Doc Hammond said, "Mollie has Scarlet Fever. It is a bad case. I do not know what will happen, but you need to keep her cool. There is little I can do for her. This is a new disease that we are just encountering.

I have seen it mentioned in English and French medical literature, but there is no treatment. Pray for her."

Eleanor walked the doctor back to his horse. "Doc, we're going to lose her, aren't we? I have known her my whole life. She is like a sister to me."

"Ellie, Mollie is lucky to have you and Thomas. I doubt she will make it through the night. Keep her comfortable and say your goodbyes. She may still be able to hear you. And make sure you clean, or, better yet, burn everything she has been in contact with and wash yourself with a good lye soap. I don't know want to be back here in the next few days to deliver more bad news."

"How much do I owe you? I will get it from the house." Ellie added.
"There's no charge for this. I did very little. Hope to see you at church next Sunday." Doc Hammond mounted his horse and rode away. Killian came up behind Eleanor on the porch.

"Miss Eleanor, um, I is sorry ta bother you. What do I tells our families about Miss Mollie, ma'am? Dey will beeze comin' out dem fields soon. Whats do I tells dem?"

"Well, Killian, our sweet Mollie will not make it. I think we should gather up the benches we use for our prayer meetings and meet together in the little field to the left of the house this evening to pray. Would you organize that for me? I need to talk with Thomas."

"Oh, yessum, I gets dem men folk and we will sets it all up. You wants it all ready 'bout six o'clock?"

"That sounds fine, Killian. If you would send someone out to get Thomas, I would appreciate it."

"Yessum', right away." Killian ran in the direction of the barn to get Thomas and to give instructions to the others for the evening's get-together. Eleanor returned to the kitchen to check on Addie and Mame. She wanted to see how close they were to having supper ready. She wanted to make certain that everyone would be able to eat and then gather by six for the prayer meeting.

"Hello, ladies," said Ellie as she walked over to the stove where Addie was standing. Mame was at the table rolling dough for biscuits. Ellie could see that Addie was quietly sobbing. Putting her arm around Addie's shoulder and pulling her close, Ellie said, "I know, Addie. A part of us will be missing soon. Mollie is like a sister to me. We've shared so much of our lives. She is such a wonderful person…." Ellie began to sob, but quickly wiped the tears from her eyes. Mame walked over and put her arms around both Addie and Eleanor. For a few minutes, the women embraced in a tender and special moment. It mattered not their social or racial differences. Everyone at Ione Skye was loved and they knew it.

Before supper could be eaten, Mollie had succumbed to her illness. The negro ladies cleaned the body according to their tradition and redressed her in her favorite dress. Jeremiah and Killian placed her in a coffin they had made that afternoon. MacKenzie placed a flower and Bible in the coffin with her, along with a picture he had drawn of his family when he was five years old.

Supper that evening was quiet. Sadness enveloped the farm like a dense fog. With James having been gone only a short time and having died the way he did, no one in this family was ready for another loss. Once the meal was finished and the table had been cleared, everyone made their way to the field for the evening's prayer service. Thomas and Eleanor stood before the group with Mary Elizabeth and Mack seated on the front bench.

Thomas began by reading the 23rd Psalms. He asked that everyone rise, and the group sang together Mollie's favorite hymn, "Alas, and Did My Savior Bleed" followed by Eleanor singing *Good Night and Joy Be To You All* as Mollie requested. Mack and Mary Elizabeth stood to read from the Bible, read-ing Ecclesiastes 3:1-15. As they read, Mack began to cry, wiping the tears away. Mary Elizabeth wrapped her arm around him and finished the reading herself.

"I wanted to say how much I will miss Mollie. She was kind to us, especially when we did not obey her. She made sure that we did our chores and completed the lessons my mother gave us. She would say, 'You dunna wanna be no ignoramous Miss Mary Elizabeth!" Everyone giggled at the touch of levity the group desperately needed. "If you want to say something about Mollie, you can stand where you are or come up here."

Jeremiah and Addie stood and walked to the front of the group. Jeremiah took ahold of Addie's hand and began to speak, "Ya'll knowd dat me and Miss Addie was friends of Mollie's Mam and Pap—Bartholomew and Miss Tabitha. We comes down to the old farm round 'bout the same time. Dey was so happy when Miss Mollie came along. She was one of the first younguns of our peoples to gets born on da farm, soes everybody done take it on deyselves to watch out over her. I think she was the purdiest little gal I ever did see, and she filled the air with the sweet sound of her voice."

Addie interjected, "I remember how much Mollie loved ta sing. Sometimes she sang a hymn and sometimes she mades up a tune. Some of 'em was real nice. I will also remember dem beautiful, amber eyes. I don't recollect seeing that color before. On da Virginy farm, Mollie started out working with me in da kitchen and keepin' da house clean when she was 'bouts 8-year old. She done made da biggest mess in my kitchen…." Addie's laughter quickly turned to tears. Jeremiah took her by the hand and led her away as her sobs became louder and more akin to wailing.

"Thank you, Jeremiah, Addie. Does anyone else wish to speak?" Thomas waited a few minutes before continuing, "If no one else wishes to speak, we will close in prayer. Please bow your heads. 'Father God, we have gathered here today to celebrate and mourn for our beloved Mollie MacKenzie. Father, we understand that you must need Mollie in heaven and that her purpose on Earth is now complete. We ask for your peace in healing our hearts as we move forward in our lives without her, especially her son MacKenzie. May you bless him with the gift of a long memory of his mother and show him mercy when grief overtakes his soul. May everyone gathered here today, Lord, commit to loving and caring for her and James' child. We are all your children, Lord. May we ever seek to do your will and forgive us, oh Lord, when we fail you. Amen. You are all dismissed now to return to your homes."

Chapter 16

Once the funeral for Mollie had taken place, Thomas and Ellie needed to discuss how best to proceed for the best of Mack. It was fortunate for them that Mack was a light-skinned boy with blue eyes. Only a few people in the area outside of Ione Skye had ever seen him. Neither of the children attended the local school and most often the children stayed at the farm when others went into town for supplies or to church. This was by design because Mack needed to be protected from gossip and suspicion as to his parentage.

MacKenzie handled his mother's death well for someone of his age. Because of his intelligence, he wanted to understand the position his life was in because of his mixed race. There came a time a couple of years later when he sought out more information regarding these questions. He had not known his father well because James was not there during his early years; and when he returned, he was only with them for a year and a half before taking his own life and then his mother died leaving him without a parent to explain the situation to him.

"Uncle Thomas, may I speak with you," inquired Mack? Thomas was in his study reviewing the farm's books and gathering monies together to pay bills.

Not looking up from writing in his ledger, Thomas responded, "Certainly, my boy, take a seat. I will be just another moment. You sound as though you have something on your mind."

Sitting down in the chair directly in front of Thomas' desk, Mack continued, "Well, sir, I wished to ask you about my parents, if I might."

Hearing the sincerity in the boy's tone, Thomas put his pen down and removed his spectacles. "Sounds serious, Mack. Do I need to include your aunt in our conversation?"

"Well, sir, maybe. I have some questions about them because…," Mack hesitated.

Thomas rose from his desk and took a few steps outside his office door. Looking into the salon and over towards Eleanor's direction, he cleared his voice rather loudly to get her attention. Eleanor looked up from her needlework, "Yes, Thomas, do you need me?"

"I do, dear. If you could join me, please?" Eleanor put her work down and walked to the office. Entering the room, she saw Mack seated in front of the desk. "Oh, Mack, dear, I did not know you were here."

"Please be seated, Eleanor. Mack has told me that he wishes to speak with us about his parents. I felt that you and I both needed to participate in this conversation. Mack, go ahead. We are here to help you."

Mack thought for a few minutes before starting to speak. "Uncle Thomas, Aunt Ellie, I know that I am different from Mary Elizabeth because my mother was a negro. I know that my father was white." Looking over directly at Eleanor, he continued. "I know he was your brother, Aunt Eleanor. I have heard some of the others say that my parents were not actually married. They've called me a bastard.

"I don't know who on this farm would say such a thing; it makes me unhappy to know that you have been called such a despicable word. One day you will be in love, and it will make more sense to you than it does now. This _is_ an unusual situation, but we will attempt to put it in terms that you can understand, okay?" Eleanor asked.

"Yes, ma'am; thank you."

Thomas walked from around the back of his desk and came around to the front where Mack and Eleanor were seated. He sat down on a settee. Mack and Eleanor turned their chairs around so that they all would be looking at each other. "Mack, I must give you a lesson on history which, I must say, I have been dreading; but you deserve to know the truth of the matter. When the first settlers came to this new nation around the year 1600, they began to farm. As you are aware from living here on this farm, it takes many people doing many different tasks to make a farm profitable. Profitable means that the farm brings in more money than it pays out in bills. (Mack nodded his head to express his understanding.) These first farmers encountered numerous hardships and many, if not most, died. As more settlers came, they desired, obviously, to be successful and so they looked for ways to accomplish that goal. Unfortunately, the decision that was made was not one that either of us or your father would have chosen; however, once it was made, it has been almost impossible to undo. At least, not without considerable negative consequences."

"Ok, so what was that choice, Uncle Thomas?"

"Mack, you understand that people often in their lives make poor decisions, right? It is like eating a second helping of mashed potatoes and gravy because it tasted so good, but later you regret it because your stomach hurts."

"Sure! I wanted a second piece of watermelon last night, but I am so glad you, Aunt Ellie told me that I could not have another. My stomach hurt from all the roast I ate!"

"Well, Mack, what happened with the farmers was similar, though the consequences to our new nation are far worse than an upset stomach. In 1620, some British merchants brought to America a ship full of negroes from Africa to work on the farms. These Africans did not know our language, customs; or really anything about us. They did not come here of their own choice; they were forced. Many did not learn until much later that these Africans were being kidnapped and sold to British merchants, sometimes by their own kinsmen. Obviously, that is something we would never have agreed to participate in because it is wrong. It is a lie by omission because, obviously, these traders realized people of moral character would not willingly and knowingly do this if they had known."

A look of shock and bewilderment came over Mack's face. "So, my momma was stolen from Africa?"

Eleanor continued the explanation, "No, your momma was not, but her parents were. Your momma was born in Virginia on Mr. Robert Fraser's farm. We both knew Mollie's family. They were good people. Mack, when Africans were brought here, they were sold to the white farmers to work on their farms. This is a situation that our family has been against, but as your Uncle Thomas said, it has been a difficult situation to deal with."

"They were sold? Like you buy something at the General Store? Could someone buy me?" Mack became visibly shaken and fearful. "Did you buy me or my momma?"

Eleanor squeezed Mack's hand as she spoke, "Years ago, when your father James and I were young and growing up in Virginia, we were raised on the farm alongside the African slaves purchased by Mr. Fraser. I know this sounds horrible. It is horrible. It was a situation where, if a farmer wanted to compete with the other farms in the area, he had to keep his expenses down. The best way to do that was to eliminate the cost of labor because that is the single largest expense a farmer has next to tools. Even if a farmer, like our fathers, were morally opposed to the practice of slavery, they eventually had to participate, or they would go out of business. It is an untenable situation, Mack."

Both Thomas and Ellie were quiet for a moment to give Mack a few minutes to think about what had been said. Then Thomas picked up the conversation, "My father felt the same way as the MacKenzies and the Frasers—he felt slavery to be abhorrent but, unfortunately, necessary. My father also chose to treat his slaves with kindness rather than with cruel discipline. I know that is why our two farms surpassed the profitability of every other farm in the area combined."

"And, Mack, dear, you will learn as you progress in your studies that slavery is not a creation of this country. Slavery has existed everywhere in the world for as long as we have written history. In fact, the word "slavery" comes from Eastern Europe where the Slavic peoples had been enslaved by their Muslim invaders. But the practice goes back even further than them. Even in the times of our Lord Jesus Christ, slavery existed. In your readings of the Bible, you will find that our treatment comes directly from the teachings of Christ."

"So, they get paid, right? I mean, if they work, they get paid. That's how it works, right?"

"In our case, Mack, we provide everything that our workers here on our farm need. We make sure that they have clothes, food, housing…whatever they need, but they are not required to pay for it. That is the way that they are paid. The term for this kind of payment is "in kind", meaning instead of cash payments, goods and services are provided."

"But what if they want something that you do not give them? How would they buy it if they do not have money?"

Thomas replied, "That is a great question. I suppose it would depend on what it is. Everyone knows that they can come to us with their concerns or to express a need. Obviously, we do not want to waste money, but we also understand that a special request might be necessary to improve their quality of life. Like maybe Jeremiah might want to give Addie a birthday gift; I would certainly help him to do that. We would want to give them what they request because that makes them happy. Happy people work hard. We want everyone to be happy."

"I think it sounds like not everyone cares like you do. Is that true?"

"Mack, as you get older you may witness events at other homes and farms that you have never seen here. Other farm owners do not believe as we do, and they can be cruel to their slaves. They often punish them for not making their daily quotas and other infractions on the farm. The farm owners are more focused on their profit than the needs of those who help them make it. Instead of finding other non-violent ways to punish, they beat their slaves. We made a decision not to discipline this way because a hurt person cannot work, and it creates hostility and resentment. We do not want this for them or for ourselves. When we encounter conflict, Mack, we both try to confront the situation in a manner that gives dignity and respect to both sides. Violence can never create respect. If you will think back on times when you or Mary Elizabeth got into trouble, we did not strike you, did we? No, we used other non-violent means to discipline you both." Thomas paused to determine if Mack understood his explanation.

"I think I understand that. Why were my parents not married? I thought all mommas and poppas were married." Mack peered intently into his aunt's face.

"That's simple really. It is against the law for an African to marry a white person. That does not mean the law is right; it is just the law. Your parents did have a small ceremony in which they pledged their love and fidelity to each other before we left to come to Tennessee. That was all that they could do, but it was not a legally binding marriage like your uncle and I have," explained Eleanor.

"I guess if they could not do anything else, that was nice. Why did it take my father so long to come here? And why did he die?"

Thomas jumped in to respond, "That's an easy answer as well. The war kept him away. When we left to come to Tennessee, he had to stay in Virginia to finish some business. He intended to come to Tennessee as soon as he concluded that business. However, we were unaware of the impending war between the colonies and Britain. Your father and his brother Donald were conscripted into the militia. Both were captured and held in prison. As soon as he was released, he came here to be with you and your mother. As far as his death goes...." Thomas became upset and could not answer. Tears began to stream down both his and Eleanor's faces.

After a sniffle and wiping her eyes, Ellie continued, "I apologize, Mack. Your father was more than my brother; he was my best friend. When we knew that we were all going to move here, he asked me and Uncle Thomas to take care of you and your mother. Your mother was like a sister to me. We had grown up together on our farm. We were all a family. After your father was released from prison, he was not the same James I grew up with. He tried to pretend to be happy, but that became too much. He loved you and he loved every minute he was with you and your mother. I think he saw too much in the war. War is a terrible thing. Unfortunately, though, sometimes it is necessary. Not only had he contracted an incurable illness called malaria, but he was also sick mentally. I don't think he could live with what he had seen and, perhaps, what he had been forced to do. It was just too much."

Mack looked down for a second and then back up, looking at Thomas, "You mean killing, don't you?"

Thomas quickly retorted, "Yes, MacKenzie." Everyone was silent for several minutes. You could almost see the questions circulating around the room in the same way they were circulating through the brains of those in the room. "Do you have any other questions you'd like to ask, Mack?"

"Yes, sir. Am I black or white? Am I a slave?" Thomas and Ellie looked with horror at each other. These were questions they hoped would never be asked of them by their nephew.

Eleanor took a deep breath, and she said a quick prayer for God to give her the best words. "Mack, you are whatever you want to be. You are a combination of your mother and your father. The term used most often for this situation is "mulatto". But we do not think of you in this way, Mack. You are our family, and we believe that you can be whatever you decide to be. Do you understand?"

"I think so. Now that my parents are dead and I live with you here in the house, will people think I am your child?"

"I suppose they may. We certainly love you the same as we love Mary Beth," inquired Thomas.

"I know. My skin is very pale, like yours Aunt Ellie. Can people tell I am black and white…uh, mulatto?"

"I do not believe so, but that does not mean that you must pretend to be something you do not wish to be, Mack. People in town have not seen you much. Your last name is different from your mother's so they would not have reason to think that she was your mother. We had her work as our nanny so that she could be with you; your father wanted you to live with us. He wanted us to care for you and educate you so that you would have more opportunities in life." Eleanor wanted to ease Mack's mind as much as she could; she couldn't bear to see him so unsure of himself.

"So, no one would know that I am not Mary Elizabeth's brother, except that my last name is Murray, not MacGregor? But my father's last name was MacKenzie. Why is my last name different?"

"They would not just assume that you are siblings. You and Mary Elizabeth are close in age, so you couldn't be siblings. He and Mollie wanted you to be raised by us if anything happened because they knew we could provide a better life for you. He also did not want you to be stigmatized by having the same last name as your mother because being the child of a slave and her master would keep you from having every opportunity in life. Your mother and her parents agreed with all of this, Mack. You are not a slave, my boy. You are whatever you wish to be." Thomas, too, was quite concerned about how Mack was going to process all the information he had been given and if there would be any cause for concern about how he might handle it all.

"Uncle Thomas, I know that you wanted to have a conversation with me about my education. I want very much to do as my father wished. I want to be a doctor. He left you in charge of my studies and I wish to proceed with the studies necessary to become a doctor." Eleanor and Thomas were both surprised by this announcement but pleased. They both feared that Mack would be too scared to ever leave Ione Skye.

"I think you have made a wonderful decision, Mack. Both of your parents would be thrilled," rejoiced Eleanor.

Just then Addie appeared in the doorway, "Ma'am, I is so sorry ta interrupt, but supper is ready."

"Oh, dear. I let time get away from me; I apologize. Let's all get washed up and get to the table. Thank you, Addie." Eleanor rose and walked quickly out the office door with Addie at her side. Thomas and Mack followed close behind, stopping at the wash basin to wash their hands before going outside to the table to eat with everyone.

A few days passed after the lengthy conversation in the office. While Thomas and Eleanor believed they had quashed Mack's fears, Mack had lingering questions. After supper was finished, the table cleared, and the workers left, Mack followed behind. Feeling someone was behind him, Jeremiah turned around to see Mack following close behind. "Boy, whats you a doin' back dere? Ain't you got some studin' ta do?"

"Well, yes, sir, but I wished to speak to you." Mack was getting hot and tired trying to keep up with the pace of the men walking back to the field. Jeremiah could tell that Mack had something important on his mind, so he slowed down and pulled Mack under a large oak tree. "Okay, son, what beeze on yo mind?" Inquired Jeremiah. "Well, sir, I wanted to ask you about my Momma and Poppa. Were you friends of theirs?"

"Why, course, boy. Yo momma and me, we was raised up together. We was raised up with Masser James, too. His daddy was our masser until we comes here ta Tennessee."

"Do you hate him 'cuz he bought all of ya'll? It ain't right to buy people." Mack asked rapidly and with conviction. "Well, now, Mack, you beeze right 'bout dat. No man ought ta beeze ownin' another, but dat's how things beeze done in dis here country, but I don't hate yo Poppa, son. Masser James and Masser Thomas, dey treats us real good. I knowd other slaves on dem other farms ain't treated like wes beeze treated here. 'Tis terrible how dem others likes us gets treated. You needs ta know dat yo Momma and yo Poppa, dey loved each other. Yo Poppa was a good man, and Miss Mollie, yo Momma, she was as sweet as apple pie. Dat Miss Mollie was a right fine woman. I won't never forgets her. Yo Poppa, he done right by yo Momma. He didn't just leave her when dey found out 'bouts you. He loved Miss Mollie. He made sure ta takes care of her. Some massers who makes babies wit a negro women just deny dem babes. Not yo Poppa. He didn't have no wife. He only loves Miss Mollie since weeze was all younguns. He wanted ta marry her, but dat ain't allowed. He did whats he could ta dooze right by you and yo Momma."

"Would it be okay, Mister Jeremiah, for me to want to be like my Poppa instead of my Momma? I mean, my Poppa wanted me to be a doctor. That's what some white people do. Would it make you mad if I became a doctor?"

Jeremiah removed his hat and wiped the sweat from his forehead while considering his answer to Mack's question. "Masser Mack, are you a axin' if I would be angry if yo becomes a doctor cuz dat is what yo Poppa wanted for you?"

"Yes, because that is something a black person cannot do. I don't wanna hurt my Momma or do anything that might make you, Killian, Jacob, Macajah or any of the negro ladies angry with me. I am not sure where I belong, Jeremiah," faltered Mack.

"Well, now, I sho do understands that Masser Mack. I thinks it'll be right fine if you becomes a doctor. We needs doctors 'round here. Ain't nobody roun' dis place gonna beeze mad if youse decides ta beeze a doctor. Youse a part of us and a part of yo Poppa's family. We wants you ta do good. If you have ta be wit dem white folk ta do good, then dat's what you do. It ain't nobody's bidness but yours."

"I want to be a doctor, Jeremiah. Thank you." Mack ran off to find Mary Elizabeth and pick up their studies. When Mack arrived in the study room, Mary Elizabeth was there lying on her back across the window seat reading a book. "Hey, Mary Beth (as he liked to call her), what are you reading?"

"*Swiss Family Robinson*, Mack. It is quite an adventure. A family gets shipwrecked on an island. It's all good until pirates show up. So, what's up with you? You're late starting your studies.

"So I am, but I was having a conversation with Jeremiah that was very important," implored Mack.

"Important? What was it about?"

Mack sat down beside Mary Beth and continued, "I had some questions about my parents, see. I just needed to know the truth of things. Who I am and such. Do you know the story, Mary Beth?"

Mary Beth sat up so that she could see Mack better. "Were you uncertain? I mean, you are my cousin. Was that in dispute in your mind?" Mary Beth wasn't quite sure how serious the conversation was and in what manner she should reply. After all, she cared deeply for Mack, and she did not wish to hurt his feelings.

"Well, I'm sure you know that Mollie, my mother, was a negro…a slave, though she and I were freed by my Poppa. Jeremiah told me that the slaves here haven't been treated like slaves on other farms. I wanted to know if I am a negro or if I am white. I cannot tell from looking in a mirror. I also wanted to know why my father died."

"Oh, well, I guess I can understand all of that. I wondered if you would come to me first, or to my momma and poppa. What did they tell you?"

"They said that I am both negro and white, something they called 'mulatto'. But they said that I can decide if I want to be one or the other or mulatto. I don't know why I would choose to be negro because they can be treated so badly. I would not wish to hurt my mother or her family by denying it either. What do you think, Mary Beth?"

"Mack, I do not think that your mother would be hurt with any choice you make, but you are correct about how negros are treated. I know that Uncle James freed you and your mother upon his death, so you are not a slave, if you ever were. Your skin is quite light. It really looks like mine, except that your skin tans more in the summertime. You also have blue eyes. I have never seen a negro with blue eyes. I don't think anyone would just assume your race. Not many have seen either one of us because we have been kept at home. I think that has been on purpose—to protect you, but also me from rumors. Our whole lives we have been told how much your parents loved each other. Everyone was raised together on the farm in Virginia. Our family is truly unique in that way. They have always been abolitionists, which is odd in the South, but it is not so rare in this county. There are many abolitionists here. What did mother and father tell you about your father's death, Mack?"

"Uncle Thomas said it was because of his experiences in the war and he had an illness. He said that some people are harmed by what they see—all the deaths. Father couldn't handle the death and having to kill. It makes sense to me. I just would have liked him to still be here with me."

Mary Beth put her hand on Mack's shoulder to comfort him. "You will always have us, Mack. Everyone here loves you, even if you are a silly ole rabbit!" She took her hand and quickly ran it under his arm pit to tickle him. The two slid to the ground and began to rough house. Within seconds Eleanor appeared at the door.

"So, how are those studies coming? I don't see much study-ing going on in here. I think it is about time to get out your arithmetic and start working. You have an hour before supper. Am I clear?"

In unison the two replied dejectedly, "Yes, ma'am." Then they began to giggle as Ellie left the room.

"Did you talk about anything else, Mack?"

"Oh yes! I told them that I wish to be a doctor. I don't want anyone else to die like my mother. If the doctor had been able to get here sooner or if he had better medicine, maybe she would have lived."

"That is wonderful, Mack. You will make a terrific doctor. I guess we'd better do as mother said." The two began their studies and did not speak of these questions again. In fact, no one ever spoke of these issues again. Mack continued to study until his Uncle Thomas believed he was appropriately skilled to sit for his examinations. After passing these exams at the young age of sixteen, Mack prepared to matriculate at the University of Pennsylvania for his medical studies which would take a year or so to complete.

Chapter 17

When the day finally arrived for Mack to leave for Philadelphia, everyone on the farm gathered to send him off. They prepared a special dinner in his honor. Addie and Mame made all his favorite foods and then packed up some of the leftovers for his travel. There were many tears shed when, at last, it was time for Mack to leave for the trip to town to pick up the coach. Thomas rode with Mack from the farm to Jonesborough. During the ride, they relived childhood stories, sang silly songs, and discussed his upcoming studies. Thomas was, of course, more of a father than an uncle. Mack felt especially close to Thomas because Thomas had been honest with Mack all those years before. Mack knew he could always trust Thomas to tell him the truth.

When the pair arrived in town, Mack got off his horse and gathered his things. A few moments passed when they knew it was time to say goodbye. It was not easy, but knowing he would be back for Christmas gave them some comfort. Mack watched his uncle ride away before handing his bags to the coachman and mounting the coach.

The trip from Tennessee to Philadelphia was expected to take nine to ten days depending on weather and any other unforeseen problems. Mack looked forward to his travel because he had never traveled anywhere before. He enjoyed looking out the window at the beautiful scenery. It was September, and the air was cooler. He brought an extra blanket for the nights spent camping along the way. He enjoyed the suppers by the fire and getting to share stories with his fellow travelers, of which there were 3. There was a gentleman named Jacob Bowman, who was a minister of some sort. He was traveling to Philadelphia to give a lecture at a Quaker Meeting House. There was also a mother and her son, who looked to be about twelve years old. They would be traveling on to New York from Philadelphia to visit her family. Her husband had recently died in an accident. The mother, named Prudence, was uncertain if they would return to their home in Tennessee. She said that she would very much like to do so, if possible.

And then there was the coachman and his assistant. Mack believed these men were incredibly brave for taking on the difficulties encountered and the risks they assumed on the trip. They stopped only to rest for a few hours, to eat, and to water and feed the horses. They were expected to travel 50-60 miles per day over treacherous terrain. In light of the situation, both men were humorous and told delightful stories.

Mack wrote in his journal about his experiences each day so that he could share them with Mary Beth when he was able to write to her. By the time he arrived in Philadelphia, a third of his journal was filled. Mack read about Philadelphia in books, but he never imagined how big, loud, and beautiful it was. He was thrilled to arrive at the coach station. He then had to walk the remaining distance to the university. He did not mind, though. It gave him the opportunity to see some of the city. He was amazed by all the people on the street going this way and that way. He wondered what all of them did and where they were going in such a hurry.

He was awed by the colorful clothing, especially the fancier ones. He felt a bit self-conscious about his clothing after seeing the top hats, ascots, and jackets worn by other young men. He began to feel intimidated and awkward. Perhaps he would not fit in. He felt provincial. Soon, however, the crowds began to dissipate, and the loudness became subdued. He finally had the university in sight, and his excitement returned. His step picked up. He was almost charging toward the door of the Admissions Building. When he opened the door, he was greeted by a young man. "Good day, sir. May I be of assistance?"

"Yes…I mean, I think so. I am here for the next term of the medical school. My name is Alexander MacKenzie Murray—Mack for short."

Shaking hands feverishly, the young man spoke again, "Oh yes, sir, please follow me. I will take you where you need to go, and I will stay with you until you are certain you have what you need. My name is Joel Sutherland. I will be in your class. I have been here a month or so taking other courses that I needed in order to matriculate in the medical school."

"It is good to meet you. How are the rooms? Do you know how many students will be in our class?"

"I believe there will be about 100. I think the rooms are adequate. You will have a roommate. We will go to a different office to find out who your roommate will be." Joel took Mack to each of the offices he needed to visit to obtain his course schedule, to pay his fees, and to find out his room assignment and roommate. Mack couldn't wait to get to his room so that he could write down everything that had occurred that day. He was afraid he might forget as exhaustion was coming upon him.

The medical students were housed in the same dormitory and ate in the same dining facility located in the same building. The medical school building was located just across the quad from the dormitory. Joel told Mack that he would come back in an hour to take him to pick up his books and other materials and then they would eat dinner together. Classes were scheduled to begin in two days. Mack was immensely thankful for Joel's attendance to his needs, many of which he not even aware of.

During dinner, Joel informed Mack that there were special events scheduled for the new medical school students over the next two days before classes began. The next day, there would be a concert on the quad given by the College of Music. That same evening, there would be a social for all the medical school students in the home of the university president. A convocation for all new students was scheduled for the first morning of classes in the university chapel. It was all so exciting for a boy from the woods.

After all the activities, Mack felt exhausted. When bedtime came, he fell asleep as soon as his head hit the pillow, but the morning came like a clap of thunder. A bell was rung to wake the students. They dressed quickly and then rushed for the dining hall. They gulped their food, took a swig of water, and then ran for their classrooms.

Students were required to wear a dark suit and an ascot or tie. Thomas, Ellie, Mary Beth took Mack to town to purchase appropriate school clothing. They all wished to be a part of the process. When Mack came out of the dressing room adorned in his university best, they beamed with pride. The suit was tailored to fit perfectly. Uncle Thomas chuckled that Mack had better watch his food intake or he'd be busting out of his pants in no time! Putting those clothes back on that first day made medical school a reality. He wondered to himself what his father and mother might have thought that day if they had been there to see him. He prayed he would make them proud.

Chapter 18

Mack was thrilled with his courses—anatomy, surgery, midwifery, as well as a course on the theory and practice of the physic. He was a diligent student, studying in the afternoon, evening, and often into the early hours of the morning. He was so dedicated to study that even his professors urged him to take time off for rest, fearing he might burn out or become ill. He could become consumed with fear over an exam and forget to eat. His roommate, Charles Addison, urged him not to worry; most often Mack received the highest marks. However, if he did not, he became sullen and depressed. Charles, who liked Mack, often brought him sweets and rolls from the dining hall. Sometimes his gang of medical school friends would rush his room, throw him to the floor, and tickle him unmercifully. It was a great stress relief.

They also introduced him to sports, specifically baseball, basketball, and later football. Mack fell in love with baseball. The gang used baseball as an enticement away from the books when such free time arose. It was exactly what Mack needed to relax. He became a skilled pitcher, and he enjoyed striking out his able competitors. He was thrilled with the idea of taking a baseball and bat home with him and teaching everyone on the farm how to play.

The medical school course was just short of a year long. At the end of the course was a comprehensive exam that each student was required to pass to graduate. No one wondered whether Mack would pass. They took bets on what his score would be. It was, therefore, no surprise when Mack received the highest score. After graduation, Mack was asked to apprentice with Dr. Benjamin Rush for a period of one year. Dr. Rush was one of the best professors in Mack's opinion and he was honored to be asked. His apprenticeship would begin after a brief visit home. Dr. Rush would provide Mack with accommodation and a small stipend for expenses. It surprised no one when Dr. Rush asked to him remain at the end of his apprenticeship.

Chapter 19

When the coach arrived back in Jonesborough, the entire MacGregor family was in attendance. When Mack disembarked the coach, he was greeted with cheers. Feeling a bit embarrassed by all the hullabaloo, his face turned bright red. Mary Beth rushed over to hug him; Uncle Thomas reached for his baggage; and Aunt Ellie picked up all the items he dropped on the ground. "Give the man some space, Mary Beth!" Urged her mother.

"Momma, I am so excited to see Mack. It's been so long. I surely have forgotten what he looks like." Cried Mary Beth wrapping her arms around MacKenzie's and they walked toward their wagon.

"I think you've grown another foot. Look at those trousers! They're filthy. I think you've put on some weight. It looks good on your, MacKenzie." Eleanor beamed with pride as they walked along the sidewalk.

"I have brought you all gifts from Philadelphia. It is an amazing city. There is so much going on there. There are people talking about the potential for war between the us and the Brits again. I have been to a few lectures about the progress with abolition. It is really something, Uncle Thomas."

"I certainly hope war does not become necessary. I do not wish that for any of us, Mack, but especially for you."

"But I can be of use, sir. I can help treat soldiers, far better than what existed when my father and Uncle Donald were soldiers. We'd be doing our duty, if such becomes necessary." This conversation would be a foreshadowing of what was to occur a couple of years after Mack began his apprenticeship. By late May 1812, war was eminent. Mack asked to speak with Dr. Rush when he arrived for work one morning.

"Dr. Rush, I need to speak with you, sir. It is a matter of great importance."

"Well, son, I think I have a good idea what you wish to speak of. You have my attention."

"As you know, sir, the United States is close to declaring war on the British. When that happens, I plan to volunteer as a doctor, if you agree for me to do so."

"As I suspected. I understand your desires. While I do not support this war, I do support you. You will learn much in service as a doctor to our military men, but I must warn you that war is ugly. You will see things that you will never be able to wash from your mind again. You must remain faithful to God and pray. My family will keep you in our prayers. I hope that you will write to us and keep us informed as to your circumstances. We have come to love you. I think it would be advisable for you to go home before this war begins and spend some time with your family. I will cover the cost of your travel home. Is there anything else you wish to discuss?"

"Thank you, sir. I too think of you, Mrs. Rush and your children as family. I never really knew my parents because both died when I was young. You and my uncle are important advisors to me. I appreciate your guidance; and I appreciate your wife's cooking!"

"Well, appreciate it one more time this evening. I will let Julia and the children know you are coming. Let's see these patients and then we will close for the day at lunchtime."

"Yes, thank you, sir."

After eating with the Rush family at lunch that day, Dr. Rush and his family accompanied Mack to the coach station. They hugged Mack and wished him safe travels home. Mrs. Rush wiped a tear from her eye as the coach pulled out. "Benjamin, will there be a war? I cannot fathom losing Mack to a war."

"Unfortunately, Julia, I believe there will be. Mack is exceptionally talented. I plan to write a letter to President Madison asking him, if possible, to keep Mack at a hospital and out of the direct line of fire, if possible. Mack is too valuable to lose."

"I do hope that the president will listen to you. Perhaps you might ask another gentleman from the medical school to write in support of your request?"

"That is a fine idea, Julia. I will ask Dr. Barton. He was of a similar opinion of our Mack. Let's go home."

The United States declared war on June 18, 1812. By the time Mack returned to Philadelphia a letter had been delivered in care of Dr. Rush from President Madison. When Mack arrived at the Rush home, Dr. Rush met with him in private in the study of his home. "Mack, I have a letter for you. I hope you may forgive my presumption into this matter, but I wrote to President Madison regarding your wish to serve in the medical corps should war be declared. This is his letter of response for you." Dr. Rush handed the letter to Mack.

"Of course, I am not offended, sir. You are far more knowledgeable regarding these matters than I. I always appreciate your willingness to assist me, sir." Mack reached for the letter and immediately ripped it open. Glancing at the beginning, he began to read aloud:

To Dr. Alexander MacKenzie Murray:

It is with my sincerest regards that I write to you in response to the requests of your medical school professors, Dr. Benjamin Rush and Dr. Benjamin Smith Barton. I have asked John Armstrong, Secretary of War, to assign you to Fort McHenry in Baltimore, Maryland, to serve as physician to the soldiers and sailors in service therein. You will receive notification of the date on which you are to report to Fort McHenry from the War Department. Until that time, please continue your training with my good friend, Dr. Rush. My best wishes and greatest thanks for your service to your nation.

Your most humble and obedient servant,
President James Madison

"That is a good assignment, Mack. Fort McHenry has just finished construction. You should have the benefit of better facilities to treat soldiers and sailors than we had during the Revolution. What do you think, son?"

"Sir, I am still trying to understand that I am holding a letter from our president addressed to ME! I am so honored. I think it would be inappropriate to state that I am excited because no one should be excited about war. Particularly because the effects of the Revolution took both my father and my Uncle Donald. I will do my utmost to make certain that I do not disappoint. I am also encouraged that I still have some time with you before I must report. I still have much to learn."

"Dr. Murray, this is the reason why you will be an exceptional doctor; you understand that you will never know everything about medicine. You will learn something new every day. Enough with the accolades, let's get to work. The lobby is full of patients waiting to be seen."

"Absolutely, Dr. Rush. I will let Mrs. Carmichael know that we are ready to see patients."

Mack reported to Fort McHenry on August 1, 1812. Practicing medicine during a time of war is exactly what you expect it to be—gruesome and tragic. Mack, unlike his father, was able to compartmentalize his work. He looked at each soldier or sailor as a fierce warrior who needed him to give them back their strength so that they could finish the battle. He understood that soldiers and sailors needed an advocate to aid them in their physical and mental recovery so that they could return to the battlefield or home to their families. If injuries were insurmountable, then he did what he could to ease their pain, repair what he could of their injuries, and, when necessary, he prayed over them in their dying moments.

In late April 1813, Mack received a letter from Dr. and Mrs. Rush. Mack was excited to receive correspondence from his mentor and his family. To his dismay, the letter was from Dr. Rush's son James. James related to Mack that his father had contracted typhoid fever and died. Mack was devastated by the loss of his professor and father figure of his early adult years. He admired Dr. Rush and he studied closely Dr. Rush's writings on mental health, diseases like dengue fever, wartime medicine, and human intelligence.

Mack wanted greatly to be a man of substance like his mentor. He knew that he could be that man in the manner in which he treated the soldiers and sailors serving in the war. By providing a high level of care to these men and by treating their spiritual wounds as well as their physical ones, Mack knew he would make the kind of difference he wanted to make. Mack had several local ministers who would take turns meeting with soldiers and sailors in the hospital, and there were nurses who would read the Bible in the evenings.

Then September 13, 1814, came. The U. S. capital had fallen, and the British were looking for their next target. It didn't take much to determine that Baltimore and Fort McHenry would be that target. The British sent their navy to the Baltimore harbor to support the attack. Over one thousand men, women and children resided at Fort McHenry. The port was blocked by a large chain and scuttled hulks. The militia manned cannons and other defensive weapons. The British determined that the only way to win the battle would be to attack at night.

At this time an American attorney named Frances Scott Key was sent out to a British ship to negotiate the exchange of prisoners with the British. The British consented to a one-for-one exchange, but just after informing the American soldiers and sailors being held on the ship, he was informed that the British would be attacking the fort with the full force of over one hundred ships. Key understood the significance of such an overwhelming force, especially against a fort that's primary purpose was to protect the port, but not much else strategically. Such an attack seemed immoral in Key's mind. The Americans aboard heard what Key had been told. They begged him to watch and tell them everything that was happening.

As the battle began that night, one of the officers aboard the frigate told Key to watch the American flag because in a short time it would no longer be flying, and America would cease to exist. Key began to pray silently as he watched the events unfold. The bombs began to fly just as the sun was setting. In a short time, Key could no longer count the bombs as they hit; there were far too many. As the sky began to turn black, smoke from the bombs began to fill the air. The British informed Mr. Key that all the Americans had to do to stop the bombardment was to take the flag down and surrender. Key responded that such a thing was not likely to happen, but secretly he was unsure. Key continued to watch as the fort took its blows, chipping away at the fortress. It seemed like a spotlight had been placed above the American flag. The barrage of over 1,500 bombs continued into the wee hours of the morning. The flag still flew tattered and torn. The flagpole leaned but it never fell.

The soldiers and sailors screamed, "Where is the flag, sir? Where is the flag?"

"IT IS STILL THERE! IT IS STILL THERE!" Yelled Key to the soldiers and sailors below. When the battle ended and the British conceded the victory to the Americans, Key rushed to the fort to find out how the flag had not fallen in the intense bombing. When he arrived and rushed to the flagpole, there he found Dr. Mack Murray assisting in the removal of bodies and men barely alive from the area. He paid no attention to the number of dead because he was in awe that these bodies were holding up a ninety-foot flagpole with a forty foot by thirty-two-foot flag atop. Key made a special effort to speak to Dr. Murray.

"Hello, doctor. I am Frances Scott Key. I know you are busy, and I do not wish to interrupt, but I must tell you how thoroughly shocked I am by what I have witnessed. I was aboard one of the British ships in the harbor last night, attempting to free American soldiers and sailors. Thank you, sir, for being here for these young men."

"It is my honor, Mr. Key. I am merely doing my duty for these brave men. There is no valor in that. I believed that, even if we lost this battle, the war would not yet be finished. When the men were told that the British meant to tear our flag from the pole, they refused to allow that to happen. There was no way they were going to take it down or to allow it to fall."

"Yes, that is what I was told. What bravery and patriotism has been seen this night! I pray you may still save some of their lives, sir. I shall not keep you any longer. I wanted to give you my regards and show my appreciation for your part in these events. God bless you sir." They shook hands and Key left the fort.

Mack spent a few weeks after the Battle of Fort McHenry at the fort caring for soldiers and assisting the hospital in the transition to a new physician. On the first of December 1814, Mack received his discharge from the War Department. Mack wrote to his family to let them know that he was well and that he would soon be home. He packed up and made his way home for some rest and recuperation. Dr. MacKenzie Murray was now thirty-five years old.

Chapter 20

"Miss Ellie! Miss Ellie! It's a letter from Masser MacKenzie! Ma'am, he's done wrote us. He's alive!!" Mame, who had been at the end of the long driveway in front of the MacGregor property when the mail rider came by, ran with the mail as soon as she saw the letter from Mack. She knew that the family would want to know. In a few minutes, Ellie appeared on the front porch.

"Mame, be careful! I don't want you to fall." Mame made her way to the house and up the stairs to reach Ellie. She was out of breath from running and she slumped down on the steps after handing the letter to Ellie. Ellie ripped into the envelope to pull the letter out. "I pray he was not injured. I…," she stammered as her eyes rushed over the letter looking for key information. "He's fine! Oh, my Lord, he's fine! He's on his way home. Mame! Quickly, we must get with Addie to plan for his arrival. We'll want to cook all his favorites."

A big smile came over Mame's face as she got up. She patted Ellie on the back and said, "Our prayers done worked Miss Ellie!" As they walked back into the house, they were met by Thomas in the foyer. Eating an apple, he looked at Ellie and Mame with a puzzled and disapproving stare.

"What on earth is all this noise I hear. Mary Beth is trying to read in the sitting room. She cannot do that with you two hollering."

Ellie gave it right back to him, "Our boy is on his way home! I think that is worth screaming about, don't you, Thomas?" She threw the letter at him as she jumped into the sitting room to tell Mary Beth about the letter.

"Mary Beth, we just received word from Mack. He's fine, and he's on his way home. I'm so happy. I was so worried about him after reading about that terrible battle at Fort McHenry." She hugged Mary Beth tightly.

"Oh, Momma! I am so happy, too. It feels like he has been gone forever. I miss his terrible jokes and pranks. I miss his books all thrown this way and that in the study. Now, Momma, we have to get ready. I will help June get his room ready. I know how he likes it. I will go tell her right now."

"That is perfect, Mary Beth. Then you can come help us in the kitchen."

"Yes, ma'am." Mary Beth looked towards the sky and spoke softly, "Thank you, Lord. Thank you for answering our prayers. I love him so much." Overhearing her words, Eleanor smiled and then walked back to the kitchen.

After telling Addie the good news, the three women began their preparations for the meals they would have while Mack was home. They make a list of the supplies they needed so that they could send Thomas to town.

"Ma'am, do you have an idea of what his plans are? Do you think he will stay here and be a doctor?" asked Addie.

"I do not know the answer to that, Addie," Eleanor replied rather sadly. She realized that with his experience and well-deserved reputation, he might be asked to return to Baltimore or Philadelphia to work. It would be a good position for a new doctor and the income would be higher than a country doctor. It was not something that had been previously discussed. "I am sure he will let us know when he arrives."

"I am sure he will. He is such a smart young man. Mollie and Masser James would be proud of their boy." Addie smiled and went back to her work in the kitchen.

Ellie thought for a moment about Mollie and James. She missed them both. She wondered to herself about Addie's comment. Would they be proud of Mack's accomplishments? Would Mollie be agreeable to Mack living and working in the world as a white man, rather than black? Then she spoke it out loud, "Addie, we, Thomas and I, have done what we believed was best for Mack in this world that we live in. Do you think we have been wrong in encouraging MacKenzie to live as a white man? We hope for a day soon when we can free you all with no fear of reprisal for you all and for us."

Addie walked back to where Ellie was standing, and she leaned against the table so that she could look into her eyes. "Ma'am, all of us knowd we gots it real good here. We hear dem stories 'bout how slaves gets treated by dey massers when we goes to church. We see da marks on dey bodies, ma'am. You and Misser Thomas been clear wit us 'bout yo beliefs and the da situation wit our people in this land. I believe you when youse tell us dat you wants us free. I knowd Mollie and Masser MacKenzie was freed when Masser James died. Dat gives us hope. You and Masser Thomas treats us real fine and dats why weeze works hard, ma'am. We knowd dat when da farm does good, weeze does too. Don't yo worry no more, Missus Ellie."

"Do Jeremiah, Killian, Mame, all of the others agree with you, Addie?"

"Oh yessum, dey do. Mmm, yessum."

That was the last time Eleanor ever asked about how she and Thomas had raised Mack. Everyone went to work hunting, cleaning, cooking, and preparing for Mack's arrival. They anxiously awaited the sight of his figure walking up the drive towards the house. That day came just four days from the day they received his letter. Upon first sight, they began to scream announcing his arrival and everyone started to run to the front of the house. June, the housekeeper, ran to the barn at the edge of the field to scream at towards those working the field to come. Eleanor was the first to make it to Mack. He dropped his bags, and they threw their arms around each other. "Mackenzie Murray, I have never been so happy to see anyone since your daddy came walking up that drive so many years ago. Welcome home! You look better than I expected."

"Well, I am not sure what you expected, but I am very well. Tired, but very well. I cannot wait to see everyone." By the time his words left his mouth, Mary Beth, Addie, Mame, June, and Thomas had made it to the front porch. The voices of those coming in from the field could be heard in the distance. Mack smiled from ear to ear. He felt truly happy, and he was thrilled to be home. "I almost feel like the prodigal son, except I did not leave for the reasons he left; nor, am I home for those same reasons. But all this…all of you make me feel so loved. Thank you."

In the days that followed, Mack rested, read, and helped on the farm. He and Mary Beth spent time together talking about his experiences in the war. "Mack, you seem much different than how your father was when he came home after the war. Why is that?"

"I saw the same horrors as my father, but I helped injured soldiers survive their injuries. Many of their lives were gravely different, but they were alive and that was important to them as well as to me. My father only saw death on the battlefield and in the prison where he was held. His situation was so grim. I was able to operate on many and help them to survive. I think that made an important imprint in my mind."

"I am so happy to hear that, Mack. What do you think you will do next? Will you stay and work in Jonesborough?"

"I have not said anything to anyone yet, so please keep this to yourself, Mary Beth. I have applied for a position in Nashville with Dr. Felix Robertson. He has opened a medical practice there. It is a larger city than Jonesborough, so there will be more opportunities to learn and grow my profession. I am waiting for correspondence from him now."

Sulking, Mary Beth complained, "Nashville is so far from here, Mack. We will never see you, unless Momma and Poppa travel to visit you there. If they haven't married me off yet. They've been looking for potential husbands," Mary Beth was obviously annoyed by the tone of her voice. Mack was familiar with this attitude having met young ladies in Philadelphia who expressed similar discontentment in not being able to set their own fates and to work if they chose to.

"Mary Beth, they only want you to be secure financially. It is a concern that you should take seriously. I have seen some young ladies, though, who have begun to work as nurses and teachers in the bigger cities. However, their lives are not as extravagant as your life here. If you wish to be a wife and a mother, then do as your parents ask. They will not force you into a marriage with someone you do not approve of. Aunt Eleanor and Uncle Thomas courted for some time before they became engaged. My mother told me when I was little that Aunt Eleanor did not like Uncle Thomas at first. They had known each other their whole lives because their parents were friends and were from Scottish families. But over time, as they became closer, they fell in love. Perhaps the same might happen to you. You and I both are on the oldish side to not already be married, wouldn't you agree?"

"Maybe. I just don't know now. Maybe I'd be alright living on my own and teaching children. It ought to be my choice," Mary Beth argued.

"Perhaps, but we don't always recognize the difference between what is good for us and what is merely temptation which could lead us towards folly, Mary Beth."

"Oh, you are just like them!" Mary Beth stormed off in disgust with her cousin. Mack just chuckled and shook his head.

Weeks passed while Mack enjoyed the hard, physical labor of working in the fields. He, Jeremiah and Killian reacquainted themselves with one another. He helped them with harvesting crops, caring for the livestock, and doing maintenance on the house and cottages. This chore brought him back to the cottage his mother and father lived in when he was a child. He had avoided it because it caused him to feel deep sadness and longing for his parents.

"Doc Mack, you ought not ta avoid dat lil house. Yo momma and poppa was happy dere. Go on in, suh, and see.

It was a happy place." Mack stared at the door trying to gain courage to open the door and go inside.

"Ok, Jeremiah. You know it really ought not to be sitting empty. Someone should be living in this old cottage," said Mack as he slowly opened the door. Mack stood at the door for a few seconds, looking around before he entered. It felt as though he was stepping back in time. He felt the presence of his parents. The cottage had been cleaned and everything had been put back where it belonged. The stove in one corner, a table and chairs in the center, and then two beds on the other…one large enough for two and a smaller, child sized one at the foot of the other. He stood there looking around trying to remember the time he spent there with his parents. It was difficult. Too much time had passed.

"Looks ova dere Doc. Looks on the lil bed. Youse see somepin' youse mights remember," encouraged Jeremiah. Mack looked back over at Jeremiah. He realized how old Jeremiah was now and how much time had passed since he lived in this little cabin. Then he looked back towards the beds, and he walked over. On the bed, his little bed, were marbles and jacks. He did remember them. Picking them up, he sat down on the little bed.

"I do remember these, Jeremiah. My father brought them with him when he came home. We played with them on the floor after dinner while Momma washed the dishes. Then he…stood up again and looked around for something else he remembered. He started looking around and under the beds.

"What youse looking for, Doc Mack?" asked Jeremiah.

"A book…a book my father would read to me as I was going to sleep every night. I don't remember where we kept it."

"Oh, I knows, suh." Jeremiah walked over and opened a cabinet. There he pulled out two small books. One was *The Reluctant Dragon,* and the other was a small book of Bible stories for children.

"Oh, I remember this one! I wanted to be a knight so I could hunt for the dragon. It was such fun. And this one, my mother insisted I read so that I would not grow up to be a heathen." Jeremiah and Mack burst into laughter. "Thank you, Jeremiah. Thank you for encouraging me to come inside. I thought I would only remember my Momma dying here, but I remember the good times also." Mack walked over and hugged Jeremiah. "You've been very good to me, Jeremiah. You, Killian, the others…you all helped me to find my place in this world, even if it is living as a white man. None of you ever judged me. If I am a good man today, it is as much because of all of you as it is my aunt and uncle. I love you all for it."

"Doc, youse our family. Dere ain't never gonna bes any question about yo identity, son. Yo folks was real clear on that 'cuz they wanted you ta have a good life. Weeze was not genst dat. But yo momma and poppa wished you to know all yo kin. Dey never denied dat neither."

"I am thankful to all of you. Well, we better get going before Addie comes looking for the firewood and we haven't split the logs today yet. She'll be furious!"

"Yo right 'bout that!" Jeremiah had a boisterous voice, and when he laughed, the whole valley could her it.

A few days later while sitting on the front porch reading a book, Mary Beth spied the mail rider coming up the drive. "Mack, Mack!," she said patting him on the arm, "The mail is comin'." Hearing her screams, Mack jumped up from his chair. "Do you think this is your letter from Nashville, Mack?"

"Could be. There has been plenty of time for Dr. Robinson to write. I guess we will discover that in just a few moments." As the rider neared, Mack walked down the steps to the drive. The rider stopped in front of Mack.

"I have a letter here for Dr. Alexander MacKenzie Murray. Is he here?"

"That is I, sir."

"Here is your letter, sir. Have a good day." The rider rode off down the drive.

"Hurry! Open it, Mack!" shrilled Mary Beth like a teen-age girl.

Mack opened the envelope, took a deep breath, and then pulled the letter out. He glanced over at Mary Beth who was so anxious she looked like she'd grab it and read it herself. "Calm down, Mary Beth." He unfolded the letter and began to read to himself. "He has extended an offer, Mary Beth! I am accepted! Woohoo!" He picked her up and swung her around in joy. He rushed inside the house to tell his aunt and uncle. Mary Beth followed in a depressed and sullen manner. She did not want her cousin to leave the farm.

Finding Thomas and Eleanor in the parlor, Mary Beth plopped herself down on the sofa. "Mary Beth, it is unbecoming of a lady to plop herself down in such a way," scolded Ellie.

"Just wait, Momma. You'll understand why in a moment," she chided.

Thomas looking at Mack inquired, "Mack, what's made you so excited, my boy?"

"Uncle Thomas, Aunt Eleanor, I have been waiting for this letter. I applied for a position in Nashville with Dr. Felix Robertson. He was in one of the medical school classes after me. Dr. Rush wrote to me while I was in Baltimore and encouraged me to consider Dr. Robertson's practice in Nashville after the war. Dr. Rush believed we would work well together."

Thomas and Eleanor jumped to their feet. "Mackenzie, that is a wonderful opportunity. Congratulations, my boy!" Shouted Thomas. "This is what we have all been working for. We will miss you, of course, but we can visit once you are settled." Thomas put his hand out to shake his nephew's hand.

"Mack, darling, I am so thrilled for you. Disregard this one's 'Negative Nelly' response. She is only dreading your departure; but I assure you she will be just fine. You have worked hard for this recognition of your expert skills and genuine care for your patients. I'm very proud." Eleanor hugged him tightly. "Now, does he say when you are expected to report to his office? We must prepare."

Looking back at the letter, Mack read it over again for that information. "He says that he would like to have me there in two weeks if possible. He also says that there is a small apartment attached to his office where I may live. It is furnished so I will not need furniture. That is a kind gesture on his part. He will deduct the cost of the rent from my weekly salary." Mack continued to read silently portions of the letter that spoke of medical issues which would only bore this group.

"That is perfect. That gives us time to gather what you need and purchase a horse and buggy for you for your travel. It will be more convenient for you to have your own rather than paying for a coach. We will go into Jonesborough to the livery and find something appropriate tomorrow."

"May I go with you, father? I would like to buy a book at the General Store," asked Mary Beth.

"I think we'll make a day of it, and we will all go into town," responded Eleanor.

On the day they went to town, they all dressed up as if they were going to church or to a special dinner at a friend's home. As they drove into Jonesborough, their eyes met those of their neighbors, many of whom they only saw once or twice a year. Of course, they knew there were rumors about them that circulated. Some called them "strange" or "those abolitionist deviants" by those who supported the practice of slavery. Still others hypothesized that they were part of some fringe religious sect because they had never seen the children in public. They saw the townspeople whispering as they tied their rig to a tree at the livery. None of the family cared about the whispers. They had long since dealt with the childish and, often hateful, disposition of some of their neighbors.

While Eleanor and Mary Beth went into the store, Thomas and Mack remained at the livery stables to choose a horse and buggy. Mack immediately saw a horse he was interested in. As he walked over to it, the livery owner hollered, "Not that one, he's out of sorts, that one. You'd best choose another."

Mack disregarded the liveryman's words and approached the stunning white stallion. As he approached, he looked directly into the eyes of the horse and whispered, "Hello, boy. I'm Mack. You are an odd boy, huh? Well, so am I." The horse raised its head and began to neigh as Mack reached out to rub his nose.

"Oh, that's not a good idea, sir. He don't care for folks much. I am considering selling him off for meat."

"Oh no, fella. You just haven't met someone you know you can depend on, have you? But you can trust me, boy," whispered Mack still stroking the horse's nose. He pulled a carrot from his pocket and fed it to the horse. The liveryman was shocked that the horse had not bucked. "See, you and I are going to be great friends. What's his name, sir?"

"I ain't gave him a name. Didn't want to since I was gonna get rid of him," barked the man.

"How much then, if you were going to get rid of him anyway? I'll give you $50 for the horse and buggy, reigns, and rig."

"Well, I guess that is fair. I hope you know what you are doing. I ain't gonna take him back."

"I don't expect you would, but it will not be necessary," added Mack still looking into the horse's eyes. "Well, now, you need a good name, don't you, boy? Let's see. How about George, after our first president? It is a quite regal name, I think." Just then the horse neighed loudly and shook his head in agreement. Everyone chuckled.

"All right, Mack, let's go meet the ladies at the store and get you another suit You'll need that and another pair of boots."

"Yes, thank you, sir. We'll be back in a little while to take this all home. Good day, sir," Mack said shaking the livery's hand.

"Thank you, Dr. Murray. Safe travels to you."

Thomas and Mack walked to the General Store to meet Eleanor and Mary Beth. When they entered the store, the other customers stopped what they were doing and stared at them. A couple lowered their head and whispered to each other, "That's him. That's the one who took care of the soldiers at Fort McHenry." Just then, everyone in the store began to clap. It took the family completely by surprise. They expected those customers to be gossiping about them, their abolitionist politics, or odd lifestyle.

"Please, please, thank you, but I was merely doing my job," announced Mack. One of the older women walked over to Mack and took his hand.

"Dr. Murray, you took care of my boy. He was in the fort working as a cook. He was injured by a piece of flying glass that struck him in the shoulder. Had you not removed the glass as quickly as you did, he would have probably lost the use of that arm, but today his arm works just fine. Thank you, sir."

Mack was taken aback by her words. "Yes, I remember your son. His name is Jack, I believe. [She nodded her head in affirmation.] The glass was quite large, and his bleeding was substantial, but we were able to remove it and stop the bleeding. I am glad to hear that he recovered well, ma'am. Please give him my best."

From that moment on, Mack was treated as a celebrity when he visited Jonesborough, something that did not happen often, but when he was there, the townspeople showered him with care and respect. He never worried again about whether the issue of his race was a topic of conversation amongst them.

Eleanor and Mary Beth chose a nice suit for Mack. Thomas aided him in choosing boots and a winter coat, which was not long away. "This winter may be harsh according to the almanac. You'll need to be prepared."

"Uncle, I am not working on a farm. I will be indoors for much of my day."

"Well, maybe, Mack, but you may be called to go out in the early morning to deliver a baby or care for a sick child. It could be extremely cold. Let's find a thick blanket as well. I don't want to assume that Dr. Robertson will provide you with everything. I think you should purchase a saddle and additional tac for George."

"I suppose you are right."

Eleanor also picked up flour, sugar, cinnamon, and some cloth to sew Mary Beth a new dress. Once everything had been added up, Thomas paid the bill, and the family went over to the hotel to eat in the restaurant.

"I don't suppose this is as nice as the restaurants in Philadelphia or Baltimore, are they Mack?" Inquired Mary Beth.

"Sure, this one is smaller, but it's the food that matters, Mary Beth," corrected Mack.

Mack and Thomas ordered roast with potatoes and carrots, while Eleanor and Mary Beth ordered roasted chicken with black-eyed peas. They all ate apple pie for dessert.

"Mary Beth, I would say this food is as good as any I had in the city, especially the pie! I guess I will have to learn to cook for myself until I find a wife."

"Well, my, my, MacKenzie, I did not know you were considering marriage," commented Thomas.

"I am not getting any younger, Uncle. I hope to work a year and have a good savings accumulated before taking on a wife, but I don't suppose it would hurt just to be looking now," he said with a big, sheepish grin across his face. Thomas patted him on the back, and they all had a good laugh as they left the store. Mack went back to the livery to pick up his horse and buggy. He was silently thrilled to be driving his own carriage as he followed his family home.

Over the next three days, the family worked on packing Mack's belongings, packing food for his travel, and reviewing the map for his course to Nashville. "This route should get you to Nashville safely. I've put two rifles and ammunition in the buggy in case you should encounter Indians or thieves along the way."

"Yes, sir. I understand the way I should go. I pray it will be an uneventful journey."

"If you don't feel comfortable, Mack, I can send one of the men with you to see you there safely."

"Oh no, Uncle Thomas. That doesn't make sense, then they'd just have to come back alone. You need everyone here working, and besides that, I am an adult."

"That's fine, Mack."

The next morning everyone awoke at daybreak. Addie and Mame made a huge breakfast so that everyone could share the meal and have an opportunity to say their goodbyes to Mack. When the meal was finished and everyone had the opportunity to say goodbye, Mack checked George's bindings, checked the rig to make certain everything was connected properly, and then he mounted the carriage. He looked back over his right shoulder at his family standing from one end of the porch to the other and he smiled and waved. Then, he jerked the reigns and gave George the command to go. The family stood and watched until he was out of sight before returning to their work.

Chapter 21

Mack's journey took him over some of the Smokey Mountains through wilderness which was desolate in places. He happened to come upon some Chickamauga Cherokee on his way to Nashville. He was somewhat apprehensive upon seeing them and their homes. He was aware of their presence in the bushes and trees along the way. He knew they were watching him. Perhaps they waited to determine if he meant them harm before making any moves in his direction. Mack drove on and made no direct eye contact with them until he needed to water George and take a break to sleep before continuing.

He found a place to stop not far from the Chickamauga Cherokee encampment. There was a stream where he watered George. It wasn't long before he sensed that he was being watched again. He spoke, "I am not here to hurt anyone. I am a doctor on my way to Nashville. I just need to eat and sleep a bit." After his announcement, he waited to see if anyone would come forward or if he would be left alone. Soon a face appeared out of the bushes, then another, and then another. In minutes there were no fewer than ten standing in front of him. He looked at the one who appeared to be the eldest. "Sir, I wish you no harm."

The elder stepped forward. His hair was dark with thin stripes of gray hair running through his braid. He wore an elaborate beaded belt around pants made of deer skin. He responded in a deep voice in almost perfect English, "We too are not here to harm you. We have a treaty with your people. I am Running Bear and these are my people. We are a part of the Cherokee people. You are welcome to join us for our evening meal."

Astonished, Mack accepted the invitation to join the group. After George was sufficiently hydrated, Mack untied him and rode with the others back to their camp. They sat together before a great fire and ate deer, corn, and other vegetables. They told him stories of their people. They danced before the fire and invited him to join in. Reluctant at first, he eventually gave in and began to dance. He was also introduced to their medicine man. He shared herbs and other natural sources of treatment. It was a thrilling evening that Mack would never forget.

The next morning as he mounted his buggy; his new friends rode alongside to keep him safe until he was out of their land. Mack was excited to report this experience to Mary Beth. He knew she would find it exciting. The more he rode, the more confident he felt. He soon found himself singing songs he was taught as a child. This helped pass the time. In no time, it seemed, he was rounding a corner just outside of Nashville. As he pulled into the town, he stopped to pull out Dr. Robertson's letter. His office was just inside the town, next to the bank. Mack rode slowly looking for the bank and, thus, for Dr. Robertson's office.

As soon as he saw the office, Mack looked for a post to hitch George to. He then made his way to Dr. Robertson's office. Coming to the door, he saw the placard with Dr. Felix Robertson's name and his hours of service. Below this was a handwritten note which said, "Temporarily Closed. Gone to deliver baby at the Wilkes' farm. Back as soon as possible. If Dr. Murray should appear, please find note under mat." Mack picked up the mat and found an envelope. Opening the note, he read, "I am sorry not to be in attendance upon your arrival, Dr. Murray. Please take this key and go around to the back and unload your belongings. I have left further information and food for you inside. I hope to be back soon. Signed Dr. F. Robertson, MD."

Mack took his rig around to the back of the building where there was an alleyway. He opened the door to the small apartment. He looked around at his accommodations. There was a nice, large fireplace with a chair and small table set close by. There was a table and four chairs next to a stove. Along the wall was a cupboard which held plates, drinking glasses, and cooking utensils. It had 6 large drawers. Next to the cupboard was a bookcase. There was a loft overhead which contained a bed, dresser, and a table with a wash basin. Mack felt content in his surroundings. Just then he heard a noise. Thinking might be the doctor returned from the childbirth, he turned to find George standing in the middle of the apartment. "George! What on earth are you doing, boy? Let's see. We need to find you some water and oats. Let me read Dr. Robertson's notes here." On the table beside the fireplace, he found another note from the doctor. It read:

"Dr. Murray, I hope that you find your accommodations to be agreeable. My wife gathered what she thought you would need. If there are other items you require, we will discuss those upon my return. You will find on the opposite side of the street the local livery. I have spoken to Mr. Guthrie regarding the care of your horse and the storage of your carriage. You may take them there and he will take care of those needs. We will discuss payment for those services later. My wife has left you biscuits, honey, butter, beans and some bacon for your supper. If I do not make it back before dusk, I will see you tomorrow morning. There is a door connecting the apartment with the office in front just behind the curtain hung on the left side of the kitchen area. There is a key for that door in your chest of drawers in the loft. I do not recommend keeping the key to the apartment and the key to the office together. We are glad to have you. Dr. Felix Robertson.

Mack did as Dr. Robertson suggested and drove George over to the livery. There he met Mr. Matthew Guthrie, the owner of the livery. As he had been instructed, Mr. Guthrie took control of George and fed and watered him. He placed the carriage in a covered area next to a corral. Mack hung around for a little while making certain that George was well. After George finished eating, Mr. Guthrie placed the horse in a stall for the night.

"Feel free to come over and see your horse. As you can see, I have others that I tend to here. Dr. Robertson instructed me to wait for his return before we discussed the cost of my services. I suppose that meets with your approval as well, sir?"

"Please, just call me Mack. I hope we will become friends. Yes, I concur with Dr. Robertson. I simply do not wish for you to feel overwhelmed by George's presence. If he becomes a burden, please let me know. The livery where I purchased George did not get on with him very well. I hope he will be no bother to you."

"Not at all. We all get along well here. I love horses and I enjoy having them around. Is there anything else I may help you with?"

"I don't suppose so yet. I guess I will go wait for Dr. Robertson's return."

"I don't know if you should expect him tonight. He's over at the Wilkes' farm. This is Mrs. Wilkes' nineth baby and every baby she's had has taken her at least 8 to 9 hours to deliver. I don't think he will make it back here tonight."

"Oh [he chuckled], I don't expect he will. Thank you, Mr. Guthrie. I hope we will get to know each other better soon."

"I do as well, and please, call me Matthew."

"Good evening, Matthew."

Matthew was correct about Mrs. Wilkes. This baby took 10 hours to arrive. Mack returned to his little cottage. He warmed up the biscuits and beans, and then cooked the bacon left for him by Mrs. Robertson. As he sat at his little table, he wondered what was going on at home. He wondered what Dr. Robertson would look like. He knew that Felix was a bit younger than he, but he was a similar student, having scored one point lower than him on the final exam.

After finishing his meal, he unpacked his belongings. After filling the wash basin with water from the pump outside, he came back inside and heated the water over the fire so that it would not be so cold. He returned to the chair next to the fireplace and read for a little while before it became too dark, and he became too sleepy to read anymore. He climbed back up the stairs to the loft and plopped himself into his bed. He was thrilled that it felt much like his bed at home. He reminded himself that he had to write a letter to Mary Beth as soon as possible to fill her in on his adventure to his new home. It did not take long for sleep to overcome him.

Chapter 22

Sunshine rushed through the windows of the apartment to awaken its new inhabitant. As if hit by a bolt of lightning, Mack jumped from his bed and rushed to shave, clean up, and dress before Dr. Robertson appeared at his door. He practically jumped down the stairs and rushed over to grab a quick biscuit with a piece of bacon from the night before. He grabbed the key to the office and made his way inside.

Once inside the office, he was impressed by its orderliness. Everything was exactly where he would want it to be. There were two examination rooms and a small reception area with chairs just inside the front door. Within a few minutes the front door opened and there appeared and adorable gray haired little lady. Removing her shawl and placing a lunch bucket down on the reception table, she spoke, "Oh, you must be the new doctor. Dr. Murray, I believe. I am Greta Abernathy, Dr. Robertson's and I guess your secretary. I meet the patients as they enter, find out what their issues are, and keep records. I hope you had a nice trip here. I think Dr. Robertson said you were from East Tennessee, in the mountains."

"That is correct, ma'am. I lived there my entire life until I went to medical school in Philadelphia. Then I was an Army surgeon at Fort McHenry."

"Oh goodness, that was a terrible situation. Dr. Robertson told me all about it."

"It was, ma'am, but there were much worse situations in other areas of the war."

"I suppose your family will miss you being so far away. How long did it take for you to arrive here?"

"They will miss me and I them, but we will write to each other. It took me four and a half days.

"Was it very treacherous? Did you see Indians?"

"There were some areas coming down off the mountain which were difficult to navigate with my carriage, but we made it without incident. I did see Indians. They were kind to me and invited me to eat with them. They rode with me past their settlement to keep me safe. It was quite wonderful, actually."

"Oh my, I would never have guessed. One usually hears terrible stories about them killing people for no good reason. I would have been terribly frightened."

"I do not know that I could say there was never a reason for them to protect themselves and their children. I suppose that they haven't always wanted to give up their land to us settlers. That might make me quite cross if I were them."

"I guess I could see that. Oh, here comes the doctor."

Dr. Robertson opened the door to find both Mack and Greta by the door. "Good morning to both of you. Dr. Murray, it is my pleasure to make your acquaintance. I apologize again for not being here when you arrived yesterday. I pray you found everything to your liking in the back?"

"I did, sir. It is perfect," announced Mack.

"We can disband the formality when we have no patients in the lobby. After all, if I recall, you are older than I. You may call me Felix, and you have already met Miss Abner…I mean Greta. Why don't you come with me to my little office over here so we can talk. Greta, do we have any appointments this morning?"

"I have only one appointment with Mr. Singer at ten o'clock, Felix." Greta beamed a huge smile at Mack, who returned her grin as if they had just shared a great secret.

"That's fine. If you will make sure that we have what we need in both exam rooms, please."

"Certainly."

Mack and Dr. Robertson walked to his office. "Please have a seat."

Dr. Robertson took off his dress coat and replaced it with an off-white jacket. "I have one of these for you in the second exam room, which most often will be your exam room." He then sat at his desk and looked over some papers on his desk. "I want to express to you how impressed I was regarding your qualifications. Of course, I heard about you from students and Dr. Rush. He was very impressed by you. I have to say, I felt a bit of envy. I studied so much for that final exam. I wanted to beat your score, but I did not. I am sure that, in your own experience, you saw doctors who barely got through their course work and then had no actual experience when coming to a practice. Dr. Barton was also an advocate for you. Moreover, I received a letter from your first line supervisor at Fort McHenry regarding the excellent care you provided while there. He spoke highly of your surgical skills, which will be of great benefit here. I understand that you were there on the evening of the British bombardment. It must have been truly staggering to witness that event."

"It was, but I was so focused on caring for my fellow soldiers and sailors that I didn't realize the extent of the damage until much later. We were able to save many using some of the newest techniques and equipment in medicine. I am sure there is plenty for me to learn from you. I have never delivered a baby…well, at least not a human one. I have delivered many a calf and lamb, though."

"Some of these young physicians come into an office like this one, see an almost middle-aged man sitting behind the desk and assume my ways are too archaic. They behave as if I need to learn from them."

"Well, I was not raised to disrespect anyone, and I was taught that learning never ends; we should learn something new every day."

"I think we are going to work well together. Now, a few minor details. We begin the day at 8:30 a.m. and, if possible, my wife Lydia would like me to be home in time for dinner with the family at 6:00 p.m. Because you are living in the cottage behind the office, there may be times when someone comes by after hours for treatment or in an emergency. I would like you to take those in most cases. If there is a circumstance in which you do not feel comfortable and wish that I accompany you, then you can come to my home and pick me up. My wife would like you to join us for dinner this evening. This way you will be familiar with the location of our home when needed in the future. Do you have any questions or is there anything other subject we need to address?"

"I think we need to discuss the issue of my horse and carriage. You indicated in your note that we would discuss that with Mr. Guthrie. I obviously will not be making a lot yet in terms of wages, though I do have some savings. I simply want to make certain that I can afford his services. If not, I would simply like to know of any other accommodation options which might exist."

"Oh yes, of course. For the time being, I will cover the cost for Mr. Guthrie. I don't want you to spend your savings. You will need those funds one day when you decide to finally get married. Once we are certain that you are happy and wish to stay on, then we will discuss that again."

"So, allow me to clarify…the cost for Mr. Guthrie will be deducted, like the rent on the apartment, from my weekly salary?"

"Not yet. We will renegotiate that in sixty days, if that is agreeable with you."

"Certainly. Are there any other chores, so-to-speak, regarding the operation of the office that I should be aware of. For instance, how medications and other supplies are handled. Oh, and do we work on weekends, except for emergencies?"

"As far as ordering our supplies and medications, Greta keeps up with those. There is a locked cabinet in each examination room which contains medications and supplies. When I first started, I did not lock up these items, but I soon discovered that they grew legs and would walk away to parts unknown. Thus, I began locking them up. As for weekends, I do like to keep those for family time, unless there's an emergency."

"For our first patient today, we have Mr. Marvin Singer. He is a 40-year-old man who suffered a head injury in his youth. Since that time, he has had frequent, sometimes debilitating headaches. I have given him a low dose of morphine to use when the pain is unbearable. This is a follow-up to find out how he has been doing." The pair walked into the examination room.

"Hello, Mr. Singer. This is my new associate, Dr. Mack Murray. He is going to be sitting in with me today, if that meets with your approval. Dr. Murray is a well-trained doctor who hails from East Tennessee."

"That's fine, Doc. Nice to meet you, sir."

Dr. Robinson inquired, "How have you been doing with your headaches?"

"Well, Doc, I ain't had too many lately. I only had to take the medicine a couple of times."

"Dr. Murray, do you have any questions for Mr. Singer?"

"Yes, sir. Mr. Singer, do you find any similarities in your headaches, such as when they typically begin, how they progress over time, or where in your head the headaches generally happen?"

"Well, now, let me think a minute. Lately, I been wakin' up with 'em. Sometimes they wake me up. Mostly, they ache behind my eyes. Sometimes my neck hurts too."

"When your head aches behind your eyes, is your vision affected?"

"I don't believe so, but I ain't been paying attention to that. I will, though, now that you have asked me that. Is that important?"

"We are learning more about the eye in medical studies. It might be that your eyes are the problem. We may need to examine your eyes before and during a headache to determine if your vision is affected. If so, glasses may help."

"I thought they were caused by my head injury when I was a kid. Are you saying they ain't?"

"As I am sure you are aware, sir, medicine is a rapidly developing science. Your headaches could very well be caused by that injury, but they also could be caused by your eyes, or even both. We just don't know enough about the brain yet. What we don't want is to treat you one way with a drug that has serious side effects when the cause is something different. I think it would be beneficial to do some examinations of your eyes. Sometimes medicine can be as much about ruling things out as it is about discovery. Are you willing to do these exams?"

"Yes, sir. If we can find out what causes them, then maybe we can do something to get rid of them."

"Exactly, Mr. Singer. It is more beneficial for you not to have to take morphine. It is a strong drug. Many medical schools and hospitals are testing new medications for pain that are not as strong but work as well. We will need you to either come in when you have a headache, or for your family to notify us at the time, so that we can come to your home to do the tests. Then we will also need to do repeat the tests when you do not have a headache."

"Yes, sir. I can ask my boy to bring me up here."

"That's fine. Do you still have some morphine?"

"I do."

"I'd also like for you to keep a journal of your headaches. I want you to make note of how bad the pain is, where the headache is located, whether your vision is affected, and any other relevant information about the headache," instructed Dr. Murray.

Mr. Singer responded, "My gal Millie can write all of that down for me, Doc."

"Ok, then, Miss Abernathy will schedule a time for you to come back when you do not have a headache. I will need to get those testing instruments ready. We do not yet have them."

"Ok, Dr. Murray. It has been a pleasure to meet you. Doc Robinson, I think you got a good one here."

Patting Mr. Singer on the back, Dr. Robertson replied, "Thank you; I agree with you. Don't forget to come in or send your boy to get Dr. Murray when you have your next headache. Otherwise, we will see you at your next appointment."

"Yes, sir. Thank you both." Marvin put his hat back on and the three men walked back into the reception area and instructed Greta to schedule an appointment. After he left, Dr. Robinson expressed his pleasure to Mack at how he handled the appointment with Mr. Singer.

"Mack, I was impressed with your attention and explanation of the situation to Mr. Singer. I had not considered that his vision might be the issue as much as the head injury could be. It is well worth the examination. How will these be carried out?"

"I will create a chart that has letters and numbers in various sizes. We will ask him to read the letters he can see with each eye covered and then together. I suspect that his vision may be impaired during a headache, but he has never paid attention to it. The key is having him repeat the steps during an episode and again when he has no headache. He may be straining to see which can cause stress in the muscles and nerves of the head and neck. This stress over time can cause headaches. If his vision proves not to be an issue, then I believe we can more accurately believe that the headaches are from the injury, in lieu of any other causes which have not yet been discovered in the medical research. I think it is a process of elimination. There are doctors in Europe who are doing more post-mortem research of the brain to discover the effects of brain injuries and how the brain works. If his vision is indeed the problem, then glasses may resolve his problem."

"That is remarkable. I look forward to assisting you on this case."

"Thank you, sir. What do we do next?"

"You will need to write detailed notes in the file about his appointment today. Make note of your recommendations are and how those recommendations will be carried out, and what you instructed him to do."

"Ok, sir."

"There was something else that we did not go into the other day when I showed you around the office. Please come with me." The pair walked down the small hallway and Dr. Robertson opened a door. As they entered the room, Mack saw an office with bookcases, a small desk and chair, as well as a chair in front of the desk. "This, Mack, is your office. I hope you will be here for a long time. I think you are a great benefit to the City of Nashville. I can tell you that I am excited that I got you and not another practice somewhere."

"Thank you, Felix. I have never had my own office. I had a table and chair at Dr. Rush's office. This is special and I am appreciative." As they spoke, they heard the door open and shut. They heard Miss Abernathy speaking and her voice getting louder. The two doctors rushed in to see what the problem was. They saw a man holding a child who appeared to be unconscious.

"Quickly, bring the child in here," Dr. Robertson urged. The father followed him into the examination room and placed the boy on the examination table. Dr. Murray asked Greta to bring water and cloths to the room.

"How long as he been like this Mr. Johnson?" "He complained of not feeling good yesterday. He looked punny and he wanted to stay in his bed and sleep. This morn-ing when my wife went in to get him up, she found him like this. I ain't been able to get him to wake up. When I picked him up, I saw something on his belly." Upon hearing this, Dr. Murray lifted the boy's shirt to discover he was covered in blisters.

"Dr. Robertson, may I speak to you a minute?"

"Certainly." The two stepped away from the table.

"Looks like smallpox, sir. We're going to need to keep him here and quarantine everyone he has been in contact with over the past week. I have already had it, albeit a mild case, but I will be able to stay with him. You and Miss Abernathy will need to be quarantined as well if you have not had smallpox."

"I agree. I will send word to the family by Mr. Guthrie. Excuse me for a moment." As Dr. Robertson left the room, Miss Abernathy arrived with the water and cloths. "Thank you, Miss Abernathy. Mr. Johnson, I apologize that I did not introduce myself to you. I am Dr. MacKenzie Murray. You are welcome to call me Dr. Mack. I am well acquainted with your son's illness. Because you came to us quickly, I think we will be able to help your son. What is his name, sir?"

"Jonathan, sir."

"How old is he?"

"He's ten. Just had his birthday last week. We had a party for him."

"Oh, you did. How many people were at the party? He may have contracted it from someone at the party. It is critical that we find out if anyone else has been sick. Smallpox is extremely contagious. Everyone who has been exposed must be quarantined until we see if you or anyone else gets sick. We will need to know the names of everyone at your son's birthday party. If you could go out to Miss Abernathy's desk and give her those names, please. We will need to find someone to inform those folks that they must be quarantined for the next seven to ten days."

"Oh no! I will go now."

Dr. Robertson went to his front window to see if he could see Mr. Guthrie across the street. Opening his window, Dr. Robertson yelled at Mr. Guthrie. "Matthew! Matthew! Come! Hurry!" Hearing Doc Robertson's screams, Mr. Guthrie came running. Once he was close enough to hear, Doc Robertson yelled again, "Stop! Stop there! Do not come any closer!" "What in world, Doc? Are you alright?" "Matthew, we have a child in here with smallpox. I need you to ride out to the Johnson farm and inform Mrs. Johnson that she must quarantine everyone in her family in her home for the next seven days. That means that no one can come in and no one can leave the home for a minimum of seven days. Do you understand? Do not go into the home or you will be exposed. Tell her that while they are quarantined, she needs to wash and clean everything in her home. She may need you to help with bringing water to the door."

"That's fine, Doc. I will take care of it. By the way, I had the pox when I was in the militia during the war. I can help the Johnsons and anyone else who may need it." "Oh, I did not know. You cannot get the pox again. This will be of great help to us because we must also quarantine everyone who was at the boy's birthday party. Come on in and we will give you that list so that you can inform them as well. I will be happy to compensate you for any work you miss." "Oh, Doc, you don't need to worry about that. I work for myself, and I will make up the work." Matthew came to the door and retrieved the list of party goers. Then he mounted his horse and rode out to tell everyone about the pox. After informing the Johnsons, he then informed the party go-ers. After that, he rode back into town and walked to all the businesses and other families about staying away from the Johnsons and those who were quarantined. He also made a list of those who had already had the pox in case they were needed to help the doctors. When he finished, Matthew returned to the medical office to update the doctors. Doctor Robinson and Miss Abernathy had begun to clean the office when Matthew arrived. "Matthew, thank you for your assistance. You will need to clean everything you have come in contact with since coming here. The virus could at-tach to your clothing and be deposited on to your equipment. Then anyone coming into contact could contract the virus. You will need to ask everyone in town to clean and pray. Also, if you could find a few ladies who have had the virus to help us with feeding everyone? We certainly do not want folks to survive the virus only to die of starvation."

"I understand, sir. How is the boy?"

"We think we have caught it early enough to help. Nonetheless, he needs prayers too."

"Will do, Doc. Do you need anything else?"

"We are going to have to sleep here. If you could round up some mattresses or blankets for us to sleep on, pillows. Ask my wife to send us some food by Albert. He has had the pox. Also, we need some more soap and ice."

"Ok, Doc, I am off to get all of this done for you. I will be back as quickly as I can."

"Thank you, Matthew." Then, Doctor Robinson returned to the examination room to check on Jonathan and Dr. Murray. "How are we doing?"

"He still has a significant fever and more pustules have appeared," remarked Mack.

"Matthew is bringing us ice. I think an ice bath might help bring that fever down. He is also getting us help in obtaining more soap, food, blankets, and pillows. I will have Miss Abernathy make a sign for the door stating we are closed until the threat of smallpox has passed. He is also contacting others in town to clean and to help with what we all need to survive this outbreak."

"Very good. Do you want me to stay with young Johnson or assist Miss Abernathy with cleaning?

"You stay here. I will handle the office cleaning with Miss Abernathy," said Dr. Robinson.

Once Matthew returned with the ice, Greta and Dr. Robertson worked on chopping the ice into pieces and filling up the tub from Mack's apartment so that Jonathan could be placed into the ice bath. When they finished, Mr. Johnson picked his son up and placed him in the tub. The shock of the cold caused a loud moan from Jonathan, though he still did not awaken. The moan scared his father.

"Are you sure that this will help? I cannot stand to hear him moan like that."

"I understand, sir, but this is what is best to bring down his fever. If we can rid him of the fever, he may awaken. If you'd excuse me a moment, I need to speak with Doctor Robertson."

"Yes, sir. I am not going anywhere." Mr. Johnson sat beside his young son and held his hand.

Mack walked to the reception area. Doctor Robertson and Greta had returned to cleaning the offices. "Doctor Robertson, may I speak to you a moment?"

"Certainly. How may I help?"

"I am certain that you are familiar with the practice of variolation with regard to smallpox?"

"I have read about it, but I have not ever done it. What do you think of its efficacy?"

"I have read the research done by Drs. Mather and Boylston in Boston. The practice was quite effective in the outbreak of 1721. I believe that, in this case, variolation would reduce the potential for a citywide outbreak which could, if not done, lead to excessive deaths."

"If you believe that is the best way to proceed, then we shall proceed. After we finish cleaning, I will have Miss Abernathy gather the needed instruments. I hope we have enough."

"Perfect. I will proceed to collect what we need from Jonathan. Once we are ready to begin the process, I will have Mr. Johnson stay with his son and monitor his progress. His fever does seem to be coming down. I hope he will be conscious soon. Once he awakens, we will know more about the status of his infection."

"Fine. Let's get to work." Mack went to the supply room to gather lancets to prick the pustules on Jonathan for transmission to those who had not had the disease. When he returned to the examination room, Mr. Johnson was leaning over the side of the tub sobbing. Jonathan was still unconscious but felt cooler.

"Is my boy going to die, Doc? I do not think I can bear that. We just lost our girl Polly a couple of years ago to influenza." "Mr. Johnson, I am very sorry to hear about that. I know how that feels. I lost both of my parents when I was young. I will do everything I can to help Jonathan. I suspect he's a fighter like his father. Don't count him out yet, sir. I have seen others come out of their comas and survive the pox." Mr. Johnson sat up and wiped his face. Mack's words seemed to have picked up his spirits. "Talk to him, sir. We do not know if a person in this state can hear or not; but if they can, I am sure he would want to hear your voice and it would be of great comfort."

"I will. Oh, I will."
Mack kneeled beside the tub to begin the process of in-oculation. Mr. Johnson became concerned when he saw all the lancets.

"What are those? Will that hurt my son? I do not wish to hurt him, Doc."

"No, sir. All I am going to do is scratch the surface of the pustules to get a little of the pus. Then we will take them and place a little of the pus under the skin of those who have never had the virus. This process helps the body's immune system to react and create immunity to the virus. I need to do this to you."

"I ain't never heard of nothing like that. I guess I'd better do it. I sure don't want to get this."

"No, you don't; your family needs you. If you are ready, I can go head." Mr. Johnson nodded his head in agreement. Mack took the lancet, and he scratched the top of the pustule until the skin broke and pus emerged. He used the lancet to pick up a sizable amount of the pus to put under the skin of Jonathan's father. Turning towards Mr. Johnson, Mack saw him turn about three shades of green and he began to gag. "Take a deep breath if you can, sir, and relax. Why don't you close your eyes, and it will be over in a minute?" "Ok, sir. I'm ready." Mr. Johnson squeezed his eyes tightly shut and gritted his teeth. Mack took the lancet and quickly punctured the skin on Mr. Johnson's arm. He then pushed the lancet under the skin making sure to get the pus under the skin.

"All done," exclaimed Mack.

"Really? It's over? You were right. It was not bad at all. What happens now?"

"We believe that this process causes your immune system to kick in and fight what we hope would only be a minor case of smallpox; you may not get anything at all. Once the symptoms resolve, you will be immune to smallpox forever."

"Really? That is amazing. Will you be going out to my house to do this for my wife and other children and my farm hands?"

"We will do as many as we can. Since your wife and everyone on your farm, all the folks that attended the party were exposed, they could also have minor cases which would also create natural immunity in their bodies without having to go through this process. If they do not show mild symptoms, then we certainly can do this process with them. I just need to collect enough from Jonathan to help as many as we can."

"Ok, I understand." Just then they heard the door to the office open and shut.

"Excuse me," Mack yelled. Not hearing a response, Mack walked out to the lobby to see who had come into the office. Matthew had returned.

Taking off his hat, he began to speak as Doctor Robertson re-entered the room. "Doctors, I did everything as you asked. Unfortunately, we have three more children who have come down with the pox. They have fever and the pustules are just appearing. I thought you would want to know."

"Yes, we need to know who those children are. We will need to get to them quickly and inoculate their families or should we bring them here so we can collect more specimens. What do you think?" Mack asked for guidance respecting the fact that Doctor Robertson's position as the senior physician.

"Time is of the essence but if we could create a makeshift hospital, maybe we could care for more of the sick. Matthew, would it be possible to bring the sick here? We need to work quickly before more breakout. Then, we need to get the word out that anyone who has not had smallpox, if they so desire and are able, they can come to the office, standing outside of course, and they will receive treatment. Before we move forward, I would like to ask everyone [Mr. Johnson, Miss Abernathy, Matthew, and Doctor Murray] to bow your heads and let us pray." Doctor Robertson began to pray: "Dear Lord, we thank you for the blessings you have bestowed on all of us here and in the City of Nashville. We have been blessed with successful businesses, beautiful families, and true friendships. We wish to lift up our city to you, oh Lord, as we find ourselves struggling right now with this serious illness. We ask for your healing hands to be upon everyone who has been affected by the virus, and we ask for the wisdom and courage to treat our families and friends. We give you Lord the glory for our abilities which come from you. We ask this in the name of your son Jesus Christ our Lord and Savior. Amen."

Both doctors proceeded to visit those families who had attended the party, and to inoculate those in town who had not been exposed and had not had the virus. It took the rest of the day and into the night and early morning of the next day to finish. The men were exhausted when they finally made it back to the office. When they entered, Mr. Johnson met them with a large smile across his face.

"What's happened to make you smile?" Asked Doctor Robertson.

"My boy is awake!" He exclaimed.
"Oh! I am thrilled. Let's go see him, Doctor Murray." The doctors followed by Daniel Johnson walked into the examination room to see Jonathan wrapped in a blanket lying on the examination table. Dr. Murray proceeded to examine the boy. He looked into his eyes, nose, ears, and mouth. He pressed on his abdomen and found it to feel normal. He looked at the pustules. His body was covered from head to toe but did not seem to have any more than before being placed in the ice bath.

Turning towards Mr. Johnson, Mack informed him, "I am happy with what I see. I think we have turned a corner in the right direction. He has no more new pox and the ones he has seem to be drying. We just need to continue to watch him and to keep his fever at bay. How do you feel Jonathan?" "I am tired and itchy, sir. My head hurts some." "That is encouraging. You just rest here. We will be get-ting supper and water soon. I'm sure that will help you feel better. We need you to stay with us for a little while." Mack patted Daniel on the back as he walked back into the lobby to speak with Greta.

"How is he, Dr. Murray?" asked Greta.

"He is much better. He will be fine. Do we have supper yet? I think he needs to eat and drink some water. We don't need him to get dehydrated."

"I am finishing up dinner now. Should be about 20 min-utes. I will hand out plates to everyone in the reception area. I don't want folks in your apartment."

"Very good. Thank you. Doctor Robertson, sir, is there anything else that I need to consider regarding Jonathan's condition? His fever has waned, and he has no new pustules, as far as I can tell. He says he has a headache and is still itchy, but the pox appear to be drying up."

"I concur with your analysis. Let's see if he can hold down food and keep his fever down. If he can make it through the night with no issues, he will be on the road to a full recovery. How much longer do we need to keep he and the other children quarantined?" Felix asked Mack.

"At least until the pustules appear to be drying up. I think we are going to need a larger space to house the sick. Do you have an idea of a good location?"

"Let's ask Sheriff Hewett to speak to Mr. Burke about allowing us to use the Saloon. We will also ask him to find more volunteers to assist in the care of the sick and to help Greta with cooking for everyone."

After moving the sick to the Saloon, hundreds of volunteers showed up to help Doctors Murray and Robinson. Greta took the lead in handing out jobs to the volunteers. Then, the doctors were able to focus on other medical care needs.

From that moment forward, Jonathan and the rest of the sick in Nashville made full recoveries, and the inoculation process prevented mass infection of the city. The day the quarantine was lifted, the townspeople gathered outside of the medical office to cheer the Doctors Robertson and Murray. The doctors came outside to see what the commotion was. They were surprised by the mass of people waiting for their appearance.

"Ok, ok...," Doctor Robertson motioned for the people to quiet down so he could speak. "Thank you all for coming here today. I want to thank the Lord for pulling us through this crisis. We give him the glory and honor for rescuing our community. I would also like to thank Doctor Murray, my new associate, for his knowledge, wisdom, and courage in facing the matter head on. Without him, this situation might not have been as successful. Further, I wish to thank Matthew Guthrie, Sheriff Hewett, Mrs. Abernathy, and all of the volunteers who assisted us in caring for the sick. for his assistance. Now, it is important to remember that you all must make sure that you have thoroughly cleaned your homes, your clothes, equipment…leave nothing to chance. When in doubt, clean it or burn it. This will help to make certain the virus does not return." Just then the crowd began to cheer again.

After this Mack had the full trust and support of Doctor Robertson. Mack focused on his work, not yet taking any time off to visit his family. When his first anniversary in Nashville arrived, Doctor Robertson presented Mack with a gift at a dinner given in his honor at the Robertsons' home. Mack always looked forward to eating at the Robertsons. The food was always delicious.

After dinner, the two men retired to the front porch where they enjoyed a glass of whiskey and a cigar. "Felix, you did not have to give me anything. I am honored to be working here. It was the best decision I ever made."

"Well, we wanted to show you how much we appreciate you, and I also wanted to encourage you to go home. Your family needs to see you as much as you need to see them. So, here is a round trip coach trip to take you home."

"This is incredibly kind, Felix. I appreciate this very much."

"I wasn't certain that I wanted another doctor in the practice with me. I appreciate the way you approach medicine and your dedication to research and advanced learning. I think I was afraid for no reason. My father, General Robertson, was a stiff, formal man. He did not believe in addressing those in his employ by their given names; he thought that being casual led to problems; but I am coming to believe that treating our practice as a family is preferable to awkward formality."

"I think that is a fine idea, though I was raised to address my elders in a formal manner until given permission to do otherwise. I used to sneak around the men who work on the farm and see if they'd let me call them by their given names."

"What happened?"

"They did not until I came home from the war. I guess that was when they finally saw me an adult."

"Where did you get your name from, Mack? It's a grand sounding name."

"It came from my father's side of the family," replied Mack hoping that brief answer would be enough to hold back any other questions.

"Hmmm that is interesting."

"Do I recall that your parents are both deceased? I hope that is not too personal?"

"No, it is not. They are both gone. My father and his brother were prisoners of war during the Revolution. My uncle died in the prison camp. After my father was freed and he returned home, he was damaged mentally and physically by his experiences. He contracted malaria in the prison camp. It took a toll on his health and mentally he could not handle being physically able to work on the farm or to be a good father. He took his life a year and half after coming home. A year later, my mother contracted influenza and died. I was raised by my father's sister and her husband on the farm that my uncle and father owned. My father was fortunate to be successful enough to provide for me financially so that my aunt and uncle would not be burdened."

"They did a fine job in raising you, Mack. They are to be commended. Did they have any other children?"

"One daughter, my cousin, Mary Elizabeth. She is a beautifully brilliant girl. She and I competed in our academic studies. She was quite unhappy when my aunt and uncle told her that her studies would end once she reached the age of 15. She is a spirited young lady."

"I suspect my daughter Elnora may become the same. She already likes to challenge her brothers. Elizabeth, on the other hand, is all girl who cannot stand to get dirty. I believe I heard your uncle speak once at an abolitionist gathering in Knoxville. I was impressed by his speech. I was excited to discover that he was your uncle when Dr. Rush wrote to me about you."

"I appreciate that. I have often told my uncle that he should pursue a political position outside of our county. Thus far, however, he has not pursued such a position because he does not wish to leave the responsibility of running the farm to my aunt, especially with the rumblings of discontent that have emerged as of late. What are your thoughts on these rumors?"

"As you know I have a philosophy similar to your family. Equality of all people is a key American value. However, we continue to find ourselves in conflict with this value so long as slavery is allowed to continue. It is a disgrace. I understand that to successfully run a farm requires compromise on this issue. It is an uncomfortable position to be in for your family as well as mine. My family, too, has been engaged in the operation of a tobacco farm for many years. However, I would prefer to find another way to get the work done while making a profit without having to use slaves to make that happen. Unfortunately, there are far more farm owners in the southern states who disagree with our position. The North, on the other hand, refuses to acknowledge the role slavery has played in their economies, as if the rest of us are oblivious to that reality. The North has been more willing to end slavery because it is no longer required for profit making in the factories; though the low wages paid in those factories and the use of children to keep those wages excessively low, almost begs the question of whether slavery exists."

"I concur." Mack felt kindred feelings budding in his relationship with Doctor Robertson. He was beginning to see his employer as more of a younger brother. He was just four years older than Felix. Mack knew he had made the right decision for himself when he decided to leave Washington County for Nashville.

"So, Mack, when are we going to find you a wife? Do you not think it is time for such a worthy pursuit? You aren't getting any younger!"

"You sound like my Aunt Eleanor. It is more important right now for me to make a name for myself in medicine. As of yet, I have not been in a position to meet anyone who interests me." Mack rebutted.

"Mack, you cannot afford to wait too long because you may miss out on the person who is meant to be with you. Fathers are looking for gentlemen like yourself; men who can provide a good life for their daughters. Much like I am certain your aunt and uncle are doing for your cousin. If you happen to fall in love with one of them is all the better." "I know you are correct. But what woman, much less her father, would choose a man who lives in a small apartment behind the medical practice where he is employed?" "You leave that up to me. If you find the woman, we will work out the living arrangements."

"We will discuss this more after I return from my vacation. I am willing to think more seriously about it."

"Agreed." The two men looked at each other, clicked their glasses together and exclaimed, "Cheers!"

"I must be going back to town now to prepare for my trip. Thank you again for your kindness. Please give my regards to Lydia. I will see you in a few weeks."

"Good evening and safe travels, Mackenzie Murray!" Mack gathered his coat and hat and returned to his carriage. On his way back to his apartment, he thought about what Felix had said. What if waiting had caused him to lose the very person he was meant for? He did not wish to miss out on a special person. He very much wanted a relationship like his parents and his aunt and uncle had. He supposed that he needed to give serious thought to the kind of woman he would want as a wife. Being a pragmatist, he decided that he would put pen to paper to make a list of those traits he preferred. It would help to focus on the important traits. He would have time to do such while traveling home.

When he returned home that evening, he wrote to his family to let them know that he would be coming home and that he would arrive in twelve days' time. He had some patients he needed to see before he left. He arranged to see everyone in two days and then he would have a few days to pack and to purchase gifts for his family and new clothes. The clothes he purchased before coming to Nashville were now worn, stained, and faded. He had not spent any money on new clothes, shoes or a hat since moving because he did not want to take time away from his job to take care of it. He now looked forward to shopping. It was the first time as an adult that he would choose his own clothing. He found it exciting.

After asking Felix for a recommendation, Mack went to the tailor, a Jewish man named Jacob Schneider. The tailor knew exactly what would look handsome on him. He chose a coat, shirt, pants, tie, shoes, and top hat. Looking in the mirror, Mack was surprised at how mature he looked, and he recalled his envy of the more affluent men in Philadelphia. Gazing at his image gave him a feeling of maturity and success. He could see a few gray hairs appearing which distressed him. In his mind, he still felt like a youngster. But he was now thirty-nine years old. Most of his friends from medical school were married and had several children. He knew it was past time. After stopping by the livery to visit George and chat with Matthew about his itinerary, he went home.

Chapter 23

The time for his trip arrived and he sat patiently waiting for his coach to arrive. He leaned his head back and closed his eyes. A few moments later he heard a melodious, high pitched voice. "Excuse me, sir." Opening his eyes, he saw a figure in front of him. He could not see her face because the sun was shining so brightly that her face was blurred by the intense light.

"I'm sorry…," moving his hand up he tried to block the sun so that he could see who was standing in front of him. "May I be of assistance? he asked.

"Please, sir, is this the coach going east towards Knoxville?"

"Yes, ma'am, it is."

"Oh good, I thought I missed it. We were late leaving to get here, and I was afraid…. I'm sorry to have bothered you." "No bother, ma'am. I was just resting. I had a late-night last night."

"Do you mind if I sit here?"

"Of course not, Miss…."

"Laura Hartwell-Todd, and you, sir?

"Doctor Mackenzie Murray, but my friends call me 'Mack'. It is nice to meet you, Miss Hartwell-Todd. Boy, that's a mouth full."

"Yes, it is. My grandfather insisted that my mother keep her name when she married my father because of some family history in Scotland. They compromised by hyphenating it. You can simply call me Miss Todd, at least until we know each other better. I believe I have heard of you. You work with Dr. Robertson, don't you? Are you traveling to Knoxville also?"

"You have heard of me? I can't imagine that. My family originated in Scotland, too. No, I will be going on from Knoxville to Jonesborough."

"Yes, Dr. Robertson is a friend of my father's. That is Washington County…it is beautiful there. My family visited there a few years ago."

"That's surprising. I cannot imagine why anyone would go there who doesn't live there. You are correct, though. It is beautiful. Why did you go to Washington County?"

"My father gave a speech to a church group. I do not recall which one."

"I see. That is interesting. A political speech?"

"He was speaking to a group of abolitionists."

"Oh, I imagine my uncle was at that meeting. Our family is active in the movement."

"What is your uncle's name, if you don't mind my asking?"

"Certainly not, his name is Thomas MacGregor. He's married to my father's sister. They raised me after my parents died."

"I am very sorry. It must have been difficult for you to lose both of your parents. Thank goodness you had them."

"I have been blessed to have an amazing family. I was young when I lost both of my parents. They have always treated me as if I was their own."

"What does you uncle do?"

"He's a planter. The farm is called Ione Skye Farm, named for two islands in Scotland where my great-grand…or maybe great-great-grandparents came from. I always get that confused. And your father…does he do anything else besides the movement?

"I thought people these days called them 'plantations' instead of 'farms'? That is such a beautiful name. My father, Henry, is a lawyer here. He represents many who disagree with slavery, who wish to see it abolished. It is not a popular position these days, you know?"

"I do. I think they have thought of the word 'plantation' as uppity. We have always been more modest, conservative people."

The conversation between Mack and Laura continued as they embarked on the coach for the trip east. While Mack had intended to use the time making note of the type of woman he wanted for a wife, he found himself sitting next to that very kind of woman. This woman was intelligent, well-spoken, and beautiful. When the coach pulled into Knoxville, he found himself not wanting her to leave, but there was nothing he could do at this point.

"When do you plan to return to Nashville, Miss Todd?"

"I will be going back in three weeks. I am visiting my grandparents. They are getting older, and I wanted to spend some time with them. And you?"

"I am going back in 3 weeks as well. Maybe we will see each other again." Mack smiled, took her hand, and gave her a quick kiss.

She blushed and responded, "Yes, it would be lovely to see you again; or perhaps in Nashville."

"Yes, perhaps we can. I hope you have a nice visit."

"You, as well, Doctor Murray. Goodbye." As she walked away, Mack noticed that she had dropped her handkerchief. Picking it up, he attempted to return it to her, but she was already gone. He held it up to smell her perfume. It had a sweet gardenia scent. He tucked it into his jacket pocket. His heart was beating hard, fearing he would never see her again. Getting back into the coach, he closed his eyes and prayed to God to help him see her again if she was the right woman for him. When he opened his eyes, the other passengers in the carriage were looking at him and smiling. He suddenly felt self-conscious and began to blush.

"What is it? Do I have something on my face?"

An older woman responded, "No, son. I think you've fallen in love." She smiled and turned her face to look out the window. Mack realized that she was not wrong. From that moment until the coach pulled into Jonesborough station, he thought about Laura. He tried to think of his family and what he wanted to do while he was home, but even those thoughts took him back to thinking of her.

When the coach arrived, it was six o'clock in the afternoon. Mack was tired but excited. As he stepped down from the carriage, Mack saw Jeremiah right away. He recalled the previous trip when Jeremiah picked him up and he noticed the gray hair and wrinkled face. Imagine his astonishment at Jeremiah's obvious advancing age. Jeremiah was moving much slower, talking slower, and his gray hair was now gone. In fact, all his hair was gone. He realized that there would soon be a time when all the people he grew up with, those he loved so dearly, would be gone. Where would home be then? He suddenly realized that he was an adult and making a home was now much more important. He thought previously that surviving war and seeing war was what made him an adult or that having a job and paying bills made him an adult, but he was wrong. While those things were important, building a family was what would truly make him an adult. He also realized that this would be even more important for Mary Beth because she was female. Her life was more tied to a family because she would have no support otherwise. He decided that he would always take care of Mary Beth until a suitable husband could be found, especially after her parents had passed on. It was the least he could do for the people who had raised him.

"Jeremiah! Hello!" Mack rushed over to give Jeremiah a hug. Jeremiah tried to pull back, worrying what the other white people would think. "I don't care what they think, Jeremiah. You've known me my whole life. You helped raise me as much as my aunt and uncle. If that doesn't warrant a hug, then I don't know what does."

"Yessuh, Docta MacKenzie. I hopes yo trip wasn too bad. It beeze mighty hot today."

"It was fine, Jeremiah. I hope Addie's got dinner ready. I am absolutely starved!"

"Oh, yessuh, she's fryin' some chicken for you. She knowd it be yo fav'rit."

"I hope everyone is well at home. We had a terrible outbreak of smallpox in Nashville. We were fortunate that no one died."

"Lawd, suh, I hopes it don't come here. Now, Doc, I is afraid youse walkin' inta a mess, but it ain't my place to tell ya." The pair jumped up on the buckboard and headed for home.

"My goodness, Jeremiah, I am sure it would be fine for you to tell me. I will know soon anyway?"

"Nah, suh, I is gonna keep dis ole mouwf shut. Youse soon see suh."

"Well, I don't know if I should be scared or not. Is it the farm? Have you had troubles?"

"Dat ain't ta main problem, weeze done real good dis summa. We's gots some new boys. Lawd, suh, deeze boys ain't like us; naw suh, dey ain't. Dey can gets my dander up. Dey wants ta argue and fights all da time."

"I'm sorry, Jeremiah. What can I do to help?"

"Dey ain't nuttin', Doc. Deese younguns don't knows how ta keep dey mouwf shut and do dey work. Dey wants ta fuss and gives us a hard time. Dey don't know how good dey gots it on Ione Skye. Yo uncle and yo daddy…dey always treats us wit respect. I knowd yo daddy and yo uncle don't do us like dem otha massers. Me, Killian, Addie, Mame, all da first negros who comes here…we ain't never been beat like dey do on dem otha farms, but deese boys don't care. Dey wanna fight."

"I see. I am sorry. I am sure that you, Killian, Jacob, and Macajah can handle it. In fact, it would be best if you try to handle yourselves before you go to Uncle Thomas. They would only resent him more. I wish I knew when slavery will become a thing of the past, but I do know that if I am able when Uncle Thomas and Aunt Eleanor are gone, everyone will be freed. And when that time comes, Jeremiah, we will make arrangements for the benefit of everyone. Those other farmers are short sighted. They only care about what is in it for them and not for the people who help support them and their livelihoods. I am sure it is difficult for all of you to see that situation on other farms and not be able to do anything."

"So, I wanna ax you sumpin', Doc Mack."

"Of course, Jeremiah. What is it?"

"When I passes on, I wants you and Miss Mary Beth ta sing dat song at my service that youse sang for yo momma and poppa. I loves dat song, Doc."

"Of course, we will do whatever you wish, Jeremiah, but I sure hope you aren't planning to leave us any time soon!" Mack patted Jeremiah on the back.

"Aw, naw suh, I ain't plannin' on it neither!" The two friends had a good laugh. Mack spent the rest of the drive to Ione Skye gazing around at the beauty of the landscape. He had forgotten how much he loved the mountains, the sounds of the birds, and the smell of the earth. He was certain that there could be no other place on earth he could ever love more.

As they drove up the drive to the main house, Mack's heart began to beat faster in anticipation of seeing his family again. It had been such a long time since he had been home. Thomas, Eleanor, and Mary Beth had planned to visit Nashville but had to cancel the trip when Eleanor became ill with influenza. Mack was concerned about her recovery and was anxious to see her.

As soon as they stopped in front of the house, Mack looked puzzled. "Jeremiah, where is everyone? I thought the family would be waiting for me."

"Well, suh, you knowd what I says before? Youse gonna fine out right now. Yo Aunt Ellie prolly ain't feeling so well.

She ain't got over dat fever . Miss Mary Beth done been seein' after her."

"Jeremiah that was five months ago. Why hasn't someone written to let me know that she is still ill. I would have come home before now. Just leave the bags on the porch. I want to go find her."

"Naw suh, dat boy'll takes 'em to yo room, Doc." Jeremiah point at his youngest boy, Charles.

"Aww, hi Charlie! Boy, you have grown a mile! That's fine, Jeremiah." Mack ran into the house yelling for his family. He ran into the kitchen. "Addie! Mame! June! Where is everyone? Mary Beth!" Soon Mary Beth appeared on the back staircase.

"Stop all that hollering MacKenzie! Mother is asleep. She did not have a good night."

Mack went to Mary Beth to embrace her, but she brushed him aside. "Mary Beth! What is wrong with you?"

"I'm tired, MacKenzie! My mother is not well. I have been taking care of her around the clock since she became ill."

"Well, I am here now, and I will help you. I would have come sooner if I had known, Mary Beth, but someone did not want me to know. I will not be blamed for that!" He took Mary Beth by the hand and led her to the sitting room. "I can tell that you are exhausted. You are at risk of becoming ill, too. You need to go upstairs and get into bed. Addie and Mame will help me. They will bring you supper later."

"I am sorry, MacKenzie. I did not mean to yell at you, but I am exhausted. I am worried about Momma. She is seriously ill. Poppa does not want to hear about it. He stays in the fields all day. He's been sleeping in his study. We're all afraid of losing her, Mack."

"When was the last time Dr. Hammond was here to look at her? What did he say?"

"He came in the beginning. He said it looked like influenza, but he couldn't be certain. He left medicine to help with the fever, but we ran out some time ago. Poppa wouldn't let me call for the doctor again. You know how much he hates to spend money."

"Well, I will handle Uncle Thomas. I have my bag, so we don't have to worry about having the necessary medicines. Mary Elizabeth, you know if God is ready for her, there's nothing we can do to change it, but that doesn't mean we don't try. I am going up now to check on her."

Slumping down into his arms, Mary Beth cried, "Oh, Mack, I am so glad you are home. I will obey your every order."

"Like that has ever happened before! Let's not worry about that right now." Mack wrapped his arms around his best friend and cousin. "Go on now, go get into bed!" The two ran mindlessly up the staircase towards the bedrooms. Mary Beth's room was the last room on the left of the staircase situated at the backside of the house. Thomas and Eleanor's room was right across the hall. Mack's room was to the right of the staircase on the front side of the house. The guest room was across the hall at the backside of the house.

When they reached the top of the stairs, Mary Elizabeth went to her room and shut the door. Mack went to his aunt's door and knocked loudly. "Yes, come in," Eleanor responded faintly.

"Aunt Ellie, it's me, MacKenzie." Mack waited a few seconds for a response. When he did not hear one, he entered the bedroom. The room was dark and there was a putrid odor.

He walked to the windows and opened the drapes letting the bright sunshine in. When he turned, Mack was terrified by what he saw.

His aunt lay in her bed covered in blankets. Her hair had turned white, and her skin was pale gray. Mack walked over to her and sat beside her. She was sleeping soundly. He touched her forehead to determine if she was still suffering from a fever. Her forehead was sweaty. MacKenzie sat for a few minutes listening to her breathing. It sounded wheezy, like crumpling a piece of paper in your hand. Eleanor's breathing was labored, and she coughed frequently. There were times during her coughing when her breathing stopped. Mame appeared in the doorway.

"What can I do to help, Doctor Mack?" "Oh, Mame, yes, we need to open the windows and allow fresh, clean air into the room. It is easier to breathe when the air is cool. We need to try to bring her fever down, as well. Let's take these blankets off the bed and bring some cool water for her to drink."

"Yessuh, I gets dat done right now."

"Before you do that, please tell Addie that Mary Beth is sleeping. I asked her to stay in her room. She is exhausted and needs rest or we'll be nursing her too! I told her that someone would bring her a plate to eat there. Oh, and Mame, if it hasn't been done, everything needs to be washed and cleaned. We need to make sure that we use hot, almost boiling water, to clean the linens and eating and cooking utensils because we must make sure we kill the germs. Do you understand?"

"Oh, yessuh, I does. I gets June on that. Addie is working on supper now. Is she gonna beeze okay, suh? We is so worried."

"I won't know for a while. Influenza is difficult to treat because we don't know enough about it. We have not made much progress since my Ma had it. We certainly need to pray for her," implored MacKenzie.

Mack stayed by his aunt's side until her fever broke. What seemed like an eternity was just a couple of days. "Mack… Mack…," Eleanor whispered when she opened her eyes, and she discovered him sleeping next to her bed. She reached her hand out to touch his head. Lifting his head slowly, he suddenly realized that he was not dreaming; Ellie was awake.

"Aunt Eleanor, you are awake! Oh, you have had us all very worried. How do you feel?"

"Well, I feel tired, but much better than before you came. I don't believe I have ever been so sick. I am so glad to see you. I hope I have not caused you any harm with your job. How long have I been asleep, Mack," inquired his patient.

"Just a few days; I was on my way home for a visit anyway. We have seen so many cases of influenza and smallpox this year. I feel certain you were run down and that compromised your immune system. You still need to rest. Let me get some fresh water for you. We need to keep you hydrated."

"I am so glad you could come. How is Mary Elizabeth? She's not ill, is she?"

"I think she is all right. I ordered her to stay in bed for the last few days so she could recuperate. We've been giving her fruit and making sure she eats. She hadn't eaten in a few days when I arrived, and she was close to exhaustion. Uncle Thomas was so concerned about you both. I don't think I have ever seen him so worried. He shuts himself down emotionally. He will be much better now knowing you were out of danger. Let me go get the water and check on our sweet Mary Beth and I will be right back. Do you think you could eat some soup? Addie made some delicious chicken and rice soup."

"I think that sounds wonderful." Eleanor looked up at Mack with an enormous smile across her face. "I am so proud of you MacKenzie. I know that your mother and father would be also."

"Thank you for saying that. I think about them both often. I often find myself learning something new or having some new experience and wishing that I had them to tell about it. There is so much I know that I would have in common with both of them. Ma would love how much I adore my horse, George. He is quite a character. And Pa and I could have intriguing conversations about medicine and agriculture. So, I guess this means that you and Uncle Thomas will have to put up with these discussions!" Mack giggled in the same mischievous way he had as a child when he played a joke or trick on Mary Elizabeth. "Excuse me a moment, Aunt, I need to go to the kitchen. I will be right back. Don't run away while I am gone." Again, MacKenzie Murray snickered as he removed himself from his aunt's bedroom.

Mack jumped down the backstairs like a little boy on the way into the kitchen to ask Mame and Addie to bring soup, bread, and water upstairs to Ellie. He also asked Mame to help his aunt to bathe. Then, he belted into the study to announce to Thomas that Ellie was finally awake, and then he hit the door of Mary Beth's room like a bolt of lightning striking the ground. He threw open her door and pounced into her room aiming to land on her bed. He missed and came crashing to the ground right at Mary Beth's feet. Looking up from the floor, he had expected to find her sleeping. Instead, he found her reading and humming to herself as she snacked on a red apple. "Well, lookie here, I thought I told you to rest. Doesn't look like rest to me, young lady."

"MacKenzie Murray! Don't you know you're supposed to knock on the door of a young lady's room! How rude you are to come blasting into my room like this!" Mary Beth rolled over giggling and jumped to her feet. "Oh Mack, are you hurt? That was a terrible fall. Do I need to get ice for your backside?"

"The only injury I have is my pride, thank you very much. I came to tell you that she is awake. She's not ready to get out of bed yet, but she's going to recover. You can go see her, but only for a few minutes. You both need to continue resting; otherwise, you both risk getting sick again."

"Oh, you cannot keep me out of there. I'll race you!" Mary Beth shoved Mack back down on the flooring leaping over him like Jack Be Nimble. She was met by Mame who was coming out of the room from bringing up soup and wa-ter. "MOMMA! MOMMA! Sorry Mame, I came to see my Momma." Mary Beth threw herself across the bed and into the arms of her mother. "Oh, I have been scared. I thought we were going to lose you and it would be my fault. I didn't know what to do, and Poppa…."

"Oh, my sweet Mary Beth… I am fine. I'm tired but I am going to be just fine. I'm sorry for scaring you so. I love you, my sweet girl!" Mack stood in the doorway watching his aunt and cousin. A few minutes passed when Thomas appeared and ran past him towards the bed not acknowledging his presence. He fell onto the other side of the bed next to his wife and daughter. Mack stood for another few minutes before deciding to go to the kitchen for something to eat.

Over the next several days Eleanor continued to strengthen. The time came when Mack needed to return to Nashville. Before he did, he asked to speak with Thomas and Eleanor about his thoughts regarding Mary Beth. "I wanted to speak with you both about Mary Beth's future. I am sure it comes as no surprise that her opportunities for a good marriage here are not great. There may be a farmer here or there who might be a good match, but I would like her to have more options, especially because, like me, she is on the older side. She should have been married before now. I thought it might be a good idea for her to come with me to Nashville. She can live with me, and I can make some introductions. Additionally, Dr. Robertson has societal connections that could benefit her, so long as she makes a good impression. If we are unsuccessful, then I can bring her home in a few months. What do you think?"

Thomas and Eleanor gazed at each other as if to confirm what they both felt without saying a word. Thomas spoke, "Mack, I think…um, we think that is a fine idea. When do you plan to return to Nashville? Eleanor and the ladies will need to look over her wardrobe to make certain she has what she needs. We don't wish for her to look like a farm girl, you know?"

"Well, there is one other thing I need to do before I return. I met a young lady during my trip here. She is in Knoxville visiting her grandparents. I thought that I might stop by

Knoxville to visit. I was hoping to send a letter to inquire as to the possibility of her grandparents allowing me, and Mary Beth of course, to stop in Knoxville overnight before continuing to Nashville." He paused looking for affirmation of his suggestion.

Again, there was a glance towards each other and then both Thomas and Eleanor spoke in unison, "Oh, we are so happy to hear this." Then they began speaking over each other asking questions so fast Mack could not respond. Who is she? How old is she? Who are her parents?" This led to a spontaneous outburst of laughter.

Chapter 24

The next morning Mack gave a letter to Killian's boy Eddie to deliver to the home of Francis (Frank) and Claire Hartwell in Knoxville. The Hartwells were a prominent Knoxville family, known to most of the elite in Tennessee. Mr. Hartwell opened one of the first textile mills in the state. He was also working with the State to bring the railroad through Knoxville. He and Claire, like Laura's parents, were also abolitionists. As he had informed his family, the note asked for their consent for Mack and Mary Beth to visit them and Laura before returning to Nashville. After reading the note and discussing the situation with his wife and Laura, Frank Hartwell agreed to an overnight visit. Mr. Hartwell was familiar with James MacKenzie and Thomas and Eleanor MacGregor. Before the gentlemen met at several abolitionist gatherings in eastern Tennessee, he had heard of them from a mutual friend of his and the Fraser's in Virginia—William Beverly. He believed them to be honest, God-fearing men and expected to find MacKenzie the same. Mr. Hartwell returned the invitation with his response noted inside to Eddie.

When Eddie returned to Ione Skye, he went straight to find Mack. He went first to the house but was told by Addie that Mack was working in the apple orchard. After stopping at the pump for some water, Eddie ran to the orchard. When Mack saw Eddie, he dropped his apples and ran towards Eddie. He ripped open the envelope to read Mr. Hartwell's response. When he read Mr. Hartwell's response, Mack jumped up and screamed, "Yahoo!" He then ran for the house to inform his family.

Eleanor had three days to prepare Mary Beth's and Mack's wardrobes for their visit. They drove into town to visit the General Store for fabric to make another gown for Mary Beth. His uncle felt Mack would benefit from another suit and he insisted that he pay for it. They also purchased new shoes for the pair and two new hats and gloves for Mary Beth. Addie, Mame, and Ellie spent the three days sewing as quickly as they could. When they finished, they impressed themselves with the quality of their handiwork. Mary Elizabeth and MacKenzie were striking in their new clothes.

Eleanor's gaze lingered on her nephew. She always thought Mack was handsome, but there was something different now. He was tall and thin, but not in an emaciated way; he was healthy. His skin with its ever so slight tan which came not from the sun, but from his mother, reminded her of a cup of coffee with milk. With his skin's richness and his bold dark brown eyebrows, his blue eyes became icy and piercing. She could not imagine any woman not instantly falling in love with him. His new clothing provided him with the elegant style of an aristocratic gentleman.

"Mary Beth, do try not to spill food on your new gown. Take small bites and, whatever you do girl, do not talk with food in your mouth! Sometimes you act like you are 13 years old!" Eleanor firmly instructed her daughter. "I cannot emphasize enough how important this family is in society. If you make a good impression on them, they may provide you and MacKenzie with finding an exceptional suitor."

"Oh, Momma! You worry too much. I know how to behave. And besides, you know Doctor Prissy Pants over here would never allow me to embarrass him!" Mary Beth giggled.

Not impressed by his cousin's flippant remark, Mackenzie returned her giggle with an expression of disapproval. "You cannot mess this up for us by behaving like a child, Mary Beth. You must be composed and think before you speak. You _are_ a lady."

With an air of sarcasm, Mary Beth retorted as she curtsied, "My pleasure, sir!"

Coming to her daughter's defense, Eleanor responded to her nephew, "Mack, you'll be wise to remember that you are her cousin and NOT her father. You will both get along better if you do." Sighing, Mack responded, "Yes, ma'am."

The pair finished packing their clothes and preparing for the trip. Despite knowing how much his aunt and uncle were looking forward to discovering their daughter's marital prospects, Mack knew that they were not ready for her to leave home. As time neared for the pair to leave for Knoxville, Mack sensed his aunt's sadness. He planned to help her through the transition with the assistance of Charlie and Eddie.

On the day of their departure, Thomas, Eleanor, Mack, and Mary Beth rode in the family's carriage. Jeremiah, Addie, Mame, Killian, June, and Boaz, along with the children Eddie, Annah, Katurah, and Charles, took the buckboard into town. After purchasing their tickets for travel to Knoxville and then on to Nashville the following day, the immediate family assembled on the platform to wait for the carriage to arrive. The others stood on the side of the station within eyeshot of the platform. Mack and Mary Elizabeth began to say their "goodbyes" and promised to write soon and often.

Mack then went back to his aunt and put his arms around her, looked into her eyes, and whispered, "I know you are going to miss her. She doesn't want to admit that she is going to miss you too. I will keep you updated on everything. We will both be fine. I have something for you that I believe may help you."

Looking puzzled at her nephew, Ellie couldn't imagine what Mack would have to help her. Mack motioned to the children to come. The children, giggling loudly, ran over to Eleanor. Her eyes widened and a twinkle appeared when she saw them running towards her. Eleanor had always loved children. She and Thomas wanted a large family, but Mary Elizabeth's difficult delivery made that impossible. The young ones stopped at her feet and wrapped their little arms around her legs and waist. Ellie knelt down so that she could look at them in the face. Looking up, she inquired of her nephew, "So what do these little babies have to do with your plan for me?"

Instead of answering his aunt's question, Annah and Katurah shouted, "Look Missus Ellie! Look what we have! Doctor Mack got it for you!" The girls motioned towards the pocket in Annah's dress.

"My goodness, girls, what could possibly be in that tiny pocket?" Annah pulled her dress up towards Eleanor pushing the contents outward. Just then a small kitten peeped out. "Well, look at you! Aren't you just the sweetest, little thing? This is for me?" Eleanor grinned at her nephew who was beaming with pride over his well-planned surprise.

Mame exclaimed, "Doctor Mack thought the kitty would help you not be sad."

Eleanor looked over at her nephew and smiled warmly. "Children, what should we name her? Let's think about it, children. Do any of you have an idea for a name?"

Annah suggested "Snowball" because the kitten was white. Katurah thought "Cotton" would be a good name. The boys were not interested in naming the kitten, but they did take turns petting it.

"I think both of those are wonderful names. Let's take a vote." Eleanor asked for everyone to respond by raising their hand for the name they preferred. The majority chose "Cotton". "Cotton it is! Now children, I don't suppose that any of you would be interested in helping me take care of little Cotton, would you?"

The boys' interest was now peaked. They whispered amongst themselves for a few seconds about how much they should charge for taking care of the little pet. The girls, in response, stomped their feet and disputed the contention that any money would be involved.

To stop their arguing Eleanor interjected, "Maybe I could get help making sure that Cotton gets plenty of food and water every day. I don't think Addie and Mame should have to worry about that responsibility, do you? And, maybe you could help with brushing her and keeping her hair from getting matted or filled with bugs?"

The children exclaimed in unison, "Yes, ma'am!" What might have been an emotional departure became a light-hearted and, perhaps, even joyous moment because of the gift of the kitten. When the time of Mack and Mary Beth's departure came, his aunt and uncle, along with their staff and farm hands, were no longer sad. There was much hugging and kissing before the pair embarked on the coach. The group remained on the platform until they could no longer see the coach. The group then separated with the negro staff returning home while Thomas and Eleanor walked over to the General Store to do some shopping.

MacKenzie and Mary Elizabeth were on their way to Knoxville. While the trip could be hot and uncomfortable, being jerked around at times from the uneven ground, Mack was pleasantly surprised when Mary Beth did not complain. For much of the trip, she did not speak but gazed out the window. Mack wondered what she was thinking, but he didn't ask. He leaned back and tried to take a nap.

After an hour or so, Mack sat back up and began looking around the carriage. "What are you looking for, MacKenzie?" Mary Beth inquired.

"Where is that basket Addie packed for us with the sandwiches, cheese, and apples?"

"Oh, that! Yes, it's here." Mary Beth leaned forward and pulled the basket from behind her skirt. She placed the basket on her lap and pulled back the linen napkin that covered its contents. "There are a few sandwiches here. Looks like ham, chicken, or sausage. Then, there's a couple of apples and some cheese pieces she cut up for us. There's a canteen with water, too."

"I will take the sausage. You need to eat something, too."

"I will. Don't boss me, MacKenzie. Worry about yourself. Nevertheless, I think I'll eat an apple and some cheese. Thank you very much." Mary Beth's tongue could be quite curt when she was annoyed.

After eating their snacks and drinking water, they returned to gazing out the window. "Mack, what do you think Scotland and Ireland look like? Do you think they are as beautiful as Tennessee?"

"I have no idea, Mary Beth. I would like to think so."

"Why do you think our grandparents sent their children here? It must have been so scary for them," posited Mary Beth.

"I do not doubt that they were afraid. Our grandfather Duncan and his brother and sister were children. I guess life in Ireland must have been unbearable or they would not have left. You know that is where that song comes from, don't you?"

"You mean the song *Good Night and Joy Be To You All*?"

"Yes," responded Mack.

"I don't know what you mean," Mary Beth said with a tone of doubt.

"Well, when Donald, Duncan, and Eleanor were about to leave Ireland, their mother, our great-great-grandmother Isobel MacKenzie asked them to stand on the dock here in America, and to look toward Ireland, and to sing the song back to her. She told them that she would hear it and know that they were well."

"I don't remember hearing that before. When would we have been told that story, Mack?" She pondered.

"I recall my father telling me the story when I was young?"

"MacKenzie, I cannot remember the story. I will have to ask Momma later." Feeling perturbed by the conversation, Mary Beth returned to her silent gaze out the coach window.

Although they were prepared for the long drive, they were anxious for their arrival in Knoxville. Neither was certain what to expect while visiting the Hartwells. As their ride continued and Mary Beth remained silent, Mack could tell that Mary Beth was in deep thought. Not wanting her to worry, he decided to strike up another conversation. "What are you thinking about, Mary Beth? I can tell that you have something on your mind."

"It's nothing serious. I wonder, though, do you think they will be nice to us? I mean, they do not know us, nor do we know them. They are so prominent; they might not care for hillbillies."

"We are not hillbillies, Mary Beth! One thing, though, I have learned about people who live in the upper echelons of society, etiquette is critical if you wish to be in their company and, more importantly, stay there. They will not want to behave in a way unbecoming of themselves because word of their behavior could get out to their peers. But that only matters if we value etiquette as well. Aunt Eleanor taught you all you need to know. You have nothing to worry over."

"So, does that make us all fake? I don't think I would want to be misled just to keep reputations intact."

"I don't think so; well, maybe not most of the time. I think there are always times when we need to show kindness and graciousness to people who may not deserve it. We should mirror their actions. Don't cause any controversy, do you understand that?"

"I do. I will try; I promise. Do you think they will consent to your courting Laura? That is what you want, isn't it?"

"It is. I hope that if I…we…can make a good impression then they will talk with Laura's parents about a courtship. This could be good for both of us. Laura's family has many connections in Nashville. They can assist us in finding you a good match."

"I hope I get a say in who that will be. I don't want some troll just because he's wealthy!"

When these words rang through the coach, its other occupants looked away or bowed their heads. Mack was embarrassed and angry. "Mary Beth! You cannot say things like that. You and I will discuss any gentleman who may present a match for you. I promise you that."

"Okay, fine." Mary Beth crossed her arms and a distinct frown appeared on her face. No one spoke again.

As the coach pulled into the Knoxville station, the pair looked around for anyone who might look like they were Hartwells. At first, they did not see anyone. It wasn't until the coach stopped at the platform and a door opened from inside the station that a handsome older gentleman and woman walked out the door out onto the platform. Just before the door closed another figure appeared in the door. It was Laura. "There she is, Mary Beth. Look…there at the door."

"Oh, that's Laura? That's her? My goodness, MacKenzie, she is truly beautiful. Look at her grandmother. She is gorgeous. I know my Momma is beautiful, but these ladies are… wow!"

Mack was engrossed in looking at Laura and quickly daydreaming of her when he responded in a whisper, "Yes…yes, they are gorgeous. "Well, here it goes cousin," Mack stepped out of the carriage and then turned to assist Mary Beth down the steps. He turned, still holding her hand, and the pair walked towards Laura and her grandmother. As they walked, Mack looked towards Laura; she was smiling at him. A negro man wearing a suit swiftly stepped in front of him.

"Suh, Doc Murray, would youse show me which bags are yours and which are the lady's?"

"Certainly, there are three bags on the top of the carriage. Those are ours. Thank you."

"I is…I mean I am, Nigel, suh. I works fo Misser Hartwell.

Smiling, the older gentleman made his way to Mack and Mary Beth. He stopped in front of Mack and looked at him with a serious stare for a few, but uncomfortable seconds. Mack could feel sweat beading up on his forehead and his heart began pounding in his chest, so loudly he believed everyone could hear it. "I believe you are Doctor Alexander MacKenzie Murray. I am Francis Byrd Hartwell; you may call me Frank. This (looking back over his shoulder) is my wife, Claire, and you have previously met my granddaughter, Laura Hartwell-Todd. We have been looking forward to your visit."

Mack put his hand out to shake Mr. Hartwell's hand. Shaking hands, Mack responded, "Yes, sir. We have looked forward to meeting you both. This, Mr. and Mrs. Hartwell, is my cousin, Miss Mary Elizabeth MacGregor."

Mr. Hartwell took Mary Beth's hand and kissed it lightly. "Welcome, my dear, to Knoxville. We hope you both will have a nice visit with us. Our carriage is just over there. I believe Nigel has gathered your things and we are ready to go." He took Mary Beth's hand and wrapped it under his arm to lead her towards the carriage. "Have you visited Knoxville before today?"

"No sir, my family has not traveled much. My family is always busy with running the farm; though, my father travels on a rare occasion to meetings around Tennessee. It is very beautiful here."

"We like it here. We have lived here for about twenty years. We came here in 1797 to start a textile mill. This was frontier then. It is not so much frontier now. We have made great strides in creating a nice town here."

"Sir, I look forward to learning more about your family. Do I detect an accent? It is faint but I hear something different in your voice that I have not heard before," Mary Beth inquired of her host.

"My goodness, you are a smart, young lady. Not many catch that. I was born in Ulster, Ireland. My family came to the colonies in 1640. Most of my family settled in the Tidewater area of Virginia."

"That is almost one hundred years before our family came to Virginia. Our grandparents came from Ulster as well. They arrived in the 1730s, I believe, and settled in Staunton, Virginia. Their son, our grandfather Duncan, moved on to the Blacksburg area, and then my parents and Mack's moved here just before the war. I recall that our grandparents were originally from Scotland. Was that true of your family?"

Chuckling Mr. Hartwell responded to her inquiry, "Well, now that is a good question. My family moved to Ulster from northern England, rather than Scotland. They considered themselves to be English. My siblings and I were born in Ulster and that was what we knew before coming here. We would probably have said Irish for many years. However, we now consider ourselves to be American. The war taught us the importance of that new identity."

"I agree. I certainly consider myself an American. I think your accent is lovely." Mr. Hartwell and Mack assisted the ladies in entering the carriage, then Mr. Hartwell embarked, and lastly MacKenzie entered. "Is it a long drive to your home?"

"No, dear. We live just a little outside of the city, but it should not take too long. I am sure you are tired of all this carriage riding."

"I enjoy looking at the landscape. It is much like home."

Mack and Laura sat opposite each other. They smiled and tried not to be too conspicuous about their excitement at seeing each other again. Mrs. Hartwell sat quietly next to her husband and granddaughter. For the rest of the ride, the group was silent.

Once they arrived at the Hartwell home, Nigel assisted the ladies from exiting the coach and then he gathered the baggage. He was met by a negro teenager who took the baggage and delivered it to the appropriate rooms.
"Your home is beautiful. I like the style of architecture. I believe it Greek Revival? I love that the porches wrap all around. We appreciate your willingness to have us, sir," Mack thanked the Hartwells.

"You are correct. You've studied architecture?

"Some. I have many interests. I was taught that learning never ends; we should learn something new all the time."

"I concur. You were well taught. We were pleased to invite you. We enjoy our home. We like to entertain our friends and family as often as we can, but it isn't often that we find ourselves in the company of young people, except when our sweet Laura is visiting. Mrs. Hartwell and the staff put to-gether wonderful parties. Miss Rose will show you to your rooms and help you in any way you may need. After you have had an opportunity to rest for an hour or so, we will gather in the parlor. Dinner will be served at seven o'clock."

"Thank you, sir." Mack took Mary Beth's hand and followed Rose, the Hartwell's housekeeper, upstairs.

"Miss MacGregor, this is your room, Mrs. Hartwell calls this the York Room, named for the village the Hartwell family came from in England. I will be back in a few minutes to help you." Walking with Mack a few doors down the hall, Rose instructed him, "This is your room, Dr. Murray. This room is called the Lancaster Room. She likes to name all the rooms. I will bring some fresh water for your wash basin and a towel. If you need anything further, you can let me know. Nigel and I run da house for da Hartwells, so anythings you needs, lets us know."

"I will be just fine, Miss Rose. Thank you. The young lady, though, may need your assistance. This is her first trip away from home."

"Oh my, I see. Yessuh, I takes good care of her. Don't you worry." Rose left Mack at the door and returned to Mary Beth's room. "Miss, I goes gets water for da basin and towels. Do youse needs anythin' else now?"

"I am fine, Miss Rose. I think I am going to rest, but you may come in with water and towels. You don't need to bother knocking."

"Yessum. I will unpacks yo bag when I comes back."

"That would be nice. You are most kind. May I ask a question?"

"Yessum, of course."

"Tonight's dinner...Will there be anyone else besides MacKenzie, myself and the Hartwells?"

"Well, Miss, I believes Mr. Hartwell done invited his partner, Misser Robert Hastings and his wife, Missus Madeline, to dinner tonight."

"Well, may I ask for your help in deciding what to wear to dinner tonight. I do not wish to be underdressed or to look pretentious. You've seen the ladies here before for this type of thing. I am sure you will know which one will be best."

"Oh, yessum. I beeze back in just a few minutes."

Both Mac and Mary Beth laid down on the bed to rest. As soon as they closed their eyes, they were asleep. Miss Rose returned and filled the basins and left towels. She unpacked Mary Beth's bag and hung the dresses so the creases would fall out. She left them to sleep for an hour, then returned to wake them and help Mary Beth prepare for dinner. When she entered Mary Beth's room, Mary Beth was already sitting on the edge of the bed and staring at two gowns. "Miss Rose, I just don't know which one of these I should wear tonight." "Miss MacGregor, both dese gowns is beautiful," Mamie walked over to the gowns and looked closely at each. "These are very well made. Whoever done sewed these is tal-ented. You should be honored to wear either of them." She stood looking at the gowns and at the young lady trying to decide which one would look best. "Ma'am, if youse was my girl, dissun da one. It will be beautiful with your complexion and the color of your eyes."

Mary Elizabeth stood and walked over to look for herself. The gown was a deep green taffeta. It had puff sleeves and an empire waistline. Once she put the dress on and stood in front of the mirror, she understood why Rose selected it. Her green eyes became brighter in the deep green gown and her skin was like milk next to her raven curls. She put on a simple gold locket necklace her mother had given her for her thirteenth birthday. Mack gave her a drawing of her parents to put inside the locket. Despite her presentation, she was visibly nervous.

When they were both ready, Rose left them to make their entrance into the parlor. As they walked down the stairs, Mary Beth squeezed MacKenzie's hand tightly. "I don't know about this Mack. I'm so nervous."

Mack stopped on the stairs and turned to look his cousin in the face. "Mary Elizabeth MacGregor, you are ready for this. You have been preparing for this your entire life, and you are gorgeous tonight. They will be enamored by your charm, wit, and most of all, your intelligence. I know I tease you, but I know how wonderful you are. They all will know it soon too."

"Aren't you worried, Mack? I mean, what if they don't like us. Will they throw us out? Forbid you to see Laura? Doesn't that frighten you?"

"I cannot worry about those 'what ifs', Mary Beth. All I can do is be myself. If they don't like me or appreciate me, then maybe this isn't meant to be. I must trust them and myself."

Taking a deep breath, stretching her neck and pulling her shoulders back, she whispered to him, "Okay, I am ready now, MacKenzie." Smiling to himself, Mack squeezed her hand and stepped off the stairs towards the parlor. They could hear voices and music. It sounded as if there were fifty people in the room. When they entered the room, everyone stood up, and Mr. Hartwell walked over to Mary Beth and took her arm from MacKenzie.

"Friends, I would like to introduce you to our new friends from Washington County. This beautiful young lady is Miss Mary Elizabeth MacGregor. The gentleman next to me is her cousin, Doctor Alexander MacKenzie Murray. He is a practicing physician in Nashville with our friend, Dr. Felix Robertson. We are thrilled to have them visiting with us this evening on their journey back to Nashville after visiting their family." Mary Beth took the lead from Laura to go over to where she was sitting and join the other ladies who were sitting by the fireplace. The gentlemen were seated at the other end of the room discussing the issues of the day. In a corner there was a small group of musicians who were softly playing music.

After about thirty minutes, Nigel entered the room, rang a bell, and announced that dinner was ready in the dining room. The group stood and walked into the dining room. Mary Beth and Mack were astonished by the ornate decoration of the room. The dining table was decorated with a large arrangement of flowers and each place was set with the most beautiful china and silver either of them had ever seen. While Ione Skye was a successful farm, the MacKenzies and MacGregors were frugal, modest people. They had some nice things in their home, but they chose to invest any extra money back into the farm rather than purchasing expensive furnishings and trinkets. The MacKenzie-MacGregor family had never been ones to entertain much because of the special nature of their family. They did not wish to put MacKenzie and his mother at risk for controversy. There was simply no comparison to the setting in which they were raised and that of the Hartwell Family.

Each person located their place at the table and stood, waiting for the ladies' chairs to be pulled out by one of the gentlemen. Mary Beth was seated next to Mrs. Hastings and Laura. Mack was seated next to Mr. Hartwell on his left, at the head of the table, and Mr. Hastings across from him. After offering thanks to God for the food before them and the successes which brought the participants together, the meal was served.

Even the food was far richer and more delicious than anything Mack and Mary Beth had ever eaten. With her first bite, Mary Beth was in love with what she was eating. She had to make a conscious effort not to inhale the food or to make any noise as she chewed; it was delicious. With each bite, she chewed slowly and then spoke with the women about her life and her family. Both Mrs. Hastings and Mrs. Hartwell appeared to be pleasantly surprised by her intelligence, thoughtful communication, and impeccable manners.

The gentlemen were inquisitive about the young suitor seated with them. "Doctor Murray, as I understand it, you were in Baltimore during this last war. Is that correct?"

"Yes, sir. Please, call me Mack. I attended medical school in Pennsylvania and after graduation, I went into practice with one of our instructors, Dr. Benjamin Rush for about six years. When we began to hear rumors of an impending war, I informed Dr. Rush that I wanted to serve our country. When the war began, I left the practice to go and serve as doctor to our soldiers and sailors, thanks to an appointment by President Madison."

"That is impressive. Dr. Rush is a fine man and, I imagine, an exquisite teacher of medicine. Did you always want to be a doctor, Mack?" Inquired Mr. Hartwell.

"Not as a boy, no, sir. I thought at one time that I would work on the farm with my uncle and father. It was after I lost both of my parents that I decided to become a doctor. My parents wanted me to either be a doctor or an attorney. Working on a farm, I helped birth, treat, and even assist in the deaths of our livestock. Being a doctor was much more prudent choice in my opinion than being an attorney. I wanted to help take care of people and, perhaps, find better ways of treating serious illnesses."

"A very honorable goal, I'd say. Wouldn't you agree, Robert?"

"I certainly would, Frank. As I also understand from Felix, he chose your application over thirty or forty other applicants. That speaks very well of your abilities. Do you plan to stay in Nashville?"

"I like Nashville very much. It is still a relatively new city in Tennessee so there is much we can do to serve that community. I am still becoming acquainted with the residents and with their needs. I enjoy my work with Doctor Robertson. He and I appear to be well matched. We are both motivated to learn more about our field and to serve our community in the best manner possible."

"I suppose you saw some serious injuries from the battle in Baltimore. That would have sent me running, I think," inquired Mr. Hastings.

"We have progressed in our abilities since the revolution and were able to save more of our soldiers and sailors through surgical procedures. I learned much during that time" responded Mack.

Mr. Hartwell, then, inquired as to his intentions on a more personal level. "I believe your cousin told me that your father and your uncle moved from Virginia to Washington County about 20-25 years ago and that they have created a successful plantation. I have been at many of the same meetings as your uncle on the issue of abolition. Are you of the same belief as he regarding our cause?"

"I certainly am, sir. The gentleman who brought my grandfather to America, Mr. Robert Fraser, against his better judgment, engaged in the purchase of slaves early on, but his intent was always to free those slaves as soon as he could. The slaves that my father owned at the time of his death were freed upon his death. It is not a particularly popular situation in our area these days, but no one in our family has ever felt a need to kowtow to popularity. My father and my uncle taught both of us that it takes more strength to stand up for our beliefs than it does to give in to what was popular. I think that is the spirit of the Scots Irish people. We are fiercely independent."

"I couldn't agree more. Would you consider moving further west? Westward expansion is happening swiftly and certainly doctors will be needed in those new territories. What will happen to Ione Skye after your aunt and uncle have passed?"

"Those are important questions, gentlemen. I am contemplating those issues which is why my cousin is traveling with me to Nashville. The most important situation before me currently is assisting in obtaining a suitable marriage for her. She and I will inherit the farm, of course. I hope that Ione Skye will still exist when our children and grandchildren are alive.

These are the issues that must be dealt with when finding an appropriate spouse for Mary Beth and myself. Our spouses will need to have input on how that inheritance is handled. I would not rule out moving westward if that is a situation my wife supports, but as of this conversation, I cannot see that happening. Taking a young lady far away from her family does not seem an especially kind way to treat one's in-laws."

"You are a thoughtful young man. I can appreciate your desires for your cousin, as well as yourself. You said that Miss MacGregor is your cousin. How are you related," inquired Mr. Hartwell.

"My father is her mother's brother."

"I believe your aunt's parents, Eleanor that is, were Duncan and Elizabeth MacKenzie, and you say, your father was Eleanor's brother. However, your last name is Murray. Why is that?"

Mack was taken aback by the question. For a second, he was afraid that he was about to be outed, so his answer must put their minds at ease. "My great-grandmother, Isobel Murray MacKenzie, died along with one of her sons and her husband before her two sons, Donald and Duncan, and her daughter, Eleanor came to America. Her children were indentured to the Robert Fraser for a period of ten years. My parents wanted to honor my grandmother because she had no brothers and her father, too, was an only child. Her father and her husband were both named Alexander. So, my parents named me Alexander MacKenzie Murray. They began calling me 'Mack' when I was about three years old."

"What an interesting story and quite an honor, I would say, to be named in this manner. A child's name is a vital part of their personality. Many people today are doing away with passing names down from their ancestors. I think that is unfortunate. I am sure you, sir, must feel honored to be so named." Mr. Hastings had a wonderful personality which Mack came to appreciate quickly. When the mood became a bit too serious, he would tell a joke to change the subject. He and Mr. Hartwell appeared to be well matched as business partners. Both highly intelligent men, but one more inclined to the social and the other inclined to business and decision making. This was, perhaps, why their textile mill was the success it was. They employed many of the people in the area. They provided their employees with housing, clothing, and food. The mill had a dining hall where employees were fed breakfast and dinner, and they had a small store where food and supplies could be purchased and deducted from their weekly pay. They provided uniforms and a laundry service.

They refused to employ children under the age of sixteen, believing that the children of their employees should be educated. There was a school on the premises. Children were taught to read, to do simple math; and, in the afternoon, they were taught skills which would help them in life. The boys were taught farming, animal care, blacksmithing, glass making, and other similar skills. The girls were taught childcare, sewing, cooking, and cleaning. It was a progressive approach for the time, which some in Knoxville disapproved of, but like Mack's family, the Hartwells and Hastings did not give weight to those opinions.

After the group completed their meal, the women returned to the parlor and the gentlemen gathered on the front porch.

"Mrs. Hartwell does not care for the smell of my cigars or that I smoke them at all. Robert, Mack, do you care to join me?"

"I will," answered Mr. Hastings. Mack, however, declined. The conversation then turned to the changing tide of slavery in the country. "I am reading more rumblings of war in Philadelphia, New York, and Boston newspapers. Some are saying that states in the South may secede from the Union if the North demands an end of slavery. If that happens, we may very well find ourselves in a war. It will not be a comfortable situation for us if that should occur in Tennessee. Washington County and our own county are more strongly associated with abolition than other parts of the state. If war were to take place, we could find ourselves in direct opposition to our fellow Tennesseans. Frank, I enjoy our conversations here on your porch," Robert commented as he continued to smoke his cigar and sip his whiskey as he rocked in his chair.

"Bob, I have heard these conversations as well. It will be difficult to find ourselves at odds with our neighbors, but I will not change my position on the matter. It is a matter of faith. However, we have a business that profits from the cotton grown in the South. We find ourselves in a difficult situation. Some might call us hypocrites. I am nearing an age at which I may consider retirement. It is a consideration that we, Bob and I, will have to discuss. Neither of us have sons, but we have sons-in-law and grandsons; I wince at the idea of any of these young men on a battlefield. I am sure you can relate to this, Mack. You cared for our boys so well during this last conflict." Mr. Hartwell was rightly concerned about the rumors of war. He could lose his business regardless of which side of the matter he was on. Men like Frank and Robert wanted to build businesses that would be passed on to their descendants. They wanted their families to build upon their legacy and to enjoy the kind of lives they were enjoying. War could destroy those goals.

"I have not heard anything directly about an impending war. I certainly do not want to have to participate in wars or to have to care for troops again in my lifetime. Dr. Robertson and I have had some conversations, but I am not in contact with anyone who would make such decisions in our State. I spend much of my time riding to see patients in the rural areas around Nashville. Dr. Robertson prefers to stay in the office in town to see patients who can come there. He has contacts in the state legislature and may know more than I. I would not be surprised if he didn't become involved directly in politics. He seems to enjoy that type of activity. I think he would be rather good at that endeavor. He cares for the community." Mack stood up from his rocking chair to stretch his legs.

"I am curious. Have you been called to care for the needs of slaves in the area you serve? Is it ever a difficult circumstance to provide them with medical care." Robert asked as he put his cigar out.

"Sir, I do not know that the situation there is much different than here. Of course, there are those owners who would never think to offer care. They will simply allow them to die and then replace them. That in my mind is an unwise decision both from a business perspective and from a moral one, but it isn't their business mind that is making that sort of decision. Many of these folks have no care for anyone else outside their own family much less those they purportedly own. There are oth-ers, like us here, who believe that providing care, appropriate housing, clothing, and education is a more Christian manner to handle the situation. As for your question, Mr. Hastings, I see those when it becomes necessary and if I am allowed. I would never deny care to anyone."

Mr. Hartwell's tone and demeanor led Mack to believe he had Mr. Hartwell's favor. "I commend you, young man, for your adherence to your beliefs. I look forward to getting to know you and your family more soon. Laura would be a fortunate young lady to be in your company. I intend to share this opinion with my daughter and son-in-law soon." Mr. Hartwell patted the Mack on the back and gave him a big smile.

"I appreciate that, sir. I am truly the fortunate one." Mack smiled and they all chuckled. "Would it be permissible, sir, for me to speak with Laura before we disband for the evening?"

The gentlemen looked at each other and responded, "Of course, my boy! I recall when I met my future father-in-law for the first time that I was terrified. You have been a good sport tonight, Doctor Mack. Hope we didn't cause you too much stress."

"It has been my honor, sirs. Now, if you please will excuse me, I would like to go to Laura."

"Yes, by all means," Frank and Robert cheered.

Mack went back inside the house and stopped at the doorway of the parlor. He attempted to catch Laura's eye so that he could motion for her to come. It was just a few seconds before she would look in his direction. She asked her mother's for permission to be excused. Upon receiving her approval, Laura stood and walked in Mack's direction. As the pair walked to the back porch of the house, they could still hear the music being played through the open windows. Though it was early summer, the air was still cool and dry, and the scent of jasmine and honeysuckle wafted around them. "This place is beautiful, Laura. I see why you love it here. I have not seen fireflies in so long. Mary Beth and I loved to chase them around the lawn when we were young."

"My sisters and brothers did that too. My youngest brother, Howard, tried to catch them and put them in paper bags. He thought he could make a lantern. Silly, isn't it?"

"The charms of childhood, my dear, are never silly; they are endearing. Would you give me the honor of a dance before the music ends?" Mack reached his hand out.

Smiling Laura turned, curtsied and replied, "Why I would be honored, sir." Mack took Laura into his arms, and they began to dance. Little did they know that there was an audience watching from the windows of the kitchen. For a few moments, the group stood watching the special moment before they decided to retire for the evening. Before leaving herself, Mrs. Hartwell spoke softly through the door of the kitchen, "Laura, just ten more minutes. You need to get your rest for your trip home tomorrow."

"Yes, Grandmother."

"You are traveling with us tomorrow, Laura? I had no idea."

"I wanted to surprise you. My parents are ready for me to return home. My grandparents thought it would be safer if I traveled in yours and Mary Beth's company than alone."

"Of course, I will take good care of you both. I suppose it is time for us to retire. We wouldn't want to oversleep and miss our coach. Would it be okay if I…." Mack desperately wanted to kiss Laura, but before he could finish his sentence, Laura stood on her tiptoes and kissed him on the cheek.

"Good night, Doctor MacKenzie Murray. We shall have plenty of time for such things very soon." With a breath she was gone and up the stairs before Mack realized what had just happened. His brain felt as though it had been picked up by a tornado and spun around like a drunk after days of drinking—dizzy and queasy. After somewhat regaining his composure, he realized he was alone, and he walked back into the house going through the kitchen where Rose and Nigel were washing the evening's dishes. Mack walked like a zombie through the kitchen and up the stairs not acknowledging their presence.

"I thinks dat boy done fell in love wit our Miss Laura, Rose," remarked Nigel.

"Youse so right. He don't even know where he be." Rose and Nigel shook their heads in agreement and laughed. Rose removed her apron while Nigel put the last few pots and pans away on the rack. "We need to gets our younguns in bed." Just then they heard the laughter of their children on the back porch and the sound of little feet scrambling away so as not to get caught.

Chapter 25

The sun came up bright the next morning. It broke through the sheer curtains hanging in the front bedrooms, forcing the occupants from their slumber. Mary Beth and Mack were accustomed to waking early to do their chores on the farm before breakfast. This morning was no different, just no chores to be done. They dressed quickly, made their beds, and gathered their belongings. Rushing down the stairs they met Rose halfway down the stairs.

"Good morning! I was coming up to wake you," she explained.

"Good morning to you too, Miss Rose. It's a beautiful day, isn't it? We have everything ready. We made the beds and took care of the wash basins. We have the dirty towels here for you."

"My goodness! You is so kind. Let me have those. Breakfast will be ready in ten minutes. Do you want coffee?"

Both Mary Beth and Mack asked for coffee with milk and one sugar. They finished walking down the stairs to the parlor to see who else was awake. Upon reaching the parlor, they discovered Laura and both of her grandparents waiting. Mrs. Hartwell was quick to greet them. "Good morning! I trust you both slept well. What a pretty dress, Mary Beth. Did you sew it?"

Mary Beth, shaking her head, announced, "No ma'am. I am still working on my sewing skills. My mother and our housekeeper, Mame, sewed this one. The bed was pure luxury, ma'am. I feel completely spoiled."

Mack continued, "For me as well. I barely recall getting in the bed."

"I don't doubt that! Rose will have breakfast ready in a few minutes. We can go into the dining room now. Nigel has gathered all your bags and put them in the carriage. We will head on over to the station after we finish eating." Mrs. Hartwell walked towards Mack and Mary Beth. With her arm outstretched to lead them into the dining room, "Rose makes a wonderful breakfast. Her biscuits melt in your mouth. I enjoyed having you both. I look forward to seeing you again when we visit Nashville in a few weeks."

"We enjoyed being here as well. You have both been kind and generous. Thank you again for the invitation. May I," Mack asked as he turned to give Mrs. Hartwell a hug. She responded with a hug. Mary Beth followed his lead and walked over to give her a hug as well.

Leaning slightly back as she hugged Mary Beth, Mrs. Hartwell commented, "My dear, I hope you find a young man worthy of your company. You are an intelligent, charming, and beautiful woman. You will be the hit of the social scene in Nashville. You are fortunate to have a gentleman like MacKenzie to assist you. I have every confidence that you will find that special someone very soon."

"You are most kind. I will look forward to seeing you again as well. I had a nice time." As Mack pulled out a chair for his cousin, Mary Beth leaned over in Mrs. Hartwell's direction and whispered, "Do we have a match between those two, you think?"

Smiling with a twinkle in her eye, Mrs. Hartwell whispered into her ear, "I think so. Mr. Hartwell plans to speak with her parents. We approve." The ladies smiled at each other and everyone proceeded to eat their breakfast.

The day quickly progressed from there. Breakfast was completed and the parties left for the coach station. After saying their goodbyes, they each climbed aboard and settled in for the long ride back to Nashville.

Chapter 26

Once the coach arrived in Nashville, the occupants of the coach were both happy and sad. They were happy to be home, but sad that they would have to say goodbye and go their separate ways. They managed to get through their goodbyes but made plans to meet soon. Laura was met by her parents' butler, Barnabas. She appeared disappointed that her parents had not come to the station to pick her up, but it was a situation to which she was accustomed. She waved to Mack and Mary Beth as she rode away.

Mary Beth turned to her cousin, "Well, what do we do now? Will someone be picking us up?"

"Sorry dear, we are not the Hartwell-Todds. We have to walk, but it isn't far." Mack picked up their bags and they began their walk to his little apartment.

"Mack, you have been gone for a few weeks. What will we do for food tonight?"

"Yes, you are correct. I do not like to eat at the tavern because sometimes the food can be bland, but for tonight I think that is what we will do. We will take care of our meal preparation tomorrow. We must be frugal, Mary Beth. I know you have never been in a situation where you had to think about money. I do okay but sometimes my patients cannot pay me in cash, so they pay me with livestock, vegetables, desserts, and other ways. I must make my funds stretch. How is your cooking, by the way?"

"What do you do with the livestock, Mack? As for my cooking, I worked with Addie and Mame in the kitchen since you left to go to medical school. Daddy said that my food was good. Momma never complained either. I think if it wasn't, she would be the first one to tell me, don't you?"
"Sometimes I have the butcher prepare the animal for me; sometimes I sell them to the butcher. You are right about Aunt Ellie; She would tell you if something was terrible. We do not know what your situation will be when we can find the right person for you. You may not have a staff right away, so being a good cook and housekeeper will be important. We would not want you to poison your husband unintentionally!" Mack burst into laughter.

"You are ridiculous, MacKenzie Murray! So, what will I do while you are at work?"

"We will have to buy you some books to read. I don't think you'll enjoy reading my medical books and the novels I have you have already read. Also for the time being, I do not think it would be a good idea for you to leave the house during the day until I can introduce you to people I know around town, and until I can provide some safety for you. The problem with living in a city like Nashville is that crime can be a problem. I need to keep you safe."

"I am not a child, MacKenzie," Mary Beth responded with disgust.

"I know that, but criminals can overpower me, Mary Beth. Many folks carry guns. You have never witnessed a crime before. It can be quite unsettling. I am planning to discuss the matter with Dr. Robertson tomorrow. At least you know how to shoot and I do have a shotgun if you need it."

"At least! Are we almost there? My feet are beginning to hurt." This was the first time since they left Ione Skye that Mary Beth complained.

"Here we are. I warn you that it is simple." Mack walked her up to the door of his apartment. Opening the door, it was so dark not much could be seen. "Wait here. I need to find a lamp. I don't want you to trip." Mack made his way inside the apartment towards the small kitchen area to light a lamp. "I'm sorry. It smells a bit musty here. No one has been in here since I left, I guess."

Upon lighting the room, Mary Beth stepped inside the small apartment. "Well, it is quaint, isn't it? Where shall I sleep, Mack? I see only a single bed here, and not much privacy for a lady."

"You will take the bed. I will make a plat on the floor. I need to go get some firewood. There is a bureau by the wall; you can put your things inside it. My clothes are in the other one. I will be back in a few minutes. Stay here, please." Mack went outside to the wood pile to gather wood to start a fire. While the days were warm, the nights were still cool.

When Mack re-entered the room, Mary Beth was sweeping the floor. "It is quite dusty in here. I will clean everything tomorrow. You are low on soap. We will need to replenish your supplies. Perhaps we should make a list of what we need from the store. Do you have a slate or paper and a pencil, Mack?" She stood looking around the room.

"That is a fabulous idea, Mary Beth. I will go next door to the office and get us what we need."

"I can make this work. It will be just fine. It is a sweet, little place. I like it. Now, let's start that list." Mack was encouraged by her optimism. He feared she would not be pleased by his accommodation and would complain. Perhaps she had matured more than he realized and was not as spoiled as he believed.

"If you are finished with that list, we can walk on over to the tavern to get some supper."

"That sounds perfect, Mack. I am famished!" Taking his arm, the pair left their temporary abode and walked around to the front of the building which faced Main Street. As they walked towards the Old Stone Tavern, people glanced towards them whispering to each other. They could feel them staring. "Is there something wrong with us? Why are people staring and whispering, Mack?"

"I am not sure. Maybe it is because they have never seen a more beautiful woman? And they've not seen me in the presence of a woman. I think they are curious."

"Maybe, but it is still rude to stare. I don't guess we look much alike, do we? I know we are cousins, but all we have in common is our dark hair. Your eyes are brighter than mine. Your skin is darker, but not too dark. I remember hearing Momma talk about our grandfather once. She said he had dark hair and light eyes. Guess that's where we get it. Has anyone ever commented on your features?"

"Once at medical school, someone asked me if I was Italian. That was amusing, but Mary Beth, please keep these kinds of comments to yourself. No one here knows about me, and it must stay that way. Do you understand?" There was a hint of panic in Mack's voice as he scolded her.

"Of course not, MacKenzie! I would never hurt you that way. You know that!"

"Of course, I do. I worry about it sometimes. There were rumors back home, you know? I cannot afford for those rumors to follow me here."

"I heard whispers a few times in Jonesborough. Talk about rude! It isn't anyone's business except yours. I thought the explanation you gave to Laura's father about your last name was brilliant," Mary Beth complimented her cousin.

"I had no idea that you heard that."

"I did. While you men folk were talking outside, I got a bit hot from sitting close to the fire, so I walked over to an open window to cool down. I heard your conversation."

"I do not know where that answer came from really. The words just came, and it seemed to satisfy their curiosity. I got lucky; I guess."

"Oh, don't be so modest, MacKenzie. You are a genius."

"I am not any smarter than you; I just have more oppor-tunities as a man." The pair entered the tavern and sat at a table next to a window. While they ate, Mary Beth glanced outside. She witnessed a man approach another on the street and strike him in the head. The man fell to the ground.

"Mack, look! That man hit that other man. He's on the ground. He's hurt. We need to do something. Come on!"

"No, Mary Beth, you stay here. I will go and help him. Do not leave this table. I mean it." Mack jumped up from the table and rushed outside. Kneeling beside the injured man, he saw blood running out of the side of his head. "Sir, can you hear me?" There was no response. He felt his throat for a pulse. People began to gather in the street. Mack looked around for the sheriff. In a few moments, the Nashville Sheriff Caleb Hewett appeared.

"Hello, Doctor MacKenzie. What happened here?"

"Hi, Caleb. I think that man over there being held by those other men attempted to rob him. When he resisted, he struck him with something. He hit him hard enough to crack his skull. He is dead."

"Well, hell, that's just the kind of day it has been. This is the third one today."

"You need help, sir. Crime seems to be increasing as more people move to Nashville."

"Don't I know it." Looking around the Sheriff Hewett shouted, "Does anyone know who is man is? I need his name and where he lives. Right now, people!" There was silence for a few minutes. Thinking that he was not going to get a response, the Sheriff began to walk away when a boy appeared by the side of the building.

"Sheriff…Sheriff, I know who he is." The Sheriff looked to see where the voice was coming from. Then he saw a boy about eleven years old.

"You do? Who is he, son? You don't have to be scared." Sheriff Hewett bent down to make the boy feel more comfortable.

"He's my father. His name is Josef Weiss, sir." The boy began to cry.

"I'm terribly sorry, son. What was done to your father was wrong. Where do you live? I will take you home."

"It is just me and my Papa. We came here a few weeks ago from Pennsylvania. My Papa is…was a peddler. My Momma and my baby brother, Ismael, died on our way here. I have nowhere to go." The boy began to sob.

Patting the boy, the Sheriff told him, "It's going to be okay; you will come home with me tonight and we will decide what to do tomorrow. I just need to let the doctor know what to do with your father's body."

"We must bury him tomorrow. We are Jewish, sir. That is our way. Please don't send me away, sir. I promise I will be a good boy." The Sheriff rubbed the top of his head and told him again not to worry. The group walked to the doctor's office. Stopping out front of the office, Mack realized that he hadn't been at the front door of the building since he returned. Looking toward the door, he noticed something different. Next to the door was a placard that read, "Robertson and Murray, Doctors of Medicine".

"Well look at that Dr. Murray. That's new. Did you know Doc Robertson was doing that?"

"I sure did not, Caleb. I have no words." Mack was shocked at Felix's gift to him.

Then, the Sheriff instructed Mack to place the body in a wooden box which he could find at Matthew's. Matthew made caskets for people, and he had an extra one on hand. He also told Mack that he knew of another Jewish family in town and that he would let them know what happened so that they could attend to the body according to their tradition. Mack agreed to help; he felt terribly for the young man.

"Where will the body stay tonight, Mack?" inquired Mary Beth, worrying he might take the body into their home.

"I will put him in the office for tonight. He will be buried tomorrow. You aren't scared, are you?"

"No! Just not something I am accustomed to, that's all. Jeremiah and Killian always took care of these things at home. I understand now why you said I need to stay inside. I promise I will."

"That's good. I cannot worry about you while I am working."

The next morning both Mack and Mary Beth were up early. After eating some biscuits, Mack opened the doctor's office to look over the schedule for the day. He moved the box to the back side of the room behind a curtain where the medication cabinet was kept so that patients would not see it when they entered.

About twenty minutes later the front door opened and Dr. Robertson walked inside with Greta following close behind. "Good morning, MacKenzie! Welcome back! We have missed you." Greta was smiling at Mack as she handed him a cake she baked for him.

"Good morning. It is good to be back. You didn't tell me about that sign out front. I just saw it last night. Does this mean that you want me to stay? And, thank you, Greta, for this amazing cake."

"It does. I don't see any reason to continue the trial period; I have seen enough. Also, I appreciated your letter informing me of the aunt's condition. I trust she is recovered?" Walking over to the coat rack, Felix continued, "Oh, I hope you want to stay."

"Absolutely, I do. My aunt is better, but she has some lingering problems with her lungs."

"Really? That is a concern. Perhaps the virus has a destructive quality to the lung tissue, or maybe it was not influenza. It might be wise to do some autopsies of any deaths we may encounter from the virus to study the effects on the lungs."

"Yes, that could be informative. I would like to introduce you to someone, if I may."

"Oh, well, of course," interjected Greta.

Mack walked over to the door that connected the office with his apartment. He opened the door and instructed Mary Beth to come. Mary Beth walked inside the doctor's office. Seeing Doctor Robertson, she smiled and waited for Mack to introduce her. "This, Dr. Robertson, Greta, is my cousin, Miss Mary Elizabeth MacGregor. She will be staying with me for a while."

"Nice to meet you, my dear. Your cousin has told me about you. You look exactly as he described you," replied Greta as she walked over to give her new friend a hug.

"Oh, my goodness! What a nice welcome. It is a pleasure to make your acquaintance. MacKenzie has told me much about you both, too. I won't hold you up. I know you have work to do. Mack, will you be back for lunch? Please don't forget that we need to do the shopping today."

"Unless I have to go out to see a patient, I will meet you in the apartment for lunch, and don't worry, we will shop today."

"It was nice to meet you, Doctor Robertson…Miss Abernathy."

As she walked back towards the apartment, Greta called out, "You may call me Greta, honey."

"You didn't tell me that you'd be bringing her back with you. I am not sure you and she should stay in the apartment; it is quite small. We may need to look for other arrangements."

"I only decided to suggest she return with me after caring for my aunt. Mary Beth is the same age as I. I was afraid that she may miss out on marriage if I did not take the responsibility on myself. My aunt and uncle should have found a husband for her, but I suspect they avoided it because they did not want her to leave the farm and them. Her opportunities in Washington County are not preferable. I thought bringing her here would be wise."

"I think you are correct, Mack. I just think that a woman of her age and her status should reside in a more appropriate abode. This apartment is fine for a bachelor, but not a lady. I will discuss the matter with Lydia this evening. I am sure that she will have some ideas. Right now, we need to get this body out of our office and then we need to figure out our day. Did the Sheriff have an idea of when the gentleman might come to take care of Mr. Weiss? I think I will take the outside calls today so that you can do what you need to with Mary Beth this afternoon."

"No, he didn't. He had not informed him yet when he and I last spoke last evening. I would think that he or they would be here soon. Their faith requires the body to be interred within twenty-four hours of death, and the body still needs to be prepared. I appreciate the accommodation today."

Thirty minutes later the Jewish gentlemen appeared at the office. They went straight to their work, and they were gone in an hour. That afternoon Mack and Mary Beth shopped for supplies. When they returned home, they were surprised to find a hot meal waiting for them and a note on the table. "This is so kind, Mack. Do you think Dr. Robertson or Miss Abernathy did this for us?"

"I suppose either is possible. Open the note and let's find out."

Opening the envelope, Mary Beth unfolded the note and began to read, "'Welcome to Nashville, Miss MacGregor. Some of our patients stopped in with this meal to welcome you.' Did you hear that, Mack? Everyone here is so kind." Mary Beth opened the lid on the pot hanging in the fireplace. "Oh Mack, it's a roast! There are potatoes and carrots. [Walking back to the table, she opened the covered plate.] It's an apple pie! Your friends are just amazing, MacKenzie! I think I am going to like it here after all. I was not sure at first. I wish we had traveled some when we were younger and I had more experience meeting new people."

"See, I told you that you would like it here. I think you are more sophisticated than you realize, but I can certainly relate to reservations meeting new people. It took me sometime to loosen up at medical school, but once I did, I made many friends. You know things of the world through all the books you have read." Mack sat in his chair next to the fireplace and read the newspaper. This became their custom as the weeks passed.

Doctor Robinson, after speaking with his wife, told Mack that he would assist him in acquiring land on which to build a home. He would help him through the entire process. His wife would assist Mary Beth with furnishings for the home and with finding a proper suitor. After the home was finished, Mack would make payments to Dr. Robinson to repay him for his expenses at a low-interest rate. In the meantime, Lydia and her children were preparing a place for them to live. The property was large, and they were moving people around so that they could create a guest house in one of their outbuildings.

It took the Robertsons about a week to get the guest house ready for Mack and Mary Beth. When the cousins were shown the little cottage, they were thrilled and thankful. They felt like they were on top of each other in the little apartment. There were two bedrooms, a living space with a fireplace, and a kitchen with a stove, table, and chairs. Lydia and her daughters decorated each bedroom in a manner that they thought each would appreciate. Mary Beth's room was decorated much like Lydia's room in the big house. MacKenzie's room was decorated in a similar fashion to Felix's study. The living area had two comfortable chairs and a settee. There was a beautiful rug on the floor, and a bookcase filled with many books. Mary Beth was thrilled with all of it, but especially the books.

The two families became extremely fond of one another. Mary Beth enjoyed getting to know the Robertson's daughters, Elizabeth, whom Mary Beth liked to call "Lizzie", and Elnora. One particular Sunday, Dr. Robertson announced that he and his wife, Lydia, were preparing for a large party at their home. The who's who of Nashville would be invited to the soirée. "Lydia and I hoped that we might use this occasion to introduce Miss MacGregor to Nashville society," announced Felix.

Mack was thrilled; Mary Beth was terrified. "Thank you, sir. I, my aunt and uncle, and Mary Beth appreciate all you have done for us both. We can never repay your kindness."

"You are welcome. I have written to your parents, Mary Beth, and have invited them to attend as well. They are planning to be here. Additionally, MacKenzie, we have invited Miss Hartwell-Todd and her family to attend. They sent a note to me of their intent to be in attendance as well. I hope that you and Miss Hartwell-Todd might also announce your engagement?" Lydia grinned at Mack eagerly anticipating his response.

"I am working in that direction. I just have a few more details to work out."

"Certainly. We have a few weeks to work out these details. I know that it will be the event of the year."

After dinner Mary Beth and Lydia retired to the parlor. They sat next to the fire to talk about the upcoming event. They looked over the latest magazines showing the newest fashions while Elizabeth played the piano nearby. Elnora sat on the other side of the room working on a needlepoint project.

"I am sure Momma will help you with your gown, Mary Beth. You are so pretty. You'd looking just darling in any of those gowns. That one (pointing to a page in the magazine) would make me look like a hippo!" exclaimed Elizabeth.

"Oh, Lizzie! You can be so extreme. I wish I had your natural curls. I must sleep with rags in my hair for days to get mine to look like your curls, and then they fall out after an hour," responded Elnora.

"So, who do you expect to be at this party? I mean, who might…." Pondered Mary Beth out loud.

"Well, let's see. I suppose Stewart Donelson and his family. He has so many children. I think nine of them are boys! Then there are the Buchanans who also have many children, except six are girls! That's 17 right there!!" exclaimed Elizabeth. The women burst into laughter.

Mary Beth and Lydia would meet several times over the next few weeks to prepare for the event. Lydia's housekeeper, Naomi, gathered the cloth needed for the gowns. They purchased shoes, petticoats, gloves, hats and ribbons. "I don't know how I can ever repay your kindness, Mrs. Robertson. There must be something that I can do for you," Mary Beth sincerely responded to her new friend.

"My name is Lydia, dear, and it is no bother. I have corresponded with your family. They have provided funds for your gown and accessories. I enjoy having you here, Mary Beth. I enjoy our discussions. I love my children, but I do enjoy adult conversations sometimes. It is our pleasure to assist you and MacKenzie. We consider you part of our family, but there is something you could do for me the night of the soiree," Lydia said rather sheepishly to Mary Beth.

"Terrific, what can I do to help?"

"Mack told us that you have a beautiful singing voice and that there is a song that is especially meaningful to you and him. I was wondering if you could sing it for our guests." Lydia was now looking at Mary Beth with a pleading look.

"Yes, ma'am. I would be honored, but don't you want to hear me sing first? What if he exaggerated my skills? What if I sound like a toad?"

"Okay, then, sing it to us now. I have no doubt your cousin does not lie."

So, Mary Beth stood in front of Lydia, Elizabeth, and Elnora, and began to sing a cappella. When she finished, the three ladies were tearing up. "Oh, Mary Beth, you are no toad, honey. I have not heard that song in a long while. My family came to America from Ireland, like yours. We sang this song too. You are so precious."

"Thank you." Mary Beth curtsied to her friends. "I'm looking forward to seeing my parents. It has been several months since I came here. That song will be a nice tribute to them and to our family. We sing it all the time. Ugh, I miss them so."

"I know they miss you too, but they know you need to be here now," assured Lydia.

"I know you are correct, but the anticipation can be dreadful sometimes," complained Mary Elizabeth.

"That is the scourge of all young ladies; we must do these things to secure our futures, which are dependent on our husband's success. Perhaps it may not always be so, but it is right now."

"When do you expect my parents? I expected them to correspond with Mack or me, but we have not received any correspondence. Honestly, I am concerned."

"I will ask Felix, dear. I would expect them, though, to be here a few days prior. You shouldn't worry." Lydia went to find her husband. Thinking about it, she didn't think they had received any correspondence recently from Thomas or Eleanor. She found Felix in his study reading. "Felix, dear, Mary Beth inquired about when her parents would be arriving. Have you heard from them?"

"Well, now, let me look." He searched over his desk for their correspondence. Putting his hands on them, he opened the one on top to look at the date. "Hmm…this one is older than I remembered. It is dated almost a month ago. Thomas indicated that they planned to be here two weeks before so that they could help Mack with the house and have time to visit with both children."

"What should we do, Felix? The soirée is next week." Lydia and Felix were quite concerned.

"Go and get Albert for me. I will send him to find them, but he must get going. Do not say anything to Mack or Mary Beth yet. I do not want them to panic."

Lydia left to find their man Albert who oversaw the home and property. Five minutes later, Albert appeared at the study. "Albert, I need you to pack up and get on the road towards Washington County. Doctor Murray's family should have already been here; we have not heard from them in some time. If you find them well, please escort them back here safely. On the other hand, if you should discover otherwise, you must get back here as quickly as you can. Now that I think about it, it would be wise for you to take at least one or two other men with you. You know what needs to be done."

"Yessuh, I dooze as yo ask, suh."

"Touch base with me before you leave so that I may gauge when you might return. This is between us, Albert. Not a word to Dr. Murray or Miss Mary Beth." Albert left to do as he had been instructed. He, along with two other men, were packed and ready to leave in two hours. He met once again with Doctor Robertson and then the group got on the trail towards Ione Skye.

The men rode for four and half hours before stopping to eat and sleep. They built a fire and cooked a rabbit with some beans over the fire. "Albert, whats dis all 'bout wit Dr. Murray's kinfolks?" Shane, a negro man about twenty-three years old, asked Albert.

"Unfortunately, Shane, I think I do. I think you two do as well." They all shook their heads in agreement and in unison they spoke, "Robbers!"

"We best be getting some sleep. We needs to get started early," advised Angus. They stored their food and wares away and then laid down to sleep.

The men arose with the sun. They mounted their horses and began the next leg of their journey. They snacked on jerky and water as they rode. They had been riding for just a bit over an hour when Albert suddenly stopped.

"What's the matter?" Shane whispered to Albert.

"I don't think we are alone." Albert got down off his horse, handing the reigns to Shane. He walked a few feet when he noticed what looked to be remnants of an extinguished fire and eating utensils strewn about. The further he walked the more he discovered. "Hey! Over here!" Albert yelled towards his men. Shane and Angus rushed over to where Albert was standing.

"Dis ain't good." Shane slowly walked toward a tree on the other side of where Albert and Angus were standing. "Albert, there's a burnt-out wagon over here." As Shane continued to walked around some scrub brush, he made a horrific discovery. "Angus! Albert! I needs youse over here! Now!"

Behind the scrub brush lay a man being cradled by a woman who was, herself, clinging to life. Albert walked over towards her; but as he neared, she began to squeal. "Ma'am, ma'am…I is Albert and dis here is Shane and dat there is Angus. We works for Doc Robertson, ma'am. He done sent us. You Eleanor MacGregor, ma'am? Dis your husband, Thomas?"

Being so weak all she could do was to shake her head in acknowledgment that she was Eleanor MacGregor. After she understood that the men were there to help, she let go of her husband's body and collapsed to the ground. Albert knelt beside her. "Ma'am, who done did dis?" Albert slowly took Thomas' body away from her, being as gentle as he could. He was not certain if Thomas was dead.

Eleanor began to weep. "Men…."

"Ma'am, we need ta gets youse up and gets some food and water. Will youse lets us help yo?"

"Yes," responded Ellie.

Walking over to Shane and Angus, Albert gave them the news, "Misser Thomas be dead. She mights beeze close too."

"What do you want us to do now, Albert?" They all knew how delicate the situation was. He sent Shane and Angus to gather wood for a fire and to a nearby stream to fill a canteen with fresh water. When they returned, Albert had wrapped Eleanor in a blanket and given her some jerky to eat. "Ma'am, dat jerky gonna youse gets yo strengf back. Youse needs ta drinks this here water, too."

They all sat together for a while to see if she could regain some energy. As tears ran down her cheeks, Eleanor looked at each of them and in a faint voice said, "Thank you."

Albert responded with a warm smile, "Yessum. We likes yo boy Mack and your gal Mary Elizabeth. Dey some goods peoples. You done raised dem kids good, ma'am. Dey is both kind and generous." Eleanor smiled back. "Ma'am, we are going to go talk over here for a minute. Do not worry. We can see you. You are safe."

Albert motioned to Shane and Angus to step over to a nearby tree. "Shane, I needs yo ta rides back and lets Doc Robertson know. Dis ain't good. Weeze stays here til we knowd she can rides back. Weeze gonna have ta tell her dat weeze gotta bury Misser Thomas here. Weeze marks it soes dat after dat party done over, weeze comes back and tote dem back to dey home in Washington County." Shane and Angus agreed.

Albert and Angus went back to sit with Eleanor. "You lookin' better ma'am. Did dem men hurts you, ma'am?"

"My head was hurting, but it feel a bit better now. Where did your friend go?"

"Ma'am, Shane done gone to tells Doc Robertson. When youse feels like it, we rides back. Ma'am, weeze gonna have ta bury Misser Thomas here for now. It beeze over a day's ride back ta Nashville. We will mark dis here place soes we can fines it again."

"I understand. You are kind to help me," she whispered trying to hold back her tears.

"We gots ta gets youse back on yo feet. Ma'am, how long dem men been gone youse think?"

Eleanor took a few moments to gather her thoughts. "Thomas thought that we were being followed. He thought it was Indians, but when we came around a turn in the road, four men came riding at us. We could see that they had guns. Thomas tried to grab his shotgun, but he was not fast enough. They shot him. I guess they thought we had something valuable to steal. They took our bags and threw everything out looking for money and valuables. When they didn't find what they wanted, they turned the wagon over and set it on fire. They struck me several times until I passed out. When I awoke, they were gone, and my husband was dead. They took our horses."

"Weeze so sorry, ma'am. We done been hearin' stories like dis 'bout robbers hidin' out on dese trails looking for people to rob. Weeze gonna stays here tonight and goes back in da mornin'."

Eleanor continued to nibble on the jerky and sip water. As evening was quickly arriving, Angus went to gather more wood for the fire and refill the canteens. As he was bending over to dip the canteen in the stream, he felt like someone was watching him. Slowly, he stood back up and looked around. A shadow caught his eye. From behind some bushes appeared a single older Indian man. Angus was not certain if he was safe until the man raised his hand and spoke.

"I am not here to hurt you," he said to Angus.

"Okay, why are you here?" Angus asked.

"I have been here watching over the white woman. I was not far away when I heard those white men riding off and I saw the smoke. I went to see what they had done. I saw her holding her husband. I did not wish to scare her anymore, so I stayed close by in case those men returned. They did not."

"Thank you. She beeze da family of some friends of da man weeze works for. He sent us to fines dem; they suppose ta beeze in Nashville."

"I can help you bury him."

"Oh yes, weeze needs help, suh. We ain't got nuttin' ta dig with," Angus said.

"I go get what is needed and come back."

"Sure, okay. What's yo name?"

"I am Running Bear of the Chickamauga Cherokee."

"Wait! Running Bear?"

"Yes, you have heard of me?" Running Bear asked turning around from the direction he was walking.

"We sho have, suh! Dat friend is Doc Murray; uh, MacKenzie Murray. He done tole us dat story of meetin' you when he comes ta Nashville. Dat IS you, right?"

"You know MacKenzie Murray? Yes, that is I—Running Bear. This woman is his mother?"

"Nah, suh, she beeze his aunt. She and her husband done raised him since he beeze a boy."

"Yes, he told my people his story. I will ride with you to Nashville and deliver you all safely to Doctor Murray."

"That would beeze so good, suh." Running Bear left for a few moments to get the tools to dig a grave. When he returned, Albert introduced him to Eleanor."

"Ma'am, dis here is Running Bear. You knows Doc Murray's story abouts meetin' an Injun when he was a comin' ta Nashville? Dis is him. He been a hidin' and a watchin' over you to keeps you safe."

Eleanor looked over at Running Bear. She stood and staggered over to him. Looking him directly in the face she said to him, "I am sorry that my people blame your people for situations like this. It is unfair. My nephew speaks highly of you. I thank you for your protection."

"You raised a good man. He did not fear us and he did not threaten us when we met him. We shared food and danced."

"Well now, he left that part out of his story. I cannot recall MacKenzie ever dancing. That must have been a laugh." Ellie, still struggling again with weakness, slumped to the ground.

Albert sat down beside her. He was concerned for her well-being. He offered her more water.

When Running Bear returned, he brought, not only digging tools, but also two rabbits for their supper. Angus and Running Bear returned to burned out wagon to bury Thomas. They marked the grave with large stones placed atop the grave. Before returning to the camp site, they removed their hats, bowed their heads, and prayed for Thomas and his family. Running Bear remained with them.

The next morning Eleanor seemed to be better, and she insisted that they leave for Nashville. Running Bear helped her onto his horse, placing her in front of him. Because they could not ride fast and needed to make more frequent stops along the way, the trip was long and draining. They arrived back in Nashville in the evening.

Chapter 27

Shane rode straight back to the Robertson's home. He did not stop except for the necessity of relieving himself. As soon as he arrived, he ran into the house to find Doctor Robertson. He found the doctor sitting with his wife in the parlor.

"Shane, you are back. What happened?"

"Suh, we done found an accident on da trail. Dere beeze a burnt-out wagon. Under a tree was da MacGregors. He beeze dead, suh, and she ain't so greats neither."

"Oh no, this is awful. But she is alive?" Lydia asked Shane.

"Yessum, I didn't sees no injury, but she ain't in good shapes neither. Dem boys is takin' care of her. Dey gonna bury him dere til after tha party. Dey gonna mark da grave."

"Okay, thank you, Shane. Go get yourself some food and water. You look tired."

"Yessuh, I rides straight here wit just two stops. Thank you, suh." Shane almost bolted out of the room for the kitchen. He was starving.

"Lydia, dear. Do you think we should postpone this soirée?"

"Maybe, Felix, but I think that should be Mack and Mary Beth's decision after they see Eleanor."

"Fine. Let's not address this matter until tomorrow. Make sure that no one in this house opens their mouth. This is not their story to tell. This is dreadful."

"I agree, Felix, dear. Will you ask the Sheriff to go look for those responsible? We ought to try to get justice for Mack and Mary Elizabeth. I just cannot believe it."

"Of course, Lydia. Sheriff Hewett will want to talk with Eleanor. I hope she can identify those who did this. There's a chance we might never catch them, but we must try." Lydia stood up and patted Felix on the shoulder.

"You are right, dear."

The following morning, Felix decided to address the matter with his guests. He was dreading it. "Morning, Mack… Mary Beth. We missed you both at dinner last evening."

"I wanted to cook for Mack. I haven't ever cooked all by myself. Lydia, you were so kind to help me with everything."

Coming back into the room and hearing Mary Beth's comment, Lydia responded, "It was our pleasure, dear." Lydia could not look at Mary Beth because she was tearing up.

"Where are your children this morning? Did you let them sleep in, Felix? Mary Beth and I thought we might take them to pick blackberries." Noticing some tension in the room and their lack of eye contact, Mack inquired, "What's going on? Is something wrong, Felix…Lydia? Have we…."

"There is no problem with us. Mack, Mary Beth, the other evening you asked Lydia how long it had been since we had heard from Thomas and Eleanor. After you retired, Lydia came to me to ask that question. When I reviewed my correspondence, I realized that they were supposed to be here already, and that we had not received any other communication. I sent Albert, Shane, and Angus to find them wherever they might be."

As Felix paused, Mack interrupted his thought, "So are you saying that there is a problem with our family? You should have told us."

"Mack, I did not want to worry you needlessly. So, I waited until last evening when Shane returned."

"What has happened?" Mack reached over to take Mary Beth's hand to support her.

"When Shane arrived, he informed us that they had come upon an accident along the trail. They found you mother, Mary Beth, under a tree next to a burnt-out wagon…."

Mary Beth then interrupted, "Where was my father, Felix?" She began to shake and cry.

"Well, honey, apparently robbers met your folks on the trail and attempted to rob them. Your father tried to defend your mother, but he was shot. [Mary Beth screamed and fell over on Mack.] When they did not find what they were look-ing for, they burned the wagon and beat Eleanor. We believe that Albert, Angus, and Running Bear are on their way back here with her now."

Hearing Running Bear's name, Mack asked, "Running Bear was there when it happened. How could he let that hap-pen to someone. I thought he was a good man."

"No, no, you misunderstand. Running Bear did not wit-ness the incident, but he heard the gun shot. He saw the aftermath and decided to keep watch over Eleanor in case the robbers came back."

"Well, thank God for Running Bear. I guess all we can do at this point is wait for them to arrive." Mack was quiet and Felix could tell that his mind was running.

"Mack, I will work today. I want you to stay with Mary Beth."

"Thank you, Felix and you too, Lydia."

That evening, about six o'clock, Angus, Albert, Running Bear and Eleanor finally arrived at the Robertson's. As they approached the home, they began to holler for help. Hearing the commotion, everyone came running to the front of the home. Doctor Robertson ran towards Eleanor to help her from the horse. Others came to gather the horses and take them to water and food.

Everyone gathered on the front porch. Lydia, the Robertson's children, Mack and Mary Beth. The house staff ran back and forth to get they thought was needed to help. Albert, Angus, and Running Bear were taken to the kitchen for food and water.

Mack and Mary Beth ran as fast as their feet would take them to Eleanor. "Aunt Ellie…." As soon as Mack began to speak, Eleanor looked up and saw him and Mary Beth. The emotions or her injuries caused her to collapse.

Mary Beth began to sob. Mack held her for a few moments before he began to speak. "Lydia, could you take Mary Beth for me. I need to go with Felix to examine my aunt." Lydia took Mary Beth and let her to the parlor.

"Thomas was simply out matched, Mack. I pray that he died instantly and did not suffer. I suppose that once they realized there was nothing valuable to steal, they beat Eleanor until she passed out so that she wouldn't remember. She may have a serious head injury."

"And my father? Where is my father, sir?" Mary Beth screamed as she went into the house. "Mack, hold on a minute. I need to finish telling you what happened. [Mack stepped back as Eleanor was carried inside by Angus.] Because of the distance, Albert, Angus, and Running Bear decided to bury Thomas there. They marked the grave and, when the time is right, we will return to his grave and take his body and Eleanor home. They did not want your aunt to witness what happens to a body after death. They had no idea how long she had been under the tree holding your uncle."

"I am concerned about her head injury. She may be bleeding inside her skull. If that is the case, she will not survive this. Would you come with me to examine her, Felix?" "Of course, Mack. Whatever you need me to do," offered Felix. He felt a sense of relief because he thought Mack might be upset with him about the situation. Having Mack ask him to assist relieved that fear.

As the men walked up the stairs to the bedroom where Angus had taken Eleanor, Mack continued, "Felix, I am indebted to you for rescuing her. They might have both died if you hadn't acted when you did. Wait, you said that the robbers thought there was nothing of value to steal, right? That doesn't make sense. Aunt Eleanor was bringing me my grandmother's ring to me so that I can give it to Laura when I propose to her at the party. How could they not have found that ring? That ring is worth a lot of money."

"Well, maybe your aunt managed to hide it, or she may not know since she passed out. Maybe that is why they beat her so badly."

"Maybe. Where is Running Bear?"

"I believe you can find him in the kitchen. I instructed the cook to feed him anything he wanted."

"Great, thank you. I will try to catch him before he leaves."

The pair met Sarah as they walked into the bedroom. "Oh, Doctor Mack, I did not know if I would see you today. I was jus gonna fine you. Looks what I done found when I takes Missus MacGregor's dress off."

Mack followed Sarah to a dresser. She opened the top drawer and pulled out a ring. Mack grabbed Sarah up and twirled her around in a circle. "Oh, praise the Lord, Miss Sarah, you are an angel!"

"Nah, suh. Alls I done was unpin it from the inside of her dress and put in the dresser for safe keeping."

About this time Mary Beth appeared in the doorway. Mack motioned for her to come. He showed her the ring. They looked at the ring and then looked over at Eleanor. "Mary Beth, she managed to keep the robbers from taking this ring. I do not know how she managed to do that. I need you to leave now so that Felix and I can examine her." Mary Beth left reluctantly explaining that she would be just outside the door.

The doctors initially thought Eleanor was sleeping peacefully, but after their examination they realized that she was, in fact, unconscious. Mack feared he might not be able to save her this time. Her body had been compromised from her extended illness. The beating may just be too much. Felix excused himself so that he could spend time alone with Eleanor.

Taking her hand in his and bringing it to his chest, Mack spoke to Eleanor, "My dearest aunt, I am sorry for what has happened to you and Uncle Thomas. I feel I have failed you. Please know, if you can hear me, that I will understand if you wish to be with him. I will always take care of Mary Elizabeth; you need not worry. I love you and I am so thankful to have had as wonderful a family as you and Uncle Thomas." As he sat, he recalled the memories of his adolescence. The times he got into trouble and how he tried to reason his way out of trouble. Eleanor never wanted to punish him, but she was often overruled by Thomas. As he reminisced, he realized that his memories would always keep his aunt and uncle close. Once he composed himself, he rose to go find Running Bear.

When he opened the door of the bedroom, Mack found Mary Beth sitting outside just as she said she would. She was sobbing. "She's going to die, isn't she, Mack?"

"She very well may."

"This is all your fault, MacKenzie Murray! All your fault. You should have been paying attention. You should have known that we had missed letters. You should have gone after them! I hate you!" Mary Beth ran from the hallway, down the stairs, and outside. Mack knew Mary Beth was not completely wrong. He had let his attention sway towards other things in his life. He hadn't paid attention to the gap in communication with his aunt and uncle. However, even if he had gone after them, he very well could have been killed too. Who then would care for Mary Beth? Although he felt guilty, he realized that Thomas and Eleanor would not have changed anything. They would want him alive to care for their precious daughter.

Mack went to the kitchen where he found Running Bear sitting at the table talking with Albert, Angus, and Shane. They seemed to be having a good time listening to Running Bear tell stories of his people and the adventures he had been on.

"Doctor Mack, I am happy to see you. How is your aunt?" Inquired Running Bear.

"Running Bear, I am so thankful you were close by. I am hopeful, but I don't think she will be here tomorrow. Her head injury is severe." Sitting down in a chair next to him, Mack began, "She is unconscious. Albert, Angus, Shane… thank you, too, for all you did to bring my aunt to me and Mary Elizabeth."

"Aw, Doc Murray, weeze sorry 'bout yo family, suh. I thought yo aunt was doin' better until we was 'bout two miles from here. Running Bear can tell you; she became weak." Albert was visibly upset, wringing his hat in his hands.

Running Bear spoke up, "MacKenzie, I held her close and could feel her heart getting weaker."

"Please know that Mary Beth and I are appreciative of your efforts to bring her to us. What happens from here is in God's hands. Running Bear, we invite you to stay with Mary Beth and me in the guest house this evening."

"I would like to stay with you." Running Bear looked his newest friends and asked them if they could show him where his horse was so that he could make sure the horse was well after such a long ride.

"Angus and I gonna takes care of yo horse. Do you wants your saddle and bag? I brings it the guest house." Running Bear nodded his head and went with Mack.

Chapter 28

After spending a few hours with Running Bear, the party of three in the guest house finally attempted to rest. Mack and Mary Beth were not successful. Their minds rushed over all the many ways the crime in the woods could have happened, and then intense sadness came over them and they would sob. It was a revolving series of events throughout the early morning hours. When the sun rose the next morning, they were tired but ready to face the day. They went to the main house for breakfast because Mary Beth did not have the energy to cook.

After they dispensed the greetings, Felix asked, "Have you thought about what you wish to do regarding the party? We have four days."

"Mary Beth and I discussed my aunt's condition last night. If she passes, as I believe she will, we believe she would want us to continue with the plans as they are. My aunt is a practical woman. Rescheduling would cause many more problems than continuing in sadness would. She would not wish to compromise Mary Beth's opportunity to find a husband at this point. I think we go forward, and we dedicate the evening to the memory of my aunt and uncle."

"I was angry at first, but after MacKenzie and I had time to talk, I think he's right. My Momma would not want to inconvenience all the people who have already made plans to be here."

Mack, taking a deep breath and thinking for a moment, interjected, "I have had some time to think about how to proceed when she passes. Mary Beth has left this decision to me. I think we should take her body to my uncle. Bury her next to him for the time being. After all the events here are concluded, we can retrieve them both and take them home to Ione Skye. Do you mind sending Albert and Angus back out there with Running Bear?"

"Certainly not. I know all of this is immensely difficult, but I think that is a good plan."

Lydia sat down in a chair next to MacKenzie. Patting his knee, she looked him in the eye to express her feelings, "Mack, I think that the idea of dedicating the party to your aunt and uncle is a wonderful idea. Felix, I will go and speak with Albert about what is to be done."

Before leaving the dining room, Lydia turned to face Mary Beth. "Mary Elizabeth, my dear, your mother will be in your memories and in your heart forever. She taught you everything you need to know to be a woman of virtue in this world. None of us get to live forever, Mary Beth. There would have always been an inconvenient time for her to leave you. No one here knows that better than Mack does. Remember how young he was when he had lost not one, but both his parents? Eleanor would want you to be the strong, courageous woman she raised you to be. You honor her by doing so" Reaching out her arms towards her, Mary Beth fell into her arms sobbing.

Mary Beth's tears began to dry, and she stood up. Dusting her dress off, she straightened up and looked at Lydia, "I know you are correct. That is exactly what my mother would expect of me. If you don't mind, I would like to go and sit with my mother. I do not wish for her to be alone now."

"Would you like your dinner brought to you there?" inquired Dr. Robertson.

"That would be nice. Thank you."

As they expected, Eleanor died a few hours later. Everyone gathered around her body one more time to pray. Her body was wrapped in linen and placed into a wooden casket that Angus had constructed for her. The casket was placed in a buckboard. The Robertson children placed wildflowers on top of the box. The family stood on the front porch as Albert and Shane drove away with Running Bear riding alongside. When they could no longer see the wagon, the family returned inside the house.

For the next three days, everyone worked diligently to make the final preparations for the soirée. The house was filled with flowers. Cooking went on almost around the clock to prepare all the dishes needed to feed the attendees. A platform was built in the backyard for a band. Lanterns were hung from branches in the trees. An enormous table was filled with enough candles to keep the lanterns lit and there were two young negro boys put in charge of that task. The silver was polished, and every dish was washed. Linens were cleaned and ironed by Elizabeth and Elnora. The yard was raked, shrubs pruned, and flowers planted around the outside of the house. The Robertsons spared no expense to make this the event of the year.

Chapter 29

On the evening of the soirée, excitement filled the house. The ladies dressed together, helping each other with their hair, gown, and jewelry. The men dressed in their finest evening suits gathered in Doctor Robertson's study for a drink and a toast for a successful evening. Fancy carriages delivered the Nashville elite to the doorsteps of the Robertson home. Staff, dressed in their finest uniforms, stood at the door to gather coats and hats to store in a room off the kitchen. Even in the South during all the months of the year, these fine ladies and gentlemen would wear coats in the evening. It was as much about style as it was about showing one's status.

People began to mingle. The sounds of talk and laughter wafted up through the roof and into the evening air. The air was dry and there was just a slight breeze. MacKenzie Murray stood on the front porch awaiting the arrival of his love, Miss Laura Hartwell-Todd. When the Hartwell-Todd carriage stopped in front of the porch, Mack walked to down assist Laura and her mother in exiting the cab.

"Miss Hartwell-Todd and Mrs. Hartwell-Todd, you are both visions of exquisite beauty," commented Mack. He leaned over and kissed her lightly on the cheek. As he was doing so,

Laura's father exited the coach. Her father cleared his throat to get Mack's attention.

"That is enough, my boy," scolded Henry Todd. His wife, Jane, who was straightening her dress, looked over at her husband with disdain.

"Relax, Henry. It was just a kiss on the cheek. MacKenzie, dear, you look handsome yourself tonight." Looking around the house and grounds, Mack could tell that Laura's parents were pleased. "Where are the Robertsons? We should find them, Henry."

"They are in the back, Mrs. Hartwell-Todd. I can show you the way." Mack took hold of Laura's mother's arm in his and led her through the house and to the backyard, with Laura and her father following close behind. Walking them right up to Doctor and Mrs. Robertson, he made their presence known. "Doctor…Mrs. Robertson, the Hartwell-Todd Family." He took her arm, handed it back to her husband, and then stepped beside Laura.

"Good evening, Jane…Henry. Laura, dear, I love your dress. The color is stunning on you. I think you and your mother must have taken a shopping trip. I will have to find out where you went."

"Thank you for the invitation. You have a beautiful home. The grounds are gorgeous," added Jane.

"Jane, you are kind. We are pleased to have you here this evening. There is food inside the house. Drinks are here on the porch. Please, make yourselves at home. Excuse me, please, I need to check with the kitchen about something. I will find you again." Lydia walked towards the kitchen looking for a serving piece for one of the trays of food.

The partygoers danced; they ate; they drank. At 9:00 p.m., Mack stood on the back porch and tapped his fork lightly against his crystal goblet to gain the attention of the party attendees. "Ladies, gentlemen, my name is Doctor Alexander MacKenzie Murray. As many of you know, I am Felix's medical partner. I wanted to thank you all for coming here this evening. When Felix and his lovely wife, Lydia, asked how I and my cousin (motioning over to Mary Beth to join him) Miss Mary Elizabeth MacGregor would feel about a grand party to introduce us to their friends in Nashville, I was not quite sure how I felt, and I know Mary Elizabeth did not. We are after all mountain people. Only on a rare occasion did our family host events such as this. We had become quite content with staying to ourselves. But we are residents of Nashville now, so after thinking about it, I realized that with new surroundings comes new opportunities. I could hear one of my uncle's long lectures about this very topic in my head. So, here we are. They have been generous to both of us in throwing this soirée tonight. Most of you do not know that just three days ago, Mary Beth's parents…my aunt and uncle Thomas and Eleanor MacGregor were killed in an attempted robbery as they traveled to be here with us tonight. (A gasp went out over the crowd.) They would not have wished to miss this evening. So, tonight we, Mary Beth and I, as well as Felix and Lydia honor their memory by dedicating this night to them. They raised me from the age of 5, educated me, and sent me off as a young man to become a doctor. If you would raise your glasses, please, and help us to honor them. To Thomas and Eleanor MacGregor!" The crowd cheered in unison.

As the crowd quieted down, Mack continued, "Okay, thank you. There is also another purpose for this gathering tonight. (Mack leaned over and whispered to Mary Beth to bring Laura over to him. He took Laura's hand into his as she stood beside him.) I met this beautiful woman, Miss Laura Hartwell-Todd, on a trip home last year. Since that time, we have spent time together with her family and with the Robertsons. I can tell you all that I have fallen deeply in love with this woman and her family. [Turning towards Laura to look her in the eye, he removed a small box from his coat pocket and knelt on one knee.] Laura Hartwell-Todd, would you do me the honor of marrying me?"

Laura was unaware that Mack planned to propose that evening. She was completely surprised. Tears welled up in her eyes and she pulled him up from his knee. "Yes…yes, Mack, I will marry you." Another collective cheer rang out from the crowd. Laura and Mack hugged as people rushed to the porch to congratulate them.

After the fervor died down, Mack tapped his glass once more. "I promise this is the last time that I will interrupt this evening. Lydia requested something special from Mary Beth for tonight. Instead, I will carry that request out. My family came to this country in the mid-last century from Ulster, Ireland. They had emigrated to Ulster from Scotland just after they married. Alexander and Isobel intended to come to America with their employers, Robert and Mary Fraser, but tragedy struck. Alexander and their young son, James died suddenly, leaving Isobel with three young children, and she was not well. Mr. and Mrs. Fraser agreed to bring her children with them, and my great-grandmother signed indentures for her children. Before her children boarded the ship she made one last request. She said, 'My precious children when you arrive in America, please turn back towards the way you came and send me a song. I will catch it and I will know that you are well.' According to my father, the children did as they were asked. This is the song they sang. It was the song that their mother sang to them every night before bed and each generation since then has sung this song to their children." And then, MacKenzie Murray, beloved son of James and Mollie MacKenzie began to sing the song that years later would become known as *The Parting Glass*.

Mary Beth, astonished by the loving gesture made by her cousin, walked to where he was, took his hand, and began to sing along. They had grown up singing the song in four-part harmony. While they may have been missing their other two parts, their voices were perfectly balanced. Years later when people reminisced about this evening, for many it was their favorite part.

While Mary Beth enjoyed herself, she did not meet anyone who sparked her interest that evening. Mack felt it best not to put pressure on her during the party to meet young men. Felix and Lydia introduced her to their friends and their sons, and she spent the evening dancing and singing. Despite her sadness, Mary Beth felt reassured that she was in the best place for the moment. Over the next year, she attended parties and was invited into the homes of Nashville's elite.

Chapter 30

After the party, Mack, Mary Beth, Laura, her mother, Felix, Lydia, and Running Bear, returned to the burial spot in the woods where Thomas and Eleanor were interred. The bodies were exhumed and delivered back to their Ione Skye. A funeral was held for the couple on the same hill where James and Mollie were buried. Eddie, Macajah, and Charlie built a tabernacle on the hill with permanent benches. Since Mack and Mary Beth had been gone, the Ione Skye family had been using it for church services. The men also built a few tables and benches so they could have picnics.

Everyone in the permanent Ione Skye family made the guests feel like family. Jeremiah and Addie, who were well into their seventies now, were in charge and they made certain that everything was handled in the exact manner as Thomas and Eleanor would expect. Laura, her mother Jane, Felix, and Lydia told everyone how wonderful their visit was despite the circumstances.

Before he could return to Nashville, Mack met with Jeremiah, Addie, Killian, and Mame. "First, I want to thank you all for the hard work and loyalty you have all shown to me and Mary Elizabeth. It just goes to show that when you treat people like family, they treat you like family. Next, because

Uncle Thomas and Aunt Eleanor are gone, that means that everyone on Ione Skye is now free." Mack paused for a moment. A look of disbelief swept over the group. "You all do understand what I am saying, right?"

Jeremiah being the natural leader, studdered, "Well Doc, I beeze supposin' dat we didn't never thinks this would happen. Nots in our lives. I done thought weeze was gonna die on dis here farm as slaves, tho we ain't never been treated like slaves."

Mack continued, "I am going to stay for a few more days to look over the farm accounts and to begin the probate of my aunt and uncle's estates. I can only stay three days. I have to work, and Laura and I have our wedding to plan. I would like to meet with everyone at the tabernacle tomorrow morning at nine a.m. If you don't mind keeping what I told you a secret; I would like to tell everyone myself. Jeremiah and Killian, if you could meet here at 8:30, please? Addie and Mame, would you mind cooking breakfast for everyone to be ready by 8:00? I know that means you have to get up early, but this is just for tomorrow."

Addie took her towel from her apron and looked Mack intensely in his eyes and then her deep alto voice blasted from her mouth, "Boy, you ain't knowd early. You lucky I don't snap this towel right on yo back side." While her sassy tone might lead some to believe her words were said in jest, Mack knew she was dead serious.

Looking back at Addie and mirroring her behavior and tone of voice, MacKenzie doubled down. "You'd have to catch me first." Everyone exploded into laughter at the exact moment that one of the teenage girls walked into the room. Hearing adults laugh like this was confusing for her.

Mack stayed up most of the night going over the farm's financial records. After doing the math, he determined what he could afford to pay each of the adults. He hoped that they would be agreeable to the terms he would propose. Mack wandered from the office to the kitchen to ask for coffee. Addie and Mame were finishing up breakfast. He grabbed his coffee and went outside to eat with his extended family.

After breakfast, the group cleared the table and then moved to the tabernacle. Mack could tell that there was anxiety within the group about what would happen to Ione Skye now that Thomas and Eleanor were dead, and he and Mary Beth were living in Nashville. "Okay, if we could settle down. This will not take long. I know the past year has been difficult, but probably not as difficult as the past few days. I know every one of you. Some helped raise me; some grew up with me; and some I have only met recently, he said looking down at one of the smallest children. I want you all to know that each of you was precious to my aunt and uncle. They valued every one of you. There have been great times, and there have been some incredibly difficult times. That is life, but what we have here on this farm that so many others do not is mutual love and respect. I am here today to tell you that you are free. You are free to do whatever you wish with your life. Of course, Mary Beth and I want you all to stay because saying goodbye is difficult. Over the next few days, each of you adults will meet with Jeremiah and Killian. Jeremiah is officially the farm manager. Each of you is responsible to him and he is responsible to me. Killian is now the financial manager. He also reports to me. He is responsible for obtaining funds from customers, paying your wages, and for paying the bills of the farm. Yes, you heard me correctly; you all will be paid for your work if you agree to our terms. Addie is the house manager. She is responsible for hiring and firing house staff, purchasing what is needed for the home, and coordinating any events we might have on the property. Mame is what I'd like to call our people person. She will act as an intermediary between all of you and management. We have never had any significant personnel problems on Ione Skye and I pray it will remain that way; but, if a problem arises, Mame is the first step to resolution. Discuss the matter with her and she will investigate and determine the best way to handle the matter. If she cannot resolve the problem, then she will go to Addie for assistance. If they cannot resolve it, Jeremiah will intervene, and he will consult with me. Are there any questions?" Mack paused expecting someone to ask a question, but to his surprise there were none. "Well, then we are adjourned. I will see you all next month."

His new managers met him at the side of the tabernacle with smiling faces. "Oh Doc, that was so good. Dem young'uns thought dey done lost they minds when you says theys free. Doc, dis gonna be real good. Ain't nothin' done changed cep tweeze gonna get paid and we is free! The Lord done blessed us; we ain't gonna leave da one who done freed us," announced Addie.

"Addie, I appreciate your enthusiasm. Jeremiah…Killian, I trust you both to handle these conversations with everyone. Take notes of any issues and we can discuss those when I return next month. Jeremiah and Addie, if you encounter a problem serious enough that you believe it warrants asking someone to leave, then I give you the authority to do that. The only stipulation that I have concerns the older folks who have been here since the beginning or their children. If they have a problem that serious, then wait for my return. Finishing his conversation and grabbing his bags, Mack left.

After returning from Ione Skye, Mack and Laura began making plans for their wedding. Felix and Lydia offered their home for the wedding, which they graciously declined. Both Mack and Laura desired to be married in the church. Mack completed the construction of their home a month before the wedding. Laura, Lydia, and Mary Beth decorated the interior with all the latest styles and decorations. Upon completion, everyone felt a deep sense of satisfaction.

Mack and Laura decided that they would return to Ione Skye after two more years in Nashville. Mack wanted to continue in the medical practice with Felix for a few more years before leaving to begin his own practice in Washington County. Moreover, he wanted to make sure Mary Beth was married before he, Laura, and anyone else returned to Ione Skye. Until that time Mack returned to Ione Skye each month. Jeremiah, Killian, Addie, and Mame were pleasantly surprised that all but three of the former slaves accepted Mack's offer. Those two were the worst of those whom Jeremiah had described a few years before. The management team felt relief that they had chosen to leave because they had never attempted to become part of the family.

Chapter 31

In the months that followed their nuptials, Laura's father's law firm hired two new attorneys. One, Ethan Somerville, was completely charmed by Mary Beth. His parents lived in Western Virginia. He attended law school at William and Mary. Mary Beth enjoyed spending time with Ethan. He spoke to her on the same level. He never assumed that she would not understand an issue that his fellows might be discussing. He appreciated her passion for reading and music. She found him easy to talk to, and she felt comfortable and safe around Ethan. About a year after being introduced, Ethan proposed marriage to Mary Beth.

Mack and Laura, with the assistance of the Robertsons, threw a huge wedding for Mary Elizabeth and Ethan. Henry Todd promised to make certain Ethan would have a job with his law firm, and that he and the rest of the Hartwell-Todds would take great care of the couple. Everyone understood that MacKenzie would have a difficult time leaving Mary Beth in Nashville when he and Laura decided to return to Ione Skye so they went out of their way to assuage his fears.

When the day came for the young Murray family to leave for Washington County, everyone gathered at the Robertsons to say their goodbyes. The Robertsons wanted to throw them a party, but Mack and Laura declined. They did not want to make their move a big event; they did not see a reason for it. Laura and Mack had twin boys, and it just did not seem like a good idea. The Murrays sold their home and its contents to the newlyweds.

Mack took ahold of Mary Beth's hand and led her over to the side of the porch so that he could speak to her alone. "Mary Elizabeth, I think today is harder on me than when I left you and your parents to go to medical school. I knew I would come back to the farm at some point, but I didn't consider how different things might be. I am so proud of you, Mary Beth…Sutherland. You are going to have an amazing life with Ethan, and you will come and visit us, and we will come back here to visit you. We are all still young and we have a good life awaiting us."

"MacKenzie, I owe you so much. You are more of a brother to me than a cousin. Your dedication to me and our family has not gone unnoticed. I appreciate everything you have done for me. You have been a blessing to the MacGregors. I will miss you, but you know that I will inundate you with letters about everything going on here; you will feel like you never left. I am so happy that you are going back to Ione Skye. The farm needs you, and our family tradition must be carried on. Never stop singing our song, Mack. Sing it to your babies every night so that they will know it." After pausing for a few seconds, she continued, "I would like to think that Ethan and I could go back to the farm at some point to live. It's where you and I belong, and so do our families." Mary Beth threw her arms around Mack. "I love you, Mack."

"I adore you, Mary Beth. You and Ethan will always have a place at Ione Skye whenever you decide to return. May the next generation be as happy and successful as we have been."

Laura and MacKenzie had two children when they returned to the farm. They would have three more; however, Laura did not survive the birth of their last child. It was at this time that Mary Beth, Ethan, and their adopted children Isobel and Duncan decided to return to Ione Skye. To make room, Mack had a second home built for his cousin and her family. Mack sold them twenty acres for their home. Ethan built a nice home, stable, and root cellar. Mary Beth became an amazing mother and wife. Motherhood suited her. She was thrilled to cook and clean her home; she loved teaching her children; and she loved being a wife.

Mack grieved the loss of his wife for a couple of years before being introduced to Katherine Burns. Katherine was previously married but lost her husband to a hunting accident. They had three children. Mack and Katherine married a year later. Because Katherine was seven years younger than Mack, she was able to have children. She and MacKenzie had four children. All of their children and Mary Beth's children were raised on Ione Skye.

Like our ancestors, we loved the land. The boys farmed, hunted, and made things needed by their family, like furniture. The girls learned womanly things. We were educated at home by our mothers and, on occasion, tutors until the government told us we had to attend their schools. We appreciated what we had, and we learned to share our blessings with our neighbors and community.

While we endured wartime, difficult farm seasons, and unexpected deaths, our family bond and the lessons learned from the past held us together. I have no idea where this journal may be found or who may be reading these pages. My purpose is to share the lessons of our experience. When Donald, Duncan, and Eleanor MacKenzie left their country on a treacherous voyage to an unknown land, they promised their mother that they would gaze into the sky toward their homeland and would send her the song she had sung to them each night. That way she would know that they were safe and well. This was the first promise they had kept. It was a commitment that they refused to fail. So, they passed it down.

They were committed to each other and to the family who had sponsored them. They set high goals for themselves. They fought for our freedom and for the freedom of those stolen from their country and families. They never forgot what family was meant to be. It isn't always easy for those who carry your name because there can be pressure to live up to the people in your past. And then there are those people who come into your life who share no blood, but because of their actions they become family. These are the families you adopt, like the Frasers, the Robertsons, and the Hartwell-Todds of the world. While the world may seem to spiral out of control, a godly family stays grounded. Love each other; forgive each other; and never forget to thank our Lord for his blessings, his mercy, and his grace.

I pray the story of our family may bring inspiration to our descendants, and that they will share these stories with each generation to come. While we do not know each other, we are a family. Know that you are loved and that the things we

have done were to give you a future ripe with the bountiful
blessings of our beloved Ione Skye.

Chapter 32

"So, is that the end of the story?" inquired Sean.

"It seems to be. On the next page is a list of the names of MacKenzies and MacGregors. It shows their names, the dates of their birth, and the dates of their death. Many of these names I don't recall hearing before," responded Alex.

Alex was quiet for a few minutes. Responding to his silence, Anne inquired, "What are you thinking about Dad?"

"I was thinking about this family...our family and the similarities that, until now, have been unknown to me."

"Like what Gram?" Hannah asked.

"Their dedication to abolition. I always had a deep need to protect those less fortunate. I worked in the Civil Rights Movement here in Knoxville, registering folks to vote. That's not a coincidence, is it?"

Ross interjected, "It sure isn't, and Anne and I have served on several mission trips to some of the poorest places in the world. We've always believed in giving back and showing God's love to those we meet."

"It sort of makes you want to find out more, doesn't it Gram?" Added Celia.

"I wish the journal had pictures. I wonder if we look like any of them?" Hannah pondered.

"Gram, do you know what happened to Ione Skye? Why didn't you live there?" inquired Sean.

"That is a terrific question, Sean. I only wish I knew the answer. I know that my father grew up here in Knoxville. I don't recall ever hearing about the family originating in Washington County or that there was a plantation called Ione Skye. I should have asked my father and grandfather more questions, but when you are young, sometimes, we overlook personal history…family history. It is sad." Remarked Alex.

Anne turned around in her chair so that she could see her father, and inquired, "Daddy, we need to make copies of these journals and give copies to everyone. I know they would appreciate a copy, and I really cannot think of a better Christmas gift, can you?"

"No dear, I cannot," responded Alex.

Ross continued the train of thought, "You know, Ann and I have spent most of our adult life learning and working with history, but I have always thought of history as being something separate from myself. I hadn't considered how my family may have interacted or participated in history or how it might do so in the future. I guess I have taken that for granted. That is short-sighted, isn't it Gram? After hearing this story…your family's story, I want to know more about my own family's story."

"Hey Dad, look at this map. Look right there. That's it. It's so cool!" Sean proclaimed after finding Ione Skye on a historical map site on the Internet.

"Sean that is amazing that you found it so fast," Celia declared.

Alex interjected, "Do you think we could re-route our trip so that we could drive through Washington, County? I would really love to see Ione Skye."

They all looked at each other with pleading faces. "Daddy, I think we absolutely can do that." The children jumped up from their chairs and screamed delight at their mother's response.

Anne, then, remarked in a most serious tone, "If you all want that to happen then we will have to go to bed early to-night because it will add time to our trip home. I do not want to hear any complaining. You got me?"

The children responded in unison, "Yes, Momma!"

The next day began with a beautiful sunrise. Anne found her father standing in the kitchen staring out the picture window at his backyard. "Good morning, Daddy. I hope you slept well."

"Yes, of course, Annie. I was just thinking about the day we moved in here. We were so excited about having a house in the country. We wanted you kids to have a big backyard to play in. It makes me wonder why my family left Ione Skye and why I never heard about it."

"Maybe hard times fell on them, and they couldn't keep it up anymore. The diary really did not tell us what happened during the Civil War. It may have been mortally damaged, and maybe they could not afford to make the necessary repairs. That happened to many plantations during that time."

"I suppose that could be true. What a terrible time that was for the country. No one came out of it unscathed. It wasn't a subject most Southerners wanted to talk about, so I guess I should not be too surprised." Alex wandered back to the kitchen counter to pour coffee for himself and his daughter.

"Maybe, if we have time, we could run over to the county clerk's office and look to see who purchased the house after Alexander MacKenzie Murray. That may answer the question for us."

"Oh, I hadn't thought of that. It's a grand idea. I better start making breakfast. I promised the children pancakes," Alex responded smiling at his daughter.

"I will go wake them now. I'm sure they will be excited about our adventure…." Before Ann could finish her sentence, her children and husband appeared in the kitchen. "I was just about to come upstairs to wake you all!"

Sean threw his arms around his mother and exclaimed, "Momma, I am so excited for today! I can't wait to see Ione Skye." His sisters joined in the hug with their brother.

"Ok, Gram is making pancakes, so you guys set the table. Ross, can you pour them milk and I will pour your coffee."

"Absolutely," Ross affirmed.

After breakfast was over and the kitchen cleaned and trash taken out, the family gathered their belongings and packed the SUV for the trip home to Virginia. Sean took his grandfather by the hand and demanded, "Gram, you sit here by me. The girls can sit in the back. I will show you how to play games on my Gameboy."

"That sounds wonderful, Sean," Gram patted him on the shoulder as he stepped up into the vehicle. Sean stood behind him in case he had difficulty; he wanted to help his grandfather.

With the closing of the last door, Anne put the vehicle in drive, and they were off towards Washington County. The drive through the majestic Smoky Mountains took about an hour and a half.

Hannah and Celia had lost interest in their electronic devices and had been talking to each other about the beauty of the landscape. Hannah inquired rhetorically, "Why would anyone want to leave here? The mountains and trees are just gorgeous. Maybe I should consider going to college near here? Maybe I will major in history."

Celia answered her softly, "You're right. I think I might do that too."

The adults looked at each other amazed at the children's opinions. Anne and Ross had never heard their children talk about their futures, academic or otherwise. Hearing the girls talk about it now made them proud. As they pulled onto the highway where Ione Skye was located Ann slowed down to look for signs. Sean pulled up the map again to try to help. "Momma, look for Fraser Road, that's where you turn," Sean directed.

"Ok, I am…I am…I am looking. Oh! Oh! There it is." Anne discovered the road to the farm, and she turned slowly. The road, while paved, was uneven and had many potholes. As they drove down the road, they passed some abandoned houses and several mobile homes before coming to a sign that read, "HISTORIC PLANTATION IONE SKYE HOME OF DR. ALEXANDER MACKENZIE MURRAY." Anne stopped momentarily to glance at her father. "We're here Daddy. Are you ready?"

Alex nodded at his daughter to go ahead and turn as tears ran down his face. "This is so special. I am so glad that we are all together to witness this place."

"I couldn't agree more, Gram," Ross added.

When they pulled into the drive, there were ancient pecan trees that lined the sides of the drive. The drive was long and ran between two large grass fields. When they came to the end of the drive, Anne stopped; she could not believe her eyes. She turned to look at Ross. He, too, was speechless. There were several minutes of complete silence before Celia invoked, "My gosh, Momma! Why don't we live here? Why would anyone in our family leave this place?"

Still shaking their heads in disbelief, the group rushed from the vehicle to the front of the home. It was an enormous house like many Southern plantations of the Antebellum period, but the style was one that the group had never seen before. The front of the house was rounded with a porch that wrapped around both sides. It appeared to have three stories. There were twelve columns that reached up to the second floor. There were many windows, one of which was made of stained glass. Just above the front door on the second floor was a balcony overlooking the front drive and yard which was immaculately landscaped.

Just as they were glancing up at the balcony, the front door opened, and a lady stepped out. "Hello, are you here to see Ione Skye?"

Alex stepped forward to speak for his group. "Hello, ma'am, my name is Alexander MacKenzie Murray III, and this is my family."

The lady's eyes opened widely as she heard his name spoken. She reached out her hand and she spoke sincerely, "Sir, I am so honored to meet you all. I suppose you know this is the home of your great-great-great-grandfather of the same name?"

Looking at his family, Alex continued his introduction, "Ma'am, I had no idea that this place existed until a few days ago. We don't understand why we were never told the story of Dr. Murray. I am moving to live with my daughter, Anne, her husband, Ross, daughters, Hannah and Celia, and son, Richard Sean Murray III (pointing at each as he introduced them). While we were packing and cleaning out my home in Knoxville, we discovered two diaries kept by the first Richard Sean Murray. We decided we had to come here. I think it is safe to say that no one expected to find this home. I am more confused as to why my parents and grandparents did not tell us about our history. This is simply breathtaking."

"I cannot answer that question, but I can tell you that you are not alone. When families go through traumatic events like the Civil War, they just want to get on with their lives and leave the past in the past. I think sometimes they assume that their descendants won't care, but I can see that for you all, it is very important. Mr. Murray, you and I are cousins. I descend from Dr. Murray's son Duncan. I think that makes us sixth cousins removed a couple of times. My name is Eleanor Grace Murray-Lyons. If you will follow me, I will be pleased to show you around the home."

"This is truly an amazing turn of events. I am astounded that all of this has transpired during a time I was dreading," announced Alex. His family gathered around him as they walked inside the home.

Each room of the home was decorated with paintings of the family Alex had never known. For the first time since they read Richard Sean Murray's journals, they could put faces with the names. There were beautiful furnishings, though not fancy, seemed perfect for the family they had come to know.

Walking out the back door towards the outbuildings, Eleanor pointed out a specific building to the right. "This building was once the cottage in which James and Mollie lived with their son Alexander. When Dr. Murray returned to Ione Skye with his young family, the cottage was renovated into what you see before you—a chapel. For a brief period, the cottage served as a laundry. Dr. Murray often enjoyed telling new friends that the building went from washing clothes to cleansing souls!"

On the opposite side of the back garden was another building Eleanor wished to point out to the group. "This building served as the schoolhouse for the children on the plantation. It was used until the federal government instituted mandatory public education." The group entered the little building where six little desks were lined up, three on each side. In the front was a table and chair. Behind the teacher's table, the wall was painted black for use as a chalkboard."

"It is so quaint Gram," proclaimed Celia. She, Hannah, and Sean plopped themselves down into the desks. "Oh, they are so small. How could they sit here all day?"

Eleanor responded to Celia's complaint, "Well, my dear, when the children were educated here, they did not go to school for five to six hours a day like you do. They were in the school for about three hours. The children were expected to help around the house and in the fields."

"I would hate that," exclaimed Hannah who was making her way out the door.

Eleanor continued, "Do you have any other questions for me? I am so honored to have met you all today. I will let you finish walking around the property on your own. I will be on the front porch if you have any other questions. There is a guestbook on the porch. We'd appreciate your information so that we may stay in touch. We have an annual fundraiser which allows us to maintain the property. If not, I wish you safe travels."

Responding for the family, Anne told Eleanor how much they appreciated her tour and the information. Ross added that, because he and Anne were historians in the D.C. area, they would be happy to assist the foundation in its fundraising endeavors. When the conversation concluded, they returned to their children and Alex.

"Dad, this has been an amazing day, but we need to get back on the road. We still have a long drive ahead." The family took one more opportunity for photographs in front of the house before loading themselves back into the SUV.

Sean, placing his arm around his grandfather, expressed what everyone was feeling, "Gram, this has been the best visit ever. I love our family."

Citations & Further Reading Regarding
The Parting Glass & Send Me A Song

The Parting Glass, previously known under other names like *"Good Night and Joy Be To You All*, was written somewhere between 1615 and 1635. The lyrics and tune, therefore, are part of the public domain. It is a traditional song which originated in Ireland and has been sung at celebrations and funerals.

For more information:

https://celticworldorchestra.com/the-parting-glass/

https://www.irishmusicdaily.com/parting-glass

https://en.wikipedia.org/wiki/The_Parting_Glass